ROYAL DESCENT

ROYAL DESCENT

GAVAN THOMSON

echo))
BOOKS

ISBN: 978-1-923441-98-9 (Print)
        978-1-923441-97-2 (EPub)

First Published in 2025 by Echo Books

Echo Books is an imprint of Superscript Publishing Pty Ltd,
ABN 76 644 812 395
PO Box 669, Woodend, Victoria, 3442
www.echobooks.com.au

'The miracle that saves the world, the realm of human affairs, from its normal "natural" ruin is ultimately the fact of natality in which the faculty of action is ontologically rooted. It is, in other words, the birth of new men and the new beginning, the action they are capable of by virtue of being born.'

Hannah Arendt,
The Human Condition,
Chicago University Press, 1958

PROLOGUE

Judge Meredith Barraclough started her concluding statement in the sentencing of Chris Frederiksen. The young man faced her below at the bar table alongside his lawyer Zoe. Behind them in the front row of the court sat Chris's wife Senty, his friend Ebbe and the Danish Ambassador Jens Jørgensen. The rest of the Castlemaine courtroom was packed with members of the media and the public. Outside gathered a throng, hundreds strong, of journalists, camera operators, photographers and the public. The police had barricaded off whole sections of Lyttleton and Hargraves Streets to keep traffic away from the crowd in the courthouse grounds that spilled into the street.

'Before I announce the sentence in this case, I thank all participants in these proceedings for their courteous and respectful contributions. I have heard, read and considered all submissions and arguments in this sentencing hearing. I have also taken into account the statements Mr Frederiksen made in Copenhagen about his actions. I also note the intense media interest in this case both domestically and internationally. As a modern judicial officer, I am informed by modern concepts and understandings that explain, if not excuse, human behaviour; criminal or otherwise. I am therefore compelled in this case to consider trauma. The report and evidence provided to the court by the psychiatrist Professor Wellard, who examined the defendant, are persuasive. He found that Mr Frederiksen had clearly experienced severe trauma and a resulting Post Traumatic Stress Disorder, commonly referred to as PTSD.'

She looked down at Chris directly after a tiny smile. He looked up at her pensively and scratched anxiously at his forearm. Tiredness marked his features.

'In referring to the events that fateful day just south of here, I acknowledge that it may be distressing to you, Sir. Further, I appreciate that you had an upbringing very different to most of us. You were shielded and protected in ways that were unusual to people who are not royalty, and this may well have made you more vulnerable to trauma. Additionally, on that sad day you were in a foreign country far from home without your usual supports or resources. You had just lost all of your few possessions. Your hosts, who you were reliant on, had abandoned you. You had also witnessed the ghastly death of your close friend and companion, the late Mr Anderson. You were in grave danger yourself and forced to run for your life. You escaped by the skin of your teeth. This all adds up, I am assured, to an overwhelmingly traumatic event for you. Such an event might lead anyone of us to do one of three things: to fight, to flee or to freeze. You chose to flee. Correction, you did not choose in any rational, deliberate or considered way. You grabbed the only resources at hand and escaped.'

The judge paused and looked around. 'Would any of us have acted differently?' she asked rhetorically. The courtroom

8

remained silent, but a jagged cacophony of voices bled in from the outside.

'Mr Frederiksen's untreated PTSD affected his wellbeing and many of his subsequent actions for some months, if not years. It may have been a good idea if he had sought help, however it is clear to me that he did not appreciate that traumatic stress had affected him. He made a series of momentous decisions, apologised fully for his misdeeds and sought to make amends. I consider that the decisions he made and the actions he took, the views of his character witnesses, and his plea and appearance here in this court display exemplary strength of character and moral fibre. I am left in no doubt about this.'

She paused theatrically to take a drink from the glass alongside her. She knew that this was the highlight of her distinguished legal career. As she looked up at the camera recording her face and her every word, she involuntarily touched her hair. She knew that hundreds outside in the street were watching her on their phones, as were thousands more across the globe, particularly 'down under' in Australia and 'up over' in Scandinavia.

She let her silence linger just a little longer, then looked the defendant in the eye again and spoke. 'My decision is based on mitigation and fairness. I record no conviction. You are free to go Mr Frederikson.'

The clerk called loudly, 'All rise!' Judge Barraclough quickly rose, nodded and glanced again at the camera. Before anyone else had a chance to get to their feet she turned and swept off.

After a wave of applause erupted in the courtroom, and a much louder tumult outside, Chris hugged his lawyer, stood and turned about. He mouthed, 'I love you,' to his wife. The future called afresh.

CHAPTER ONE

Twenty thousand kilometres away, Christian Glucksberg probably first had the thought, at age 15, that led him to the Castlemaine Courthouse. He was at the Copenhagen Zoo with his grandfather Prince Henrik, or Henri as he preferred to be called, that cool and windy November day. They were there to open the new elephant enclosure with suitable dignity and ceremony. But his heart was not in it. He felt sorry for the two elephants. He could not help thinking of such intelligent and peaceful giants imprisoned in a dark enclosure in Scandinavia as a cold, dark winter approached. No doubt the staff did their best to provide an 'enhanced, stimulating and enriched environment' for the noble beasts, as the PR announcement chirped, but still. He caught the eye of the young bull and held it for ages. It was as if the elephant was wanting to tell him something important about his own future.

He listened carefully and heard the animal clearly warn him, 'you are also a young bull and may be destined for a life in a zoo. I want to go back home to Thailand. Although I was mistreated badly by my keepers, I miss my home so much and the winters here will be unbearable.'

Chris saw a tear fall from the elephant's large intelligent eye. The prince's personal security detail, a policeman called

Ebbe Mosegaard, stood nearby and Chris turned to him and with a frown and commented, 'Maybe I will end up a bit like that elephant. It is so sad. Why would the Thai King just give it away? And why would Grandma agree to accept it?'

Ebbe shrugged and replied, 'Well I don't know why, but Monarchs have to give gifts to other Monarchs often, and the more exotic the better, but at least you will get the Order of the Elephant!'

They both laughed at the irony. The young prince realised the Thai King would have known about the Danish royals' liking for elephants. Indeed, the Order of the Elephant was the country's oldest and most distinguished honour. He liked Ebbe and wondered if he had also seen the elephant's tear. He was a lot less stuffy than so many of the other court and security officials that surrounded his family.

CHAPTER TWO

Chris started his campaign in earnest in the winter of 2025, his second year of university. His arguments were both rational and emotional.

'A year off would make me a more mature, more independent, well rounded young man with better social, language and practical skills, plus,' he argued over dinner one evening from a script he had committed to memory, 'I will get time and space to recover from the residual traumas of my Covid illness, and the bullying at school.' He did not actually have long Covid or residual trauma, and the bullying was years ago, but it was worth a try.

'But Christian, all that is well in the past,' his father replied, 'I do not see why you cannot just go there as yourself. Get a job or go to university down there. After all I went to Harvard as myself and your cousin Nikolai went to Sydney as himself.'

Mary, his mother, interjected, 'But you seem to forget, dear, the problems you had with the media in the US. Didn't you have to live in a secret location off campus? I am sure you told me that.'

'Well yes,' Frederik admitted, 'the media were savage. But Mum pulled a few strings, and I was able to get some privacy in my apartment. The authorities over there were great. They really looked after me.'

'But Dad, I don't want any of that attention. I just want to be left alone,' Christian implored and looked from his father to his mother eagerly.

But the only replies from his parents were shakes of the head.

He realised his campaign was getting nowhere so next he enlisted his sister Isabella. He convinced her that if he could get permission then this would set a wonderful precedent for her future. They had often talked about Australia and how much they wanted to go there, and they always spoke of it in English. It developed into a semi-secret activity they shared when their parents were not around. She told Christian she would speak to their parents.

By the spring of 2026, Chris sensed a softening of resistance, so he brought up Peter the Great, King Gustav Adolph of Sweden and Emperor Napoleon.

All three, he pointed out, had granted themselves the liberty of going incognito amongst their people for different periods of time, to see, while staying unseen. And nobody could ever suggest that these furloughs impaired their reigns. On the contrary, he argued, it made them better leaders of their people.

But his father with a broad smile, countered forcefully. 'Napoleon was no king, just a horrid, little Corsican upstart and military dictator. And I ought to know. I am half French. While you are only one quarter French!' He went on, 'and he caused the bloody English's vicious and unprovoked attack on Copenhagen in 1801.'

But he did concede that Peter the Great and Gustav Adolf

both passed muster. Indeed, he had pointed out to Christian some years earlier the pillar inside Roskilde Cathedral where Peter's great height was scratched during a Danish visit. It towered over the other royal markers so much that Frederik suspected the Tsar was standing on an apple box. All he said about the great Swedish King was, that although he might have been a military genius, he was a poor father as his daughter had abdicated the throne and fled Sweden.

At his 20th birthday dinner on October 15 that autumn, Chris decided to play his trump card. It was not an offer he wanted to make at all, but he was getting nowhere. His parents knew well that their eldest child had lost all interest in military service after his initial training despite his forefathers' long tradition of honourable postings and brave deeds; indeed, he had expressed distinctly pacifist, ever anti-military views. He told them before he had no interest in learning to take orders, fight and kill. So, he hoped his trump card would work.

Just before dessert in the grand old dining room of Frederik VIII's Palace at Amalienborg, Chris raised the topic again, and again his parents objected in the same terms: his safety, his education, his isolation, his family duties and his public duties as well as the expense. Chris sensed their opposition was perhaps not quite as vehement as last time and thought the right moment was now.

He smiled at Isabella and offered, 'If I promise to join the military again when I get back would you allow me to go?' He could see immediately that his father showed interest.

'Which service would you join?' he replied.

'Is that a yes then? And would it matter?' Chris asked, trying to hide his rising sense of hope.

'Well, I am sure you would be welcome in my old frogman unit, and it would make me very proud,' his father said. 'But I reckon any service would be good for you. It certainly was for me.'

'So, is that a definite yes?' Chris repeated.

'It's a definite maybe,' his father countered with a grin. Chris saw his parents exchange a meaningful glance. His hopes rose further, but he realised he had left himself horridly exposed.

'I would prefer the Air Force actually, but only for 12 months,' he added.

Now Isobella spoke up, 'Oh come on, Father. You know he is making a big concession. Don't be so difficult. He is an adult now. If he decided to go without your permission, there is nothing really you could do to stop him.'

Before her husband could reply, Chris' mother piped up; her eyebrows raised. 'Coming from you Christian that sounds like a very big deal. I know the military has never interested you after your first go. So, you must be really keen to get your year off,' she conceded, but she was looking at her husband not her son.

'I sure am. And I will come back and learn to fly,' Chris replied. He wanted to add, 'and shoot and kill,' but he bit his tongue.

King Frederik had wanted to refute his daughter's claims that there was nothing he could do, but instead he just said, okay. 'As you no doubt suspect young man, your mother and

I have been discussing this with each other for a while now, and with our advisors too, and we think it might be okay. Your grandmother is of the same opinion. But before we agree to this folly of yours, I want to know have your really thought it through? Remember, Napoleon and Peter the Great did not have thousands of followers on social media to keep happy, not to mention the damn media. You can't just disappear without a trace. Even a few months out of the public eye would cause a scandal,' his father warned.

Chris knew he was right, and he had no response as he slumped in his chair. 'I don't think I have,' he admitted. 'I haven't thought about that. I would need a cover story.'

'You sure will,' his mother agreed, 'a very plausible story that does not need regular pictures, interviews, media releases and posts.'

'That sounds impossible,' Chris conceded, crestfallen. He chastised himself for his stupidity. The plan looked doomed.

'Well, this is what your grandmother thinks,' Frederik began with a half-smile. Chris was taken aback; the old Queen knew of his plan. Maybe all was not lost. His father continued; Chris was all ears, 'Mum thinks you need to be sent to a military academy in the United States for a year. A special institution where in you will study international relations, diplomacy, military strategy and leadership.' Frederik added, 'Mum may not be our monarch any longer, but she is willing to pull a few strings just for you.'

'And the yanks still owe us a few favours after they tried to get Greenland. That was such a disgrace,' Mary stated.

'Indeed' Frederik responded, 'and we will need to get the experts to concoct the occasional picture and story.' He sounded almost enthusiastic now, 'you will need tight security over there and measures to deter journalists.'

'Well, Christian, that's the plan. What do you reckon?' his mother asked.

'We are prepared to help you with this giant deception although it will cost the state a lot of money. Hoodwinking the media for a year will be most rewarding. Fake news all the way,' Frederik added, and recalled the many subterfuges in the early stages of his courtship with Mary. Like father, like son, he thought with a hint of pride as he recalled the trysts with his mother across two continents.

Chris was taken aback, 'I had no idea. I reckon it is a great plan. I must thank Grandmother as soon as I can. And I will do all I can to make it work. Thank you both so much!' He got up beaming and embraced his parents.

'Fantastic! Thank you so much for such a wonderful birthday present!' Then, in his best Aussie accent as he went to hug Isabella, he proclaimed, 'I'm going down under. I am going down under. Bring it on mate!'

His parents laughed together as the two siblings embraced. Isabella who had remained silent throughout the negotiation then asked her brother another question. 'What will you call yourself? You can't use your real name.'

Chris realised she had a point, 'I have no idea,' he answered.

'Well, I have a suggestion, how about Kasper Frederiksen?' she proposed.

It struck an immediate chord. 'I like the sound of that a

lot. And it is in honour of my dear father,' he added grinning.

Prince Christian had finally got his gap year, and, after Covid19, this had been the hardest battle he had ever fought.

It took some time, but Chris eventually received a new identity in the physical forms of a passport, a driver's licence, a bank card, a person ID card, a vaccination certificate, all in the name of Kasper Frederiksen. He also had to take a brief trip across the Atlantic to pose for a whole set of pictures at the American Foreign Diplomacy Academy in Pennsylvania while shaking hands with staff, sitting in the cafeteria, chatting with fellow students and studying in his room. The officials who had been let in on the project at the Foreign Ministry back home would take care of the details and he could follow his fake progress at the academy while away.

Chris decided to become a Woofer. He joined the WWOOF organisation which stood for either Willing Workers on Organic Farms or Worldwide Opportunities on Organic Farms. A Woofer works on a host property unpaid but in lieu of wages is given accommodation and food. Chris had heard about Woofing from friends at university who had been Woofers in various parts of Europe and further afield. He read that Woofing had been around for forty years and was popular among backpackers and other travellers.

Isabella and Chris eagerly scanned the list of WWOOF hosts in Australia. He was looking for a place where he would meet interesting people, do interesting things and stay in an interesting place. There were many possibilities. They made a short list. Most hosts were families with farms of different kinds and sizes down the east coast and across the south to Western Australia. A few were quirkier; a cactus farm, an emu farm, a horse stud for Icelandic ponies and couple of rare plant nurseries.

Then they saw a listing for a host called Commonplace in Victoria, down south in Australia. It was one of a few communes, or intentional communities as they were also called, that hosted Woofers in Australia. It called itself a social change organisation and was looking for people to help with gardening, catering, property maintenance, cleaning, tree planting, childcare, office administration, event management and land conservation. Quite a lot, the siblings mused. Chris thought he would make a go of those jobs but the bit that caught his eye was at the bottom. 'Woofers may be able to attend workshops and other events conducted by the hosts free of charge.' Chris and Isabella then quickly found the Commonplace website and trawled through it keenly. Commonplace lay about twelve kilometres south of Castlemaine, a town in central Victoria, situated on 150 hectares of cleared land but with some residual bush dotted with ironbark and river red gum trees.

The pictures showed a range of buildings of different sizes; external and interior views, as well as gardens, trees, and smiling people. Chris saw that it offered a range of services to the public as well as a workshop and retreat venue for organisations, workers, clients and users in the community health, self-help, environmental, social housing, charitable, philanthropic, and community development sectors.

Isabella was adamant, 'this is where you must go Chris!'

Later, she confided in her brother that she also hoped that she would be allowed to do something similar in a couple of years, but as things turned out this did not eventuate.

CHAPTER THREE

Early morning, late January 2027, Kasper landed at Tullamarine, Melbourne's airport. He had not been to Australia for five years and felt tired and jet lagged after the 25-hour journey from Denmark. His plans for the first three months of his gap year were firmly laid. He also had in place his cover story. With the help of his family, he put this together over dinner one night. It was a lot of fun, and Frederik and Mary were keen contributors. Kasper Frederiksen was a Danish university student from Copenhagen studying Sociology, History and Geography. He was the son of middle-class parents, Annette and Jens. They lived in Gentofte in a fully detached home. His Australian mother was working in marketing, and his Danish dad was a senior bureaucrat in the naval section of the defence department. He retained his three siblings but changed their names. They became Lene, Tove and Anders.

At age 21, Kasper stood a lanky 192 centimetres tall. He was proud to have outstripped both his statuesque father and grandmother. He had a solid build but was not overly muscular. His face was classic pan European, reflecting his Danish, French, Swedish, Scottish and other European genes. He thought he looked like no-one and everyone; a nondescript. He had changed the cut of his light brown hair.

It was longer now, just below his ears and he sported a scruffy moustache. His appearance was styled upon on how he and Isabella imagined the average Danish backpacker would present themselves.

Of course, he had concerns that he might be recognised by Danish tourists or some Danophile Aussies, but decided that all he needed to do was agree that he did have the misfortune to share the looks of Prince Christian. It was a burden he had to bear. His mother had given him a few pointers on Australian English but admitted that she was rusty. They agreed that he did not get to hear much of it at Amalienborg Palace, or at university, but he was glad that he had been raised trilingual. Both his parents and grandparents had insisted, and anyway, it was what most educated Danes achieved. Apart from his fluency in Danish, English and French, he could also get by in German and the other Scandinavian languages, except for Icelandic.

From Tullamarine, Kasper caught the airport train to Sunshine station and changed to the Castlemaine train on the Bendigo line. The smells and sounds of Australia engulfed him, with pleasure, on that hot summer day. Not so happily, he remembered the flies, as his personal entourage of blowies descended. At the Castlemaine station he was met by Fran in an old Ford 150 utility truck; an assortment of empty 44-gallon drums, tree stakes, grocery shopping and rolls of fencing wire in the back. Fran, short and round with long dark hair, was about 50 years old. She wore faded denim shorts, a tee shirt and thongs, and on her head perched a big, battered Akubra hat.

She beamed a warm welcome, gave him a hug, and stated keenly, 'Welcome to Australia mate, and welcome to Castlemaine, the centre of the universe. I'm Fran, one of the Commonplace members. How was your trip up from Naarm?'

He was a little taken aback at the physical welcome and mumbled, 'thanks, it is great to be here,' but then had to ask, 'what is Naarm?'

'Oh, that's the Aboriginal name for Melbourne. We try to use it around here.'

Kasper just nodded, He lowered his bag into the back then remembered at the last moment to go to the left side of the truck. Fran tore off in the old Ford to Commonplace and they arrived in the warm evening sunlight. Sounds of much hilarity came from a very large building. Monday night, at the commune, was games night.

'Welcome to the highlight of the week! The Eyrie is our main building. The walls are made of earth.' Fran added as she ushered him quickly into a large room. 'This is our Great Room.'

Kasper saw about 14 people of many different ages, shapes and sizes, frantically chasing each other around the room while four stood stock still with their legs wide apart.

'Great, it's Scarecrow Tiggy,' Fran cried and rushed into the melee, 'Feel free to join in,' she yelled back over her shoulder to a bewildered Kasper.

Not knowing the game, he felt a bit overwhelmed. Instead of joining in he dropped his bag against a tall, earthen wall and sat on a long, padded bench that ran alongside it. He wondered what on earth he had let himself in for.

After a while, he got the hang of the game. Whoever was 'It' had to catch and tag another player. As soon as someone was tagged, they had to stand still, and with legs wide apart yell for assistance because if another player dived between their legs without being tagged the scarecrow was back in the game. Hence all the screaming and pleading from scarecrows. But diving between someone's legs while being pursued by 'It' greatly increased the risk of being tagged. Kasper realised that someone had to risk being tagged to liberate a scarecrow. Eventually, as he watched, everyone but 'It' was reduced to scarecrows and the game ended. Several players slumped to the floor in exhaustion as the shouting subsided.

The next game was in distinct contrast to Scarecrow Tiggy. And right up the alley of a jet lagged, newly arrived Dane. Dead Fish was the game and the rules were simple. A middle-aged man in a red singlet and khaki shorts volunteered to be 'It' and everyone else lay motionless on the floor. Kasper joined them. He could manage this. 'It' had the task of getting the dead fish to move; even the slightest movement meant the fish had to get up and join 'It' as a human tormentor. The last dead fish was the winner. Tactics were both fair and foul: whispering, fanning, shouting, blowing, joke telling, insulting and heavy breathing were all permitted; touching and spitting were not. Though spitting was often a grey area because when shouting and blowing occurred at very close quarters some spittle escaped incidentally but perhaps not always accidentally. Fish were known to protest that they only moved to avoid such spittle. But all sports have grey areas in the rules.

Kasper found that he was doing very well. He lay there perfectly still and retreated into himself; eyes closed and eye lids heavy from his weariness. His mind turned back the years to a lovely spring day he had spent as a boy with his father, sailing the Øresund, the strait which forms the Danish–Swedish border. He felt peaceful, serene and relaxed. Sleep was close as his present surroundings retreated, and the noise and other stimulation faded away. It turned out well for him as he was the second last fish to move, and he was pleased he had not won. Lots of attention would have been embarrassing. He finally flinched when eight-year-old Ivy blew into his ear and unleashed a mighty shout, 'WOOFER!' Others gathered around her, and he instinctively opened his eyes and jerked his head. Loud applause and cries of 'well done you' followed.

Community games ended with a ritual group activity called a Whoosh. All players, Kasper included, formed a circle, holding hands around the ring with arms lowered. Slowly the circle inched inwards and closed as people slowly raised their arms. At the same time, they all began to utter a deep, throaty sound, like a howling wind, growing louder. Finally, the circle closed in tight with everyone's hands now together high in the air. When they could progress no more, the voices came to a loud crescendo and a mighty 'WHOOSH' rang out.

Now, one of the children called out, 'Can we play community games again tomorrow night?' but Fran got in first and called for everyone's attention before people headed to the dining room and kitchen for drinks and snacks.

'I want you all to meet Kasper, our new Woofer. He has

just flown in from Denmark. A huge welcome to you Kasper and we hope you enjoy your stay.' Kasper did not speak. He just smiled and raised his right arm in a brief wave.

Everyone clapped and Fran turned to Kasper and stated, 'I'll take you to your hut first. Feel free to come back down later. And tomorrow someone will show you around. We don't expect you to do any work for a couple of days. Unless of course you want to. So please feel free to sleep in and settle in.'

Kasper gathered his bag and day pack and followed as Fran led him up a slight hill at the back of the building. The sun had just set with the western sky ablaze with every shade of red and orange. He took in the smell of eucalyptus and a strange birdcall he did not know. He remembered a painting of a sunset like this his mother had back home on the wall in her study.

The wooden hut was small with a single bed, a two-person sofa, a desk, chair, cupboard, bookcase, wardrobe, and a pedestal fan, On one wall, a hand basin with a single cold-water tap. On the table, a torch, insect repellent and a desk lamp. A mosquito net hung above the bed from a circular frame attached to the ceiling. Kasper looked around then down. 'But the floor is just dirt,' he exclaimed with a frown. 'Is that allowed?' He was certain he had not seen any mention of dirt floors on the website.

Fran laughed and replied without irony. 'It's clean dirt, keep it swept, and you'll be right.' Kasper was annoyed but was too tired to argue.

'I'll leave you to it mate, please feel free to piss outside,'

Fran suggested, 'it is a liberating experience. The toilets are in the main building, the Eyrie. This hut is called the Brown hut. I hope you get a good night's sleep,' she finished, and left him alone.

He mumbled a thank you and closed the door. He did not want snacks or drinks with the others. First, he pulled the curtains across the single window and put his phone on its charger. Next, he took off all his clothes and fell on his bed. Personal hygiene could wait. Day one of his gap year really starts tomorrow, he thought, as he lowered the mosquito net and fell asleep, in no time at all.

He woke at 3:30 am with a start and wondered where in the world he was. The host of memories from yesterday rushed in; he felt most satisfied and went back to sleep. By 5:30 am he was wide awake and sent a message to his sister: 'Arrived safely at Commonplace, okay but strange place, earth floor in my hut, friendly people, very warm. Say hi to the others. More to follow.' Isobella replied almost at once, 'I want details.' Kasper smiled, that was so like her, but she would have to wait.

He got dressed and left his hut. It was quiet. The first rays of dawn light lit the eastern sky. He sat on a bench and watched the dawn ascend. Unfamiliar bird calls soon welcomed the new day, and he thought he saw animals rustling in the bush nearby. He was very pleased to see two grey kangaroos shuffle around selecting grasses before retreating into the bush.

After breakfast, a boy called Sam confidently advised Kasper that he would be showing him around Commonplace this morning. Sam looked about ten and was dressed in a pair of khaki shorts, a pair of black elastic sided boots and a hat. He was talkative and proudly showed Kasper over the property like an old hand, pointing out the various buildings and the two caravans, the kangaroo-proof vegetable garden and orchard, eucalyptus trees plantations, a large dam with pier and pontoon, the creek, the solar array, the wind turbine, water tanks and the back gully. Sam gave a potted history of the property including permaculture expert David Holmgren's principles used in the design and placement of the buildings and gardens. Finally, he showed Kasper proudly around the Eyrie and had all the facts at hand; 110 squares in area with 25 rooms comprising, twelve bedrooms, two kitchens, three bathrooms, three toilets, two offices, the great room, a pantry, a laundry and a phone booth. At one bedroom he stopped and nonchalantly stated, 'that's the room I was born in.' At the phone booth he pointed out the landline as if it was an archaeological specimen and commented, 'Sometimes it even rings!'

Back outside they spotted in the distance a mob of eastern grey kangaroos. Kasper mentioned that he had seen two of them by his hut earlier that morning. Sam replied casually, 'Well one was probably Sinbad, he is very tame, but watch out, he likes to box with men.'

'Box with men?' Kasper exclaimed. He had seen boxing kangaroos on film but assumed it was a circus act.

'Yeah,' Sam explained. 'The bucks fight all the time. Poor Sinbad tries to practice his boxing skills with humans as well as the other bucks. I avoid him when he comes up to me looking for a fight.' Kasper wondered how he would manage going toe to toe with Sinbad. Sam had lived at Commonplace all his life and did not go to school. He was home-educated. He wanted to be a paramedic or a professional basketballer when he grew up. Kasper was hard pressed to service Sam's curiosity and the detailed questioning about his own life and had to embellish his cover story on the spot. Finally, he had to say 'enough' to Sam and retreat to his hut for a rest. Sam sauntered off to the dam cheerfully after his final burst, 'Next time I will show you my wedgetail eagle feathers. They are awesome. Oh, and one other thing, if you go down by the creek, you might spot a koala. I did a couple of times. See ya.'

Kasper lay on his bed wondering if all Aussie kids were so precocious and inquisitive, while feeling guilty about the string of lies he had just told a child. But that was the price he must pay to stay undercover. So far, it was worth it.

CHAPTER FOUR

As Kasper had discovered, Commonplace was blessed with its own mob of eastern grey kangaroos. They roamed freely across the property with only the orchard and vegetable garden protected by a three-metre fence that was often put to the test at the height of summer when the only lush green grass was around the septic and grey water outlets that watered the plants inside the fence. Mostly the kangaroos avoided humans and hopped away without much fuss but occasionally, especially when they were scared by dogs or humans, they would tear off in fear and panic.

The roads in the Mt Alexander shire were a killing ground for kangaroos and other wildlife, mainly from drivers who did not slow down from dusk until dawn when the crepuscular creatures were on the move or grazing along roadsides.

The Mt Alexander Wildlife Sanctuary took in injured kangaroos, and joeys whose mothers had been killed and where too young to survive. But as the human population of the shire grew, road traffic increased and land free from housing and human activity shrunk and so the kangaroo death toll climbed; from road deaths, dog attacks and senseless hunting. Animal rescue volunteers were kept very busy attending the scenes. They had to carefully examine the pouches of dead or dying mothers for joeys that had survived.

Raising joeys by hand was very rewarding but it took skill, resources and time. Increasingly, the local sanctuary became full and foster parents in the community had to take in the excess joeys.

The children of Commonplace were dead keen to raise joeys, but wiser heads insisted that it was not the right place for them. Too many visitors would find them far too attractive. Joeys were not pets and the less human contact they had the better. Indeed, it was illegal to keep them as pets. But the children, led by Sam and his sister Eve, persisted, finally winning a concession. If the local sanctuary could find no other option, and if the children did the training, they would agree as a last resort. But only on a trial basis and only if the joeys were released as soon as possible to join the others. Then the inevitable happened and the adorable Gretel and Sinbad arrived, much to the delight of the children.

Once Gretel was old enough and could join the mob she never came back to the Eyrie, but as a male, Sinbad had a much harder time. As a juvenile buck kangaroo, he was finding himself up against a rigid male hierarchy based on might not equity. It was only the alpha male who was able to mix and mate with the mature females and he protected his privilege ferociously. Young males spent much of their time fighting with their peers on their slow ascension to become a challenger for the top job and the right to mate. Sinbad was no exception except that he was in the privileged position of being able to practise his boxing skills with males of both the roo and human kind.

Kasper was wary when Sinbad first approached him for a

sparring session. He had no desire to fight with a kangaroo or any other creature and tried to walk away but Sinbad insisted. Without too much effort Kasper was able to defend himself from the jabbing paws and the kicks from the hind legs. Sinbad was still learning to use his tail as a fifth limb and to rock back on it to deliver powerful kicks from his legs in that uniquely kangaroo way. Sometimes he just fell over clumsily but got up and tried again. The challenge for Kasper, or any other man who Sinbad took on, was to knock him over enough times while avoiding the treacherous claws. After a few falls Sinbad would submit and hop off unfazed. But very quickly he got bigger and better.

Late one night Kasper awoke to what sounded like old men coughing outside his hut. Puzzled he got up to investigate and there were three kangaroos in conversation. Two hopped away when they found they were disturbed but the third came forward. It was Sinbad and without invitation he came inside and lay on the earthen floor. Kasper was only too happy to give him a pat and a rub under his chin. Sinbad was very fond of a chin scratch and rolled his head and his eyes back in total pleasure.

Sinbad spoke sadly saying 'You know it is so bloody hard for me to grow up. I now know I am a roo, not one of youse Notails but the others won't accept me or let me join in. Even Gretel hates me now. They keep picking on me and fighting me.'

He looked forlorn and all Kasper could think of in response was, 'Well as you get bigger and stronger you will be able to beat more and more of them. Then you will earn your place and the respect of others. Maybe one day you will be the King Kangaroo.' He hoped it would work out for Sinbad and thought of his own unhappy school days. But he knew he would never have to fight to be respected by most Danes. It was his right from birth.

Sinbad appeared to accept this and flicked his ears in appreciation, then raised his right paw for Kasper to shake before he shuffled to the door. Kasper let him out of the hut. From then on Sinbad would pay him the occasional nocturnal visit and their connection deepened. Sinbad grew bigger and stronger, and his fighting prowess developed fast. Everyone who knew him commented that Sinbad was becoming a big, strong buck and he knew it too.

With hindsight it was inevitable that it would come to a head, but nobody foresaw it in time. Kasper had been rendering the outside earthen walls of the Eyrie with a new coat of red clay one Friday. After work he retreated to the large dam to wash off the render and sweat. He floated freely enjoying the bird life in the sky above him. He was starting to recognise some native birds. The water was cool with the occasion patch of cold streaming up from below. He lay there in peace and solitude and appreciated that he was becoming accustomed to the physical labour.

As he began to wade ashore, he saw a male kangaroo break away from two others and head towards him. It was Sinbad of course. Kasper was not well placed to defend himself if Sinbad wanted to fight. He was right near the edge of the dam, unarmed and unclad. He felt exposed and vulnerable. He stayed in the water hoping Sinbad would go away but after what seemed like ages, he decided he needed to get past the kangaroo somehow. The fight for Kasper to keep his guts and genitals away from Sinbad's claws began. Sinbad had the higher ground and pressed forward as Kasper tried to manoeuvre himself higher up the bank. But Sinbad kept him downhill, and Kasper realised he only had two options; get Sinbad to submit or for himself to flee. Neither seemed possible and so Kasper struggled mightily to protect himself from the onslaught of kicks and claws. Mastery of the fifth limb was now Sinbad's who used it to unleash volleys of powerful kicks at Kasper's viscera.

He suddenly had the crazy thought that he had come all this way only to be killed in a boxing match with a lovable tame roo who visited for chats at night. What would Queen Margrethe and the Danish aristocracy possibly think? Slowly a strategy appeared to him. He started inching along the bank towards the boat shed. There were his towel and clothes as well as a rubber dinghy and a pair of oars; his possible defences. He was tiring fast and still had metres to cover. Could he make it?

Sinbad seemed to show no signs of exhaustion; he was clearly up for more. Kasper now bitterly regretted counselling Sinbad to fight for the kangaroo throne. It was now or never. He waited for Sinbad to rear back again onto his tail then he shouted at Sinbad, 'Stop Sinbad stop. You will kill me!' Sinbad paused a moment; Kasper dashed the last few metres to the boatshed. He knew Sinbad had hesitated, but he could hear and smell him at his back. Kasper made it to the shed. He grabbed an oar and spun around to see Sinbad again rear back to launch another volley of kicks. This time Kasper thrust the oar at the roo's midriff and backed up the dam bank to higher ground. Sinbad could not grab the oar, so Kasper used it to knock him off balance. The tide of the battle had turned. Sinbad came for him again, but each time Kasper poked him with the oar while backing away. Three times the roo was knocked down and got up for more. But on the fourth occasion he had had enough. Off he hopped, and Kasper felt a wave of relief wash through his naked body. He had survived. With enormous relief he called to Sinbad, 'thanks for letting me go free,' as he dressed before dragging himself up the Eyrie for a hot shower and a cold drink.

Afterwards the news of this fight spread around the community. He was asked about it by all and sundry, and it kicked off the debate which came to be known ironically as the Kangaroo Court. All agreed that it had been a mistake to raise Sinbad at Commonplace, as he now posed a real threat to all human males as most of them, he could now outbox. And many human males of all shapes and sizes passed through the community and those from the city would be defenceless. They could all imagine the headlines in the Castlemaine Mail, *"Man killed by Pet Kangaroo on local Commune."* Something had to be done about Sinbad before someone was hurt, or Goddess forbid, killed.

After a long and spirited debate that covered such themes as animal rights, human rights, ecological principles, and the evolutionary and gendered nature of violence, three options arose. They were across a spectrum. One was simply to let Sinbad be. He had every right to do his thing and if it made males scared then they had to make sure they went around in pairs and carried a weapon whenever Sinbad was nearby. Some women of Commonplace embraced this option and pointed out it was what members of their gender had been doing to stay safe from male violence for at least two millennia. But there was no real clear division along gender lines.

The second option was to kill Sinbad and eat him. There were a few carnivores in the community and kangaroos from the mob had been on the menu before. The final option was to take Sinbad away from the property to an animal sanctuary with other eastern greys. This would give Sinbad a new chance to assimilate and survive with his own kind.

Although his opinion was sought, Kasper did not have much to say throughout the debate. He enjoyed observing the passion and learned a lot about what the participants thought and how they debated. It was animated but mostly orderly. There was also a commitment to finding an option that they could all accept. He was happy with two of the options, but he wanted his friend to live. He had no desire to eat Sinbad. Memories rushed back to a time when he had first seen horse meat in a Copenhagen butcher shop. He loved horses and did not know that the Danes ever ate horse but there it was. He did not partake.

He also came to appreciate why there were no pets allowed at Commonplace and how that rule had to be rigorously enforced when visitors would turn up with their beloved dogs, despite the rules. Surely, Rover was an exception! It was often hard to insist that they leave, but the land was the home of kangaroos, wallabies, wombats, echidnas, antechinus and reptiles. All these creatures were at grave risk from domestic dogs and cats and from the feral dogs and cats that had escaped domesticity and now roamed the countryside.

Consensus about Sinbad's future was finally reached, Sinbad would be relocated if they could find a sanctuary that had room for him. They could not just take him away and release him somewhere else. He would be a sitting duck for the small number of redneck male locals who believed that shooting roos with high powered automatic rifles with telescopic sights was sport. Kasper was pleased with the decision but wondered how they would be able to transport Sinbad. This had not been discussed, so he decided to ask. Simone explained, 'We had to take him to the vet's a couple of times when he was younger. The first time we carried him to the car; he seemed to enjoy the ride. The second time we coaxed him to the back of the station wagon with a few of his favourite pellets. Guess what? He jumped right in!'

At this, Kasper did not hesitate, 'Can I help move him?' The others nodded and Simone replied. 'After your encounter by the dam, that would be fitting. First, we will look for a sanctuary. If we find one, can you keep an eye on Sinbad? Sometimes he hangs around the cars. We think he might be keen on another drive. When he's there, grab someone else and spring into action. There is a good chance he will co-operate with you. You're certainly his biggest fan!'

CHAPTER FIVE

Eric Anderson was a tall, muscular young man, aged 24. He stood 1.90 metres and had russet hair, a long face and a very fair complexion. Maybe he had Viking blood as he was a Scot and grew up in Edinburgh. Music was his talent and passion, and he could play the piano in his sleep – and often dreamed that he did. Eric had a peripatetic nature and his musical talents allowed him to travel, work and play around the world. He had qualified as a music therapist and especially liked working with older people. And they loved working with him. In his repertoire he had hundreds of songs, and he carried the sheet music with him in a big thick folder. Old songs brought a lot of joy to people who had dementia or were just lonely and depressed. The neural connections relating to music were deep and permanent, and he had seen first-hand that music was more than a source of joy; it was an effective therapy for many psychological ailments.

For four years, Eric had been living in New York and working as a music therapist in a couple of aged care homes. It was fun but it was time to move on, and he came to Australia to visit his father. His parents had separated when Eric was two years old, and he had grown up with his mother, brother and sister in Scotland. His dad, Magnus, was an academic historian who specialised in ancient civilisations. He was particularly interested in Old Europe, the Neolithic era in southern Europe that flourished along where the Danube now flows, long before the arrival of the Indo Europeans. He, and others, claimed it was an age of peace, egalitarianism and goddess worship without warriors, wars or kings, and it lasted for a couple of thousand years. Other historians, of course, disagreed, but Magnus was convinced by the growing body of archaeological evidence and was renowned in his field for his scholarship and erudition.

Magnus had been in Australia for ten years and had tenure at the University of Melbourne, the oldest and most distinguished seat of higher learning in Victoria. He had become a naturalised Australian and had not seen his son Eric for five years. Both were looking forward to the reunion. Their first two meetings were a little tense. Eric had not fully forgiven his father for abandoning him as a child and moving to the other end of the earth. He was hoping that he would be able to tell his father of his resentment and perhaps forge a closer relationship.

Sadly, this never happened. There was a misunderstanding about schedules. Magnus had to attend a professional conference in San Francisco just two weeks after Eric arrived in Melbourne. Magnus could not get out of it as he was presenting a paper on the Etruscans, a tribe from the Italian peninsular with roots in Old Europe, and it was a feather in his professional cap. What he did not know at 65 years of age, was most of his cardiac arteries were very badly occluded and he had no idea he was in such bad shape. The night before he was due to give his paper, he had a massive, fatal, cardiac arrest in his hotel room. He did not get the chance to ask for help and his body was discovered the next morning in the bathroom by a shocked staff cleaner.

The news took five days to reach Eric. He knew something was wrong as his father had stopped communicating, but this was the worst possible news. Now he could never reconcile with his father. Instead, he was left to mourn his death and regret what might have been, and to bring his father's body home to Melbourne. Magnus had no partner and no other family in Australia. And he left no will. The next month for Eric was a maelstrom of airline officials, foreign office officials, lawyers, undertakers, cemetery officials and clergy. Eric resented all of it but fortunately he was able to call on some of his father's close colleagues in the history department, though the responsibility and duty fell solely to him.

The funeral and cremation were miserable affairs with just a few friends, a few colleagues and one family member. His father was no extrovert with a big circle of friends. His mother and siblings had offered to come but he knew they would prefer not to. When he was clear that he could manage without them, they found reasons not to come.

When the rites were over, he needed a retreat, somewhere he could escape responsibility and reflect on all that had happened. He knew that an inheritance was coming his way eventually, but he had to be frugal until then. Commonplace appealed to him; he had been a Woofer before. He arrived in mid-April, autumn, as the temperatures fell, bushfire risk abated, and the grass greened. For most people living in southern Australia, it was a time to relax; the absolute best season.

The old piano in the Great Hall of the Eyrie was good news to Eric. He had not played for a while and missed it, so set to work tuning up the veteran goanna. It had not been played for a few years and needed some TLC. Word had got around that Eric was a pianist and was fixing up the old piano, so he was being asked for updates on when the piano would be ready. There was an agreement at Commonplace not to have televisions in the common areas although they had infiltrated some of the members' own rooms, and there was an unspoken agreement that a sing-along around the piano over the long winter evenings would be a very positive development. Eric was happy to oblige. For him it was a form of healing, his own music therapy.

Community Singing was soon added to Friday nights on the calendar and was a great success, even attracting some of the locals from the towns nearby where many friends of Commonplace lived. Beatles songs from the 60s and 70s were perennial favourites, even with the young. Soon Eric agreed to join a local rock band known as the Hairy Backs, which had two Commonplace members, Luis, on drums, and Elspeth, on bass. They played gigs in the Commonplace great room on special occasions or on no occasion at all. Kasper and Eric became good friends and stayed in the adjoining huts; brown and orange.

CHAPTER SIX

All Commonplace members, residents, visitors and a few townsfolk who self-identified as cis or trans male were invited to attend the monthly Men's discussion group, known with a touch of irony, as MAGI: Males against Gender Injustice. Kasper and Eric were invited. MAGI met at the Five Flags Hotel in Campbells Creek where moderate social drinking was the custom. There was a topic each month for discussion, and someone made a short presentation to get the ball rolling. Attendance was patchy and depended on the topic and what else was going on. The topic for May was 'What does an anti-patriarchal strong man look like in this patriarchy?' A regular attendee, Bob, a social work lecturer at Latrobe University, some 40 kilometres to the north in Bendigo, was the presenter. Kasper was very interested and agreed to go but Eric said no.

Twelve men gathered in a side room off the main dining room with drinks and snacks at hand. An open fire kept them warm as Bob took the floor. He first welcomed Kasper, the only newcomer, then began. Bob meant to provoke and had some success. His presentation was simple. He listed on butchers' paper attributes that traditionally are associated with manly virtue – toughness, decisiveness, stoicism, ambition, virility, hard work, physical strength,

43

rationality, objectivity, loyalty, patriotism, steadfastness, competitiveness, mastery and fearlessness. One by one, he described how each represented a threat to the physical and mental wellbeing of men, women, others, children, peace and the planet.

Kasper had not heard such an analysis or critique before. King Christian X, his forebear, leapt into his mind. Surely, he was much loved by his people for most of these attributes. But then again, that was nearly 80 years ago when the country was under occupation by the Germans. Surely things have changed. Or have they? These attributes he did not have but was quite certain he was expected to acquire and display them if he was to rule his people successfully. The history books were full of glowing eulogies to strong kings, the conquerors and the brave, as well as condemnation of weak kings, the conquered and the cowardly. Denmark had its fair share of both.

The debate centred on whether these attributes were all bad or just bad in excess. If they were so bad what other attributes were desirable. Some men spoke a lot and others not at all. Bob started a list as others threw up suggestions – sensitivity, flexibility, co-operation, creativity, scepticism, compassion, fairness, earthiness, light heartedness, curiosity, fun loving, gentleness and optimism were listed. Kasper saw that the two lists stood in great contrast.

Bob took up the challenge again, 'You might have realised, as I surely have, that we will not bring down the patriarchy and establish justice and emancipation for all by just using those piss weak things on the second list,' he said.

Kasper and others laughed, and someone said, 'We need them both!'

Bob seized the moment, 'Absolutely right, Andrew. We need them both. But can we have them both? Have we got them both? I mean personally. Do any of you have them both? Are they mutually exclusive? Can we be both competitive and co-operative?'

'Not at the same time,' Andrew added, 'But there is a place for both. I was a real wimp as a lad. I was about 16 and went to St Arnaud to play footy one Saturday. In the visitors' change room there were some motivational posters hanging on the wall. One said, "When the going gets tough the tough get going!" I remember thinking that made a lot of sense. Blokes who act so tough would be useless when it came to the crunch, so they would decide to leave. That night, I told my dad of my clever insight. He burst out laughing, called me a total effing idiot, and clipped me over the ears. I had got it completely wrong!'

Many laughed and Bob spoke up again. 'Team sport is an interesting example. The champions are the players who can ruthlessly take charge of the game when it must be won, but if they refuse to co-operate on other occasions, they will lose admiration and may be forced out of the team.'

Kasper was compelled to speak. 'Yes, but I had a teacher who was competitive all the time!' Jacob Larsen, whom he loathed, was always sarcastic and 'right'. But maybe he was just like this with the students. Perhaps he had to co-operate with other teachers.'

'Yes,' someone else agreed, 'but I know men, my father

included, who were always tough bastards. They would not know flexibility or compassion if they tripped over them.'

'Well, we are never all one thing,' Bob opined, 'even Hitler was a lovely waltzer, but if we have learned to be tough bastards from our fathers and follow in their footsteps we block out the softness and we find it very hard to act otherwise when the occasion demands it. Like when our children need a hug.'

An older man, Brian, spoke up for the first time. 'Yes, and if we have grown up to be meek and mild, and one day the situation calls for us to be a real tough bastard, then we are just as useless.'

'Yeah, well that was me,' Andrew replied, 'I was such a wimp and so terrified of male authority. Still am, now I think of it,' he added with a grimace.

'It's horses for courses,' someone offered. 'And the more horses you have, the more courses you can ride.'

'But surely horse riding is the patriarchal abuse of another sentient species?' Bob interjected.

Some groaned and others chuckled.

'Try telling my daughter that!' Brian added. 'She's horse crazy. Costs me a bloody fortune.'

Kasper thought of the horses in the royal stables back home, and of his great, great grandfather King Christian X defiantly astride his horse Jubilee on daily rides through Copenhagen during the bitter German occupation of World War Two. No security could be seen when he was mobbed by thousands of cheering Danes and the German soldiers watched in amazement. Jubilee was a horse for a course but

46

would not have enjoyed a daily ride through the throng. But then, how would he possibly know what Jubilee was feeling?

At a quarter to ten, the evening ended with no clear resolution. No one seemed to care. Then a toast was made to Bob for his presentation followed by the recital of the MAGI pledge. The men stood in a circle with hands on their hearts. Some also made the Scouts' salute with their left hands as they recited with great mock reverence:

I will do my duty by Mother Earth and my planet. I will do anything I like but never cause harm or use violence. I will laugh, sing, dance and have fun. I will seek to learn, to love myself and all other living things, and to brush my teeth every night, as long as I have them. Ahwomen.'

After the pledge, half the men stayed for coffee and supper. Kasper stayed and listened to the high-spirited banter. He had not had much experience of all-male company before. He preferred the company of females, but this had been okay. No one teased or bullied him, or anyone else.

Kasper was a little tipsy when he returned to his hut in a jovial mood. Australian beer was stronger than Danish. He sent his sister an email and concluded that he was looking forward to the next men's group. He reported to Isabella that the topic would be: 'What is male mal-employment and how can we stop doing it?'

He dreamed he was riding a big brown mare through Castlemaine. All the locals had come out to watch him when the horse suddenly demanded, 'Get off me now! She needs to ride much more than you.' He dismounted and saw a little girl standing shyly beside her big father. Without a moment's hesitation he scooped her up and placed her in the saddle. The mare said, 'Take the reins and lead us to safety.' The little girl beamed with pleasure and pride as Kasper led them to the playground in Victory Park.

CHAPTER SEVEN

Ten days after the Kangaroo Court verdict Simone told Kasper there was a place available at the animal sanctuary near Dunolly so the relocation could be attempted. Kasper was most pleased and started keeping an eye out for Sinbad. One Sunday afternoon, a week later, Kasper had just returned from a run with Eric and noticed that Sinbad was up near the car park. Maybe the job was on; the relocation team had to spring into action. Kasper called Eric and the two of them approached the station wagon. Sinbad stood nearby looking with interest at the two Notails. Kasper opened the tailgate of the Holden station wagon and gestured. It was like an invitation to Sinbad. He came shuffling up, eyes ablaze, and with encouragement from Eric by means of a lift of the tail Sinbad climbed into the rear compartment as readily as any family dog. The two men looked at each other in amazement.

Kasper carefully closed the tailgate. Sinbad looked very content. Eric jumped into the driver's seat as Kasper got in behind on the rear bench. Sinbad sat in the very back of the station wagon; all was ready. Each was in his rightful place and off they drove. For about half the fifty kilometre journey out, past Maldon and Mt Tarrengower, to the sanctuary, all went smoothly. But Sinbad was a social soul. He wanted closer company and clambered over the back seat to sit alongside Kasper despite his opposition. Getting the tail over was tricky but he managed it after a struggle and settled down next to Kasper looking mightily pleased with himself. His first drive in about two years. All was fine as they travelled on, but about ten kilometres from their destination Sinbad made his next move.

Kasper tried hard to stop him and yelled to Eric; 'Watch out. He is coming over. I can't hold him!' Sinbad wanted a promotion.

Sinbad made his move and climbed into the passenger's seat next to Eric. Again, the tail was an impediment. Kasper tried to stop him by hauling on it, but to no avail. Sinbad was too strong and determined. He looked even more pleased with himself in the passenger seat sitting proudly alongside the driver. The two men could not hide their amusement as they noticed the looks on the faces of approaching motorists. Sinbad was a model passenger at first. But that soon quickly changed when the precocious young buck began to appreciate that he was a superior driver to Eric and needed to take the controls. He reached for the steering wheel and the gear shift with his clever paws. Kasper hung over the back of the seat and pulled his paws away while Eric tried to drive while batting away those same insistent paws.

The car slowed. Clearly this was dangerous driving. They just managed to keep Sinbad restrained without running off the road. Kasper had the horrid thought of being intercepted by the police. Finally, with much relief, they reached the sanctuary gate and Eric stopped the car. Kasper opened the gate as Eric drove in and closed it behind them. Ahead, behind a high fence, they spotted Sinbad's new family; other eastern greys. The men both got out and opened Sinbad's door. He did not budge. A woman approached from the building near the gate. 'Hi, I'm Bess. This must be Sinbad,' she said. 'what's he doing there?'

'He wanted to drive!' Kasper exclaimed before he introduced the three arrivals. 'Now he won't get out.'

'Wow! Just let him sit there for a while,' Bess replied. 'He's adjusting to his new surroundings.' She led the men across to the high fence where two of the other kangaroos now stood, their ears twitching. 'We'll just stand here for a while near these two and see what he does,' she suggested.

Finally, Sinbad jumped out and approached them. He sniffed Bess then the other roos through the fence and she let him into the enclosure with the words, 'Sinbad, this is your new home. We hope you enjoy it.'

Kasper wished Sinbad goodbye and good luck. He thanked Bess while handing her an envelope with a large donation. She asked if they would like to look around but both men said no. As soon as the station wagon returned to the main road both men simultaneously launched into a tirade of swearing and laughing at the danger, ridiculousness, and bizarreness of what they had just gone through. Kasper exhausted his Danish vocabulary of curses, oaths and blasphemies and then went through his English repertoire with a few 'merdes' thrown in with even a pair of 'scheisses'. He was a Scandinavian polyglot after all. Eric had less of a range but made up for it with volume and vehemence. Finally, Eric had to stop the car as they dissolved into infectious laughter.

Over dinner that night they told of their adventure, and for days after, Kasper's thoughts and worries were with Sinbad. Would he be okay in his new home? He phoned the sanctuary twice to enquiry. Sinbad was fine. But Kasper thought of visiting whenever he went near the dam.

CHAPTER EIGHT

Each autumn, Uncle Darcy and Auntie Gwenda, Aboriginal elders from the regional Dja Dja Wurrung nation, conducted a weekend workshop at Commonplace called "First Nation Truth Telling and Justice." It aimed to 'allow people of colonial European and migrant backgrounds to explore the truth of invasion, colonialisation and dispossession, and the path to justice.' The cost to attend was 600 dollars which included accommodation and all meals, with 70 percent of the income going to the Dja Dja Wurrung association. Kasper was allowed to attend free of charge but later made an anonymous donation. He knew very little about Australian history apart from the broad facts of European 'discovery' and 'settlement.' The Indigenous history was unknown to him, but he was keen to learn.

22 participants attended, mostly from Melbourne for the Friday night dinner with a difference: bush tucker. The weekend started with a smoking ceremony to cleanse and welcome before the meal. The leaders lit a bundle of green gum leaves from the property and generated much blue grey smoke. Uncle Darcy carried the smoking leaves to each person in turn and carefully blew smoke from the head to toe of each person. He explained that the smoke purifies a

person's body and spirit and wards off evil spirits. 'With this ceremony we offer you our respect and best intentions. You are cleansed and opened to good spirits.'

The dinner menu included yabbies, yams, cumbungi roots (an edible bullrush), witchetty grubs, and wattle seed cake, with the highlight being kangaroo tail.

Uncle Darcy had shot one of the young bucks from the local mob the day before and he roasted the tail in the traditional way in the hot ashes of a fire pit outside the Polygon, a large building about 300 metres from the Eyrie where the workshop was held. Some people, perhaps vegetarians or vegans, or those not game, would not eat any of the kangaroo, but Kasper got in line. He quite liked the taste; lean and tender; he looked forward to telling his siblings.

Uncle Darcy spoke over dinner of the long symbiotic relationship between kangaroo and Aboriginals, and the millennia of hunting and kangaroo management practised by his people. Knowledge, skills, fitness and courage was needed to bring kangaroo to the menu before the arrival of guns. He also mentioned the nutritional benefits of roo over beef and lamb. Then Auntie Gwenda took over and with passion told of the destruction that the hooves of cows, sheep, pigs, goats and horses had wrought on the fragile and essential plants, soils and watercourses of the country. She was not happy that white fellas were now eating kangaroo and that it was found in some supermarkets. She found the hunting and killing of kangaroos for meat to be cruel and unnecessary. She hoped that roo would never replace beef and mutton. She did not mind a lamb roast with mint sauce now and again. Uncle Darcy confessed that he had a weakness for bacon; they both chuckled.

Kasper was surprised to learn that kangaroo was eaten in Australia. He was reminded of the time he had first seen whale meat in an Icelandic restaurant. He knew horse was eaten in Europe and Grandpa Henri praised it, but Kasper had no interest whatsoever in trying it after he had seen it in a Copenhagen supermarket. After dinner they stayed up around the fire for a while with food the common and safe topic of conversation. When he was asked what the Danes ate he extolled the many culinary virtues of potatoes, mackerel, salmon, fish eggs, fresh peas and sausages. And of course, Danish pastries. He felt compelled to tell the history of these famous items; how the Danes call them Viennese breads because when Danish bakers went on strike and Viennese bakers were imported from Austria to break the strike, they baked what they knew best and soon the Danes were queuing up for these marvellous Viennese breads.

The next morning they visited sites of significance around the district. An ancient volcano, was first. The Aboriginal leaders related eyewitness accounts of it erupting around 12,000 years ago when the mountain threw rocks at its neighbour, Mount Tarrengower, some forty kilometres away. At the Guildford plateau they stopped and were shown that the rocks thrown by Lalgambuk at Tarrengower now formed this stony upland. They visited scar trees and birthing trees, water holes, murder sites, grinding stones, village and corroboree sites.

Outside the original Castlemaine Court House, in

Goldsmith Crescent, they were encouraged to touch the gnarled old gum trees where, from 1851 until 1865, Aboriginal prisoners were chained in the blazing sun before being administered British justice. In a language they did not understand, and in trials where they could not give evidence in their own defence, or in any other legal matter, because they were unable to swear on the Bible. Inside the stark, stone lock-up, behind the current Castlemaine courthouse and the old 19th century Castlemaine goal, they inspected the prisoners' cells, and the gallows site where ten hangings occurred between 1865 and 1876. Nobody lingered. All were places of death, detention, sorrow and injustice.

As they passed the Castlemaine Police Station, Auntie Gwenda recalled a recent tragedy. In 2017, a Yorta Yorta woman, Tanya Day, was arrested after falling asleep on a train to Melbourne. She had been drinking and fell, hitting her head on a cell wall multiple times. The police left her lying on the floor with a serious head injury for three hours. She died in police custody, having not received medical help. Auntie Gwenda called it a blatant case of racial profiling and neglect.

They returned to Franklinford, near the ancient volcano Lalgambuk, renamed Mount Franklin in 1843 in honour of a colonial governor of Tasmania. The Aboriginal name for Franklinford was Larrnebarramul, the land of the emu.

They gathered at the site in a field just west of the Franklinford church and hall. A small, rusty sign hung on the roadside fence in the shape of a boomerang. The place was of great and sorrowful significance for Auntie Gwenda and Uncle Darcy.

'We have brought you here to tell the sorry story of this sad site. It is the story of the 1840s, the first ten years of the arrival of the British, the theft of our Country and what became of us,' Auntie began. 'Some charitable members of the British government were concerned about our death toll from disease and felt we needed protection, and the "benefits of Christianity and civilisation," their words, not mine. So, in 1841 they chose the land around here on what they called Jim Crow Creek to form the Loddon Aboriginal Protectorate. The local squatter Mollison did not mind but other colonists did. Then they appointed a Methodist missionary, Edward Parker, to run the project and called him Assistant Aboriginal Protector. He moved in and tried to attract our people to this place and keep us here. By offering food and medicine he had some success in the beginning.'

Uncle took up the narrative, 'We sure needed both. By that time western diseases were rampant. The deadly smallpox epidemic preceded white fellas' arrival. Then, when the invasion of our Country began in 1837, they brought, along with the guns, bronchitis, influenza, measles, TB, scarlet fever and those two old favourites, syphilis and gonorrhoea. We had no immunity to any of them. Western medicine had no answers either. Anyway, Parker set up a typical English farm with white overseers, farm hands, builders and bullock drivers. He was clear about what needed to be done. Through farming, he would civilise and Christianise us. And in his words, we would be "reclaimed." What could possibly go wrong?'

'In the beginning our people were pleased, they called

Parker "Marmingorak," or father. We came in the hundreds; a refuge with food was too good to refuse. So, in 1844 for example, 316 visitors were recorded,' Auntie continued. 'But few chose to stay and take up farming. We came and went with the seasons, with work opportunities on the stations and for our traditional practices on our Country. We had our own culture to follow. And besides, all that Christian evangelism stuff Parker sprouted was just plain weird to our folk!'

Uncle took his turn, 'Parker's grand scheme was failing and he knew it, though he also knew it was not his fault. Guess who he blamed? He needed to bend us to his will, but we would not bend. So, he started railing against our beliefs, our kinship practices and our culture. It got even nastier when he falsely accused us of killing some white men. So, it is no surprise that our elders stood up to him. They vigorously opposed all attempts by Parker to assume authority over their people. The result of this breakdown in relations, just seven years after it all began, was that only 27 residents remained. This core group, loyal to Parker, did become farmers and Christians, but were losing their Aboriginal culture. After just eight years, in 1849, the government conceded that the protectorate scheme across the colony had completely failed and began closing the Loddon protectorate. Parker protested to no avail. They rewarded him anyway with a private lease over much of the land, keeping just a small area as an Aboriginal reserve. That's accountability for you! But in an unusual act of kindness, one family headed by Beembarmin, called Tommy Farmer by Parker, (I know, I know!) was granted 21 acres of land and stayed farming for a few more years.'

'But that is not the end of the story by any means,' Auntie continued. 'Our population had been halved during the 1840s through disease, as well as from infertility from venereal diseases, often following rapes. Remember, this was before the gold rush had even started. It began in 1851. The numbers at Franklinford continued to fall and by 1863 there were only 38 of us left. Of course, other Dja Dja Wurrung members had avoided Parker's farm and found jobs with white bosses such as shepherds, servants, labourers, woodchoppers and stockmen as the gold rush took off, but we were very few in number by then. So, by the 1860s the authorities decided on a different approach. The new view, which was really an old view, was that Aboriginal people were akin to children. We needed isolating from whities for our own good. Laws were enacted to give the authorities total power over Aboriginal lives. Contact between us and white people was now considered harmful. We had to be kept apart and controlled, preferably by missionaries. To quote one luminary at the time; *"the blacks should, where necessary, be coerced, just like we coerce children and lunatics."* So, there you have it. We got coerced!'

Uncle wound up the story, 'After the Corranderrk Aboriginal Reserve was set up near Healesville to isolate and control Aboriginal people from across Victoria, about 20 of our people, including Beembarmin, were forcibly removed from right here and sent there in 1864. The stealing of our people had begun. This little boomerang on the fence is all that remains. But we survived and never abandoned our Country. Thank you all for your kind attention.'

The elders formed the group into a circle and lead a

minute's silence in memory and honour of the ancestors of their mob whose lives were so tragically disrupted in the 19th century and since. Kasper felt the tears well in him as he imagined those forced from their tribal land for another virtual prison, Coranderrk reserve, near Healesville, north-east of Melbourne. Others were weeping, too. A tall black woman he had seen a couple of times before at Commonplace placed her hand gently on his shoulder.

He mumbled, 'thank you. I am sorry.' Immediately he wondered why he had apologised. It had just slipped out. He felt foolish.

She replied, 'I come from Africa. You can call me Serene.'

'I'm from Denmark. My name is Kasper.'

Finally, they all walked solemnly down the road to what was left of the village of Franklinford and gathered around a large, ugly square monument the size of a large fridge, made of concrete and rocks. Auntie read the inscription:

"Edward Stone Parker 1802–1865 Regional Pioneer Protector of Aborigines established the Loddon Aboriginal Station, Homestead, Church and School near this site in 1841. His devoted service remains a challenge and inspiration. April 1966."

'What is wrong with this glorious dedication?' she asked.

Uncle Darcy burst out laughing, then yelled out, 'everything Auntie, everything! Parker; such an inspiration! He stayed on right here in Franklinford and died at the age of 62! He's buried just over there in the whitefella cemetery under a huge monument!' He pointed to the southwest then jigged about in a mixture of exasperation and exuberance. Everyone laughed. Then silence fell.

Back at Commonplace in the evening, the focus was on spiritual connection to the earth and its living creatures. The elders told of Bunjil, the wedge-tail eagle, the creator who descended from the sky, breathing air to form the earth and all living creatures. He then taught humans how to live in harmony with the land before ascending back to the sky where he watches over the land and its people. They spoke of the crucial significance of knowing your Country, of being owned by the land, not owning the land; of being in the land, not on the land; being a custodian of the land, not an exploiter or developer.

Each person was asked to address two questions: 'What mob are you from? Where is your land?'

These questions threw Kasper. The leaders suggested thinking about where you feel at home, where you feel grounded, where your heart lies, where you belong, where you want to be buried, who you belong to, what is in your tribe. A number of palaces rushed into Kasper's mind. Each year the family rotated through Amalienborg, Fredensborg, Graasten and Marselisborg in Denmark, and also stayed in grandfather's Château de Cayx, France.

So many magnificent royal edifices, but did he belong or feel at home in any of them? And his tribe? It was his family but not all of them, certainly Henri and Isabella, his few friends from school and Uni as well. But he often felt that he was different, an outsider. As his turn approached, he was tempted to pass, then he remembered his pony. Flikflak, the Welsh pony he received as a christening present from the Danish Parliament in 2006. Flikflak lived in the Royal Stables that were part of the complex known as the Christiansborg Palace, or just Borgen. Danish kings had lived there in centuries past but now it was the home of the parliament, royal reception rooms, ministries and other bits and pieces including the stables. He loved his pony, and between grooming and riding him, would spend many happy hours telling Flikflak all about his life and his worries. In the stables with the horses, he felt at home. Maybe this was his place, where he had belonged. Any wonder he could never eat horse! But those days were gone. Since Flikflak was gone, the stables held little attraction.

'My Mum is, or was, an Australian, so I am having a gap year here, from Denmark, to see if this is a land where I might belong.' So far so good, he thought. 'I am of mixed Danish, Australian and French heritage. I love my parents and my two sisters and brother. I also loved my granddad and my pony before they died, years ago. I moved around a lot as a child and didn't really feel at home anywhere. Except in the stables with my pony Fremfram,' he remembered to rename the pony at the last moment, just in case some curious stickybeak amongst the participants googled the name 'Flikflak'.

The sky was clear that Autumn night. Perfect for star gazing. Later, Uncle Darcy gave the group a quick lesson on the Dja Dja Wurrung language: 'We are the people who say yes, yes,' he said, with pride. 'If you literally translate 'Dja Dja Wurrung' into English you get 'yes, yes tongue'. We are a positive people.'

Uncle Darcy looked up and named some of the major star groups in the night sky. Kasper saw, for the first time, that the stars in the southern hemisphere were totally different to those in Denmark. Uncle Darcy finished his talk with the dreaming story of Barramul, the emu. A young man, Djanmari, challenged the emu to a flying contest by promising to reveal a secret, kept sacred, if the emu won. Barramul; powerful, vain and arrogant, accepted the challenge and was tricked. The other animals helped take away his wings, so emus could no longer fly.

'Where you see the Southern Cross, we see Barramul, the great, dark emu,' he explained. 'He reminds us that too much pride can lead to humiliation, especially when we crave what we have no right to.'

Uncle Darcy pointed out the shape of the emu crouched there, not a constellation, more a subtle mix of darkness and cloud. Kasper was very pleased to identify the five famous stars of the cross right there in the south, just like on the flag. Slowly Kasper could make out Barramul. He knew now he would recognise the dark emu again with ease and promised himself he would look for it each night before going to bed.

CHAPTER NINE

On Sunday, when the participants arrived in the Polygon, the two leaders had already hung Australian, Aboriginal and Torres Strait Islander flags on the wall. Auntie Gwenda welcomed them to the final day of the workshop and promised them some hands-on fun. Kasper listened half-heartedly as she summarised the British invasion and colonisation of half the planet and many more lands than Australia. She named: Ireland, Hong Kong, USA, Malaysia, Myanmar, India, Pakistan, South Africa, Guyana, the West Indies, Fiji and New Zealand and asked the participants for any she had missed. They called out; Canada, Gibraltar, Malta, Sri Lanka, Afghanistan, Vanuatu, Kenya, Egypt, Palestine, Zimbabwe and Belize, but Auntie said there were many more. 94 countries in total are or had once been British colonies, she announced. The sun never set on the British Empire.

This was not a hands-on workshop, Kasper thought. Auntie Gwenda thundered on about the fundamental prerequisites for these conquests: racism, religion, greed, social inequity, poverty and militarism, couched in terms of progress, civilisation, discovery, conversion, and service to king and country. Kasper new little of British history. He vaguely remembered learning how wicked Lord Nelson had once attacked Copenhagen and destroyed the Danish fleet for some obscure reason and of course there were all his distant relations in the British royal family. He realised, anew, he was connected to the British on his mother's Scots side.

Uncle Darcy turned to the Aussie flag and gave his summary of Australian European history. He spoke of the First Fleet, the lie of 'terra nullius', the wars of resistance against overwhelming odds, he told of Buckley, Batman and Bearbrass, and the British invasion of Victoria. First the explorers, then the squatters and convicts, all with their sheep, fences, poisons, diseases and guns arriving on his mob's Country from 1837, to grab massive tracts of Aboriginal land. But already the Dja Dja Wurrung and the other tribes of the great Kulin nation had been devastated by the pestilence of smallpox that preceded the white squatter's arrival on Country.

Increasingly, Kasper was not following, nor really listening. This had nothing to do with him. Surely modern Australia was a free and democratic country with justice and opportunity for all? Well, that's what he had been led to understand.

Darcy kept on, describing how his people had no immunity to the European diseases especially smallpox which brought widespread death and disfigurement of his people. Before the first white colonists had arrived on his Country most of his people had already died from smallpox. Then came the ruthless and murderous campaign of the squatters and colonialists to dispossess or kill the tribes, alongside the associated tasks of Christian conversion, 'civilising' and pacifying.

Kasper let this wash over him. This was what he had already heard at Franklinford. Instead, his thoughts turned to the attractive, black woman sitting just two seats away. She had been so friendly yesterday. What was her name again? He wondered where in Africa she was from. She spoke with a warm, lilting accent. Why was she here? Fantasies of romance and intimacy with her entertained Kasper briefly, but his rational, reasonable self dismissed them quickly when he realised the challenges of any lasting romance between a Danish Prince and a woman like her. An Aussie commoner as the queen was quite a challenge to the Danish aristocracy so the prospect of Mary being followed by a black African queen would be beyond the pale. But still, it was a welcome distraction from the lecture he was finding hard to take. He glanced her way quickly. And again. This time she must have sensed his gaze and caught his eye. Embarrassed, he looked quickly away but not before he noticed the slightest smile form on her lips.

Uncle Darcy was still in full flow. With the discovery of gold in 1851, miners flocked to the gold rich Forest Creek Diggings in their tens of thousands from all over the world. Although Chinese miners were barred from disembarking in Victoria, they walked from South Australia in their thousands. At the peak there were 40,000 inhabitants living in tents, shacks and cottages on the numerous diggings of Forest Creek, the first white name for Castlemaine.

Kasper was now angry. He could feel the tension in his hands and feet. How dare this arrogant black man tear down the achievements of European civilisation, he thought. He had been brought up to honour and cherish his European past. Then a realisation struck him. This was the first time in his life he had been lectured to by a black person. Maybe he was feeling so angry because he was racist enough to think that he had nothing to learn from a black man.

Campbells Creek, the southern part of Castlemaine, once a separate town, had a Chinese settlement of five thousand miners alongside the area called Little Copenhagen where Danes and the other Nordic settlers congregated. Now Kasper's ears pricked up. He wondered how much the two populations mixed? He wanted to know more about the Danish miners.

Uncle Darcy continued his monologue. Kasper was tuned in. It took about 40 years for all the alluvial gold to run out and most of the miners moved to other occupations but by then they had devastated the local environment. The land was denuded of trees and resembled a moonscape. But no white invader was concerned, Uncle Darcy said with bitter irony. Fortunes had been made and deep lead mining rumbled on, way down below the surface, right up to the end of the 20th century.

The group listened without interruption to Darcy's story until an argument broke out. A tall, older male named Rodney, raised an issue that Kasper had also wanted to raise but had not wanted to risk embarrassment. Rodney claimed forcefully that surely British settlement had not been all bad. Indeed, had it not brought all the advantages of western culture; learning and technology; literature, science, medicine, transport, housing, clothing, arts, music, overseas travel, agriculture, sport, democracy and so forth. Everyone now wanted to have a say. Some agreed, others objected. Kasper followed the debate keenly while he waited to see if the African woman would say anything, but she sat quietly. A shouting match had broken out, but a polite one.

Auntie Edna restored order by stamping her foot and declaring, 'well I am not giving up my hairdryer and microwave after we kick out the whites. The clock cannot be turned back but we can be wise about what we keep and what we reject, especially now we know that the planet is in such peril.'

Uncle Darcy followed gravely, 'The way I see it is, that because the European colonisation of the continent has been so pervasive, we cannot really compare it to any alternative. All I know is that this land is totally unsuited to almost all European agricultural, mining, housing, fishing, and recreational practices. I say this because of the gross extinction of native plant and animal species, the destruction of the environment and native habitats, the depletion of soils and the pollution and poisoning of the land and water. On balance, I see European civilisation as a curse. But I reserve the right to keep my computer, mobile, and motorbike. Oh, and satellite navigation!'

'What about religion? So many Aboriginals have become devoted Christians, like me,' June, a middle-aged woman asked. A good point, Kasper thought, surely Christianity was a positive force.

'So what?' someone else challenged.

'Well, my Aboriginal sisters and brothers became Christians for good reason.' Auntie Edna replied. 'They were forced onto missionary stations and converted at the end of a whip. You heard what Parker was trying to do; for some of us it worked. If only the Messiah was a black woman and not a Bjorn Borg lookalike,' she added only half in jest. 'If you have been shot, bereaved, dispossessed, subjugated and impoverished, the Christian promise of love and salvation is mighty appealing. Especially if you had to convert to get a feed, a bed and avoid a beating. And it is something you can adopt without having to fight the white authorities. But of course, some of our great leaders like Sir Douglas Nicholls used their faith against the fundamental hypocrisy of white Christians in their dealings with us Blacks.'

Kasper thought of his future role as head of both state and the Danish church, and of his faltering faith. How could he ever be true to such roles, he wondered?

Auntie Gwenda wound up the discussion by proposing a thought experiment. 'If Australia had remained a sovereign country of federated Black nations back in the 19th century and into the 20th, with full control over immigration, trade, defence, foreign policy, and all the other powers that governments possess, what parts of western culture and technology would the country have allowed in, if by some miracle we could stop European incursions and invasions? Draw up a list of what the elders would have chosen based on their accumulated wisdom from 60,000 years of continuous culture. Japan or Thailand might be interesting examples to consider because they have never been colonised by white Europeans.' Kasper thought this was a clever idea and something he must tell Isabella about. She would be very interested.

Uncle Darcy took the floor and gestured behind him. 'So, we have our three flags, Aboriginal, Torres Strait and Aussie. Two are staying and one is going. The National Flag Committee is working hard to find us a new national flag. But I see flags as classic symbols and practices of European imperialism. You know all that stuff – salute the flag, raise the flag, fly the flag. So much symbolism and so much heightism.'

'What's heightism?' Someone asked.

'Well, it is a western cultural phenomenon where 'up' is better than 'down', 'high' is better than 'low' and 'tall' is better than 'short'. I call it heightism. When it comes to flags it is all set out in the Flag Act. No flag can be flown above the Australian flag – which has the good old Union Jack in the upper left corner not the lower right.'

Auntie spoke up, 'Notice on the map how Australia is down the bottom of the world. Europe is up there in the top left corner. I love those corrective world maps that have Australia upside down, top and centre.'

Uncle asked the group, 'so how would you change our flag?'

To everyone's shock the response was immediate. Justin, a young, long-haired man in a red shirt leapt up and wielding a pocketknife, rushed at the Aussie flag. 'I'm gonna cut that fuckin' Union Jack right out of there. I hate it.'

Nobody reacted, such was the surprise. Then Uncle Darcy rushed over to intervene. 'No way mate,' he yelled as he jumped between Justin and the flag. 'Not in our workshop you don't.' After a brief struggle he disarmed Justin and ushered him outside.

'Wow!' Auntie exclaimed, 'that old Union Jack sure got young Justin riled up. But we can't let him damage our flag for two reasons. One, it is disrespectful to us and our reputation as the workshop leaders, and secondly it violates the Flag Act. But let me ask you all. How many others would like to see that bit of our flag go? Hands up.'

Kasper saw most hands go up as he glanced furtively at the black woman in the group. Serene, he had remembered her name. Her hand rose too. But he was totally torn. Such conflicting thoughts spun in his mind.

Before he could decide, Auntie spoke again. 'Okay, that is a huge majority. And how many of you want it retained?'

Kasper kept his hand down again. Rodney was the only objector. He was keen to explain that his parents back in Surrey were traditional loyal monarchists and loved King Charles and Queen Camilla and he just did not want the Union Jack to go. 'It is our history and our tradition. Whenever I see the Union Jack, I get a feeling of pride and a little awe. And I have joint citizenship, so I am still half British.'

Uncle Darcy had returned with Justin and gently ribbed Rodney, 'Good for you, mate. But here it's not the Union Jack anymore. Down in Australia it had been rebranded the Australian Ensign.' It was a telling point, but Rodney still demurred.

Kasper remembered that as a Danish Royal he was not allowed to hold joint citizenship of another country which was why his mother had to give up her Australian citizenship when she married his father. And he realised that if he ever married a non-Dane she would have to as well. Would any woman ever want to do that for him, he wondered?

The leaders left the flag issue there. They took the group outside and invited them all to make fire, the traditional way. This was an essential skill and rite of passage for First Nations people, Uncle Darcy explained, while giving each person a hardwood stick in a small wooden cradle with a length of twine and some very fine wood shavings. He demonstrated once and they all saw the shavings readily burst into flame.

Making fire looked so simple but was so devilishly hard, Kasper soon discovered. He tried and tried as he felt his hands grow blisters. A few of the others had already succeeded and finally he too saw that first little plume of smoke. He blew gently and coaxed it into a tiny flame. He was now a firelighter, and he was elated. Ten others had achieved the feat and smiled broadly.

Outside, Kasper discovered billy tea and damper and was delighted when the African woman came up to him. 'My name is Serene. How was all that for you? I saw you made fire.'

'I remember your name from yesterday but my head is spinning. In Denmark I knew nothing of this. My mum was Australian, but I never learned about all this. How about you?' he asked.

Serene frowned, 'Well I am from Southern Africa. I am black. You probably worked that out,' she added with a quick grin. 'I did not know the local history, but I sure know about invasion and brutality, especially from the British. Nothing new there. The flag exercise: I loved it. Just brilliant! And you were a star! Or should I say a dark emu? What's on the Danish flag?' she asked.

Kasper thought for a moment, 'just a boring red cross on a white background. With a bloody history,' he added, surprised at his new negativity about the precious Dannebrog.

'Do tell,' she prompted.

'Well 800 years ago, King Valdemar had a vision on the eve of a battle. He saw a white cross in the evening sky. Soon after, the flag helped Denmark win a battle over the Estonians. Our brave soldiers had their backs to the walls trying to colonise and Christianise those heathens and God decided to throw down a flag to them. The Danish soldiers grabbed it and went on to win. Of course. It did not seem to matter to God that they were invading another country at the time,' Kasper said, shocking at how vehemently he had spoken. He would never say that at home. Was he just trying to impress her, he thought?

Serene chuckled and he realised just how cynically he had spoken about his country's beloved emblem. A flag he had worn, flown and waved hundreds of times with patriotic pride.

Then he added sarcastically, 'and coincidently it resembled the flag of the enemy in that war. God may have borrowed it on the day.'

She smiled. He noticed her beautiful smile and was about to ask her about her nation and flag, but time was up, so they all went in for the last session. He felt a growing desire to find out more about her.

The final session was about the future. Everyone was asked what close connections they had with Aboriginal people in their lives. Again, Kasper felt left out. Some of the group said they gave money and supported campaigns, others had

Aboriginal work colleagues, some had bought Aboriginal art and music, had attended rallies and concerts or been on exposure tours to Aboriginal communities but this was not what was being asked. Serene did not contribute. It took a while for almost everyone to concede that they had few if any personal connections with Aboriginal people.

'What is this about?' Auntie asked.

Silence fell across the room. People lowered their eyes and sat in silence. The heavy silence seemed to continue for ages.

Finally, a soft voice broke the silence, 'Shame!' was the single word uttered.

'That's right,' Auntie Gwenda replied, 'so many of you lovely, right minded, compassionate, white Australians are crippled by shame. We often call it white guilt. You need to acknowledge your shame and guilt as soon as possible and get on with it. Let us try to help.'

June spoke up again. 'I can't accept that I have this shame. Where I live there are just no Aboriginal people to meet. I just never meet any in my life.'

'Well, you may be an exception June.' Auntie responded. 'I did say many, not all. But I would ask, how do you know you have not met any? We can be very hard to pick at times. I congratulate you for coming to meet us.'

Kasper sensed that Auntie was right, certainly about white Australians but maybe about him too.

Auntie and Uncle then rose and approached the nearest sitting participant. They stood back and front and placed their palms on the person's shoulders.

Then they each recited in turn, 'It was not your fault. You

are not guilty for the past and you can address your white racism from this day on. We want your friendship. We embrace you. Take your shame and let it help you make change.'

One by one Auntie and Uncle repeated the ritual around the circle. The atmosphere in the space grew heavier and heavier. Some people wept, others lay on the floor, most sat in silence.

For the first time, Kasper felt his Australian heritage keenly. His maternal ancestors had come here, too, as part of colonisation. But he also realised he felt shame about his privilege, his status, his birthright – his entitlement as a royal prince. Obviously, he benefited from Danish colonialism, conquest and violence, he realised. A sudden urge possessed him when he felt the four hands on his shoulders to come clean, confess and be absolved as his real royal self. But he fought it down. He was not just thinking about Australia but about the victims of Danish racism, colonialism and invasion: the slaves in the Danish colonies in the Danish Virgin Islands, the indigenous Sami people during the long Danish colonisation of Norway, the Greenlanders under the Danish flag, still. Perhaps his newly felt shame about these foul deeds might be eased by the four hands.

They came to Serene last. She was asked to stand up and got special treatment. They did not place their hands on her shoulders, instead they embraced her wordlessly, then Auntie Gwenda said, 'Black Sister, our ancestral spirits are still walking with us across our sacred Country, now and for thousands of years, and they welcome and embrace you, too.'

As they pulled back Serene yelled, 'INKULULENKO!' at

the top of her voice. Kasper was most impressed, although what she shouted, he had yet to learn.

The sombre spell was broken and the others clapped and cheered. Kasper beamed with the others. What a day to remember. But it was not over yet. A large rectangular piece of cloth had appeared on one of the walls. It measured about three by five metres. Kasper wondered what it was for?

Uncle Darcy reached into his box and pulled out a large container filled with a rich red colloid. He explained, 'we offer you the chance to mark your presence on our Country with your handprint. Ochre is an important ceremonial medium in our culture. It has been mined and traded across the continent for at least 40,000 years. It has lots of ceremonial uses and this is one. Dip your hand in. Make sure your palm is well covered; stretch it out and apply it hard to the wall. Who would like to leave this mark on this canvas to signify their visit to our Country and attendance this weekend?'

Kasper hung back as the others took their turn. He had a plan for posterity. He noted where Serene put her print and when it was his turn, he placed his left palm adjacent, but not so close as to be obvious. He pushed hard then carefully removed his hand. There stood his unique mark. Only his hand would ever truly fit that print, he understood, as he cleaned the ochre from his hand.

The weekend ended with a confession from the leaders. They apologised for the didactic lecturing they had both delivered, and Auntie asked the participants how they had found these monologues. Four people agreed that they had felt angry about being lectured. Rodney said he had been furious and felt like walking out. Kasper mustered his courage and said, 'I was angry too. But then I realised I had assumed that a black man in Australia had nothing to teach me. I was so wrong.'

Uncle Darcy replied with a big grin, 'Yes, you are a wise young man. You have got the point. We deliberately wanted you all to feel what it might have been like to be lectured by and from the point of view of dispossessed and colonised people. We have had to fight like crazy to get our voices back and have been copping white colonial lectures, full of lies, for over two centuries and it bloody hurts. Thank you all for staying the course!'

Uncle and Auntie got a rousing ovation and Auntie Gwenda finished with the parting words, 'Remember we have never surrendered sovereignty of this land. You are walking on Dja Dja Wurrung Country. You are welcome, so have no shame but remember well, this always was and always will be our land, so pay your rent.' Then there were further thanks, exchanges of phone numbers, promises of further contact, handshakes and hugs all round.

All of those who had come for the weekend headed off and Kasper went back to his hut to lie down. Dinner was not until 7 o'clock and he had a lot to mull over. Now he marvelled at the generosity and strength of the two leaders. He realised how lucky he had been to attend. He thought of the countless generations of Aboriginal people that had walked across the land he was on and the resilience and strength they have needed to survive the white invasion and to continue the oldest living culture in the world. For the first time in his life, he felt a real sense that he was half-Australian. But it was a realisation that came at a price. Now he knew he was part of the invasion and colonisation of a First Nation peoples both as a Dane and an Australian. But at least he had a small connection to two generous and gifted Aboriginal elders who had laid their hands on his head. And with Serene.

He thought also of all those generations of Aboriginal people living rich lives without the need for European reading, writing, science or the wheel; without kings, queens or hereditary aristocracy, and in relative plenty, peace and justice. Nothing in Denmark's relative brief history of a few thousand years could compare with the timelessness of the world's longest continuous culture. He also thought about Serene.

At 7 o'clock he went down to the Eyrie for a dinner of dahl and rice followed by apple crumble and custard. He immediately saw that Serene was at the dinner table too. Of the 12 diners that evening they were the only two who had attended the workshop. They sat together. Sam asked him how he found the weekend.

He thought carefully. 'It was an amazing weekend. I have learnt so much. I even found out that there were Danes here for the goldrush.'

Luckily someone immediately asked, 'And how did the roo go down? You were eating the national symbol, you realise.'

'Well, it was okay, but I think it might have been better wrapped in Danish bacon,' he answered with half a grin. 'At least it was not Sinbad.' The others chuckled, to his relief. He immediately regretted making that last comment.

It sounded far too flippant and crass. But he could not retract it.

Kasper was happy the conversation drifted off to Aussie rules football as the new season was underway. Sport was quite a common topic over dinner, but he knew little about Aussie footy or about cricket either. Twice he had been asked which AFL team he supported and when he replied that he did not have a team, the Richmond Tigers and the St Kilda Saints were forcefully recommended, but he did not want to choose without careful consideration.

As dinner drew to an end he and Serene exchanged looks and left the big dining table when they first politely could. Without any prior negotiation they walked off down to the garden below the Eyrie together. Kasper was very pleased how this had just happened naturally. Night had fallen and the stars were bright in the sky. Together they looked for the Dark Emu.

Serene was the first to speak and asked, 'are there indigenous people in your country?'

Kasper replied, 'I don't really know. The first Scandinavian people came from the south and east well after the last ice age. I now realise that they may well have colonised and enslaved the first peoples. I need to find out.'

'I would not be surprised.' she commented, then added, 'and the first people probably had black skin.'

'Well, we colonised later on,' he recalled his thoughts from the workshop. 'There are the Sami people in Norway and across Lapland, where the Danes ruled for centuries and the Greenlander people that Denmark still controls. I ought to mention the Virgin Islands in the Caribbean that the Danes once colonised and filled with African slaves. And then there were all the slaves the Danes kept for centuries during the Viking times. I think that's all.'

Then he added, 'After the workshop I now realise that my ancestors would almost certainly have been slave owners, but no one has ever talked about it.'

'Well, the Viking shows and movies seem to gloss over slavery too.' Serene agreed. 'Slavery does tend to get that treatment by white people.'

'I guess the Danes can more easily forget our racist past as not many of the descendants from our colonial past are living in Denmark. Not like here,' he mused.

'Yes, it is very different in Africa too,' she agreed. 'The results of slavery and colonisation are everywhere where I come from,' she added. 'I mainly know about the British and Dutch colonialists in my homeland. Oh, and the Indians and Gandhi!' she said with a laugh.

'Really? What has he got to do with Africa?' Kasper asked. He had been exposed to a little of Gandhian Nonviolence teachings at school.

'Well, he was one of the thousands of Indians who settled in southern Africa as subjects of the British. He went there in his early twenties to practice law and stayed for over twenty years. Finally, the racism he faced got too much for him and he went home to confront the British in India,' she explained.

Kasper finally got to ask, 'Serene, I'm sorry I have not asked before, where do you come from?'

She said, 'I come from the Kingdom of Eswatini.'

Apologetically he said, 'Sorry, but I have not heard of such a country.'

She laughed and replied, 'many have not. Swaziland to you.'

It did ring a bell for Kasper, and he said, 'Oh right.' But little else about the country could he recall.

Serene went on, 'We are just a tiny, landlocked African country. And before you ask, we do have a wonderful indigenous flag with no Union Jack. When we gained independence from Britain, we already had our own king. The Brits had kept our kings in place, but they had to pay homage to the British monarch to stay on. Not like poor Australia. When independence came in 1968, the King refused to have anything British on the flag. So, we have ended up with a shield, arrows and a staff; traditional things, though still male fighting objects. But it is quite cool really. I do not mind it.'

There was so much more he wanted to find out about her, and he had one burning question.

'May I ask you what you shouted earlier, when the elders hugged you? It sent a chill up my spine,' he ventured.

'Freedom!' She replied with a grin and raised both arms in the air. 'I want freedom for my people and me.'

He wanted to keep the conversation going. What had brought her all the way from Africa to Commonplace? But he was so tired and the last thing he wanted was to outstay his welcome. 'That's fascinating. Thank you for the wonderful company and conversation but I need to get some sleep,' he said warmly.

Serene said goodnight and added, 'I am going away for a

few days, but I will be back. If you like, I would be happy to help you look for any Danish ancestors you may have from the gold rush.'

'Really? Oh great,' he responded. He knew all his Danish ancestors and was certain none had made their way to Castlemaine, yet he was so pleased at her offer he almost embraced her. He made do with extending his hand in his proper, well-bred Danish way. She shook his hand with a hearty laugh, and he headed up to his hut. He could not stop smiling as he looked at the bright southern stars and the Dark Emu. It has been quite a day. He fell asleep very quickly, almost as soon as his mosquito net landed.

That night, he dreamed of Flikflak. Only the pony was black and had a trunk like an elephant. The poor horse was hobbled and spoke to him in a language he did not understand. Was it Welsh or Sami perhaps? He tried to get the hobbles off, but they were welded in place.

Suddenly the dream changed, and he was in Kenya on a Danish sisal plantation. He was the supervisor and wore a safari suit and a pith helmet while carrying a long cane under his right arm. He had a 303-rifle slung over his left shoulder. He was trying to get his black workers to salute him, but they refused. Then an elephant appeared off to one side and the workers all turned and saluted the elephant. The elephant looked a bit like Flikflak!

CHAPTER TEN

One month after the weekend workshop, Kasper and Serene visited the Castlemaine Historical Society in the Old Court House. He had arranged to meet Michael Rasmussen, an amateur historian and local authority on his Danish compatriots from the time when the local goldfields were famous for the untold riches that could be found at the end of a pick or bottom of a pan. Michael was a big, round, burly man with a mop of curly blonde hair and a beard to match. Like a typical Viking, Kasper thought, as they shook hands and he introduced Serene.

Kasper tried a few lines of Danish, but Michael shook his head. 'Sorry mate. Danish died out pretty much by the second generation in my family. I always wanted to learn it but never have. Maybe one day,' he suggested.

'Well perhaps I could teach you,' Kasper replied. 'But only if you tell me about the Danes in Castlemaine first.'

'Okay,' Michael said. 'Well, hundreds of Danes, almost all young men, came here in the 1860s and 70s. Many more Danes came than any other Scandinavians, at that time. The Danes got hammered by the Prussians in the Slesvig–Holstein wars and Denmark lost about one fifth of its territory. The Danish economy collapsed. Defeated Danish soldiers felt they had to leave, especially those from the land Denmark lost. I suppose they were refugees. They could get a ship from Hamburg and sail directly to Melbourne. It was a time of great Danish poverty and emigration."

Kasper remembered learning about these terrible Danish defeats but had forgotten which member of his family occupied the throne at the time. His recollection was that Denmark's military was not up to its vaulting territorial and colonial ambitions in the 19th century and paid a heavy price.

'It must have been such a huge decision to move to the other side of the earth back then. Like going to another planet. They must have been so desperate,' Kasper commented.

'Or very adventurous,' Serene proposed. 'Gold can be a huge attraction.'

'Indeed, it was and still is around here,' Michael agreed. 'The Chinese name for Australia back then was Golden Mountain.'

Kasper asked, 'Was Campbells Creek where the Danes lived? I have heard this.'

'Well, most of them moved around the goldfields. As soon as the surface gold dried up in one creek gully, they would decamp and rush to the next one. Mostly, they lived in tents in the early years, so it was not hard to move about. But at one time more than 500 Danes did camp at Campbells Creek as well as drink, shop and socialise there,' Michael stated.

'Why Campbells Creek?' Serene asked.

'Not everyone was a miner,' Michael said. 'Businesses sprang up like crazy to cater for 30,000 hungry, thirsty people here at the height of the gold rush. That's a lot of customers and many miners had sudden riches. So, the Danes set up blacksmiths, grain stores and other businesses as well as the general store and the Five Flags hotel. In fact, another hotel from the time, the Copenhagen Hotel, is still standing at 55 Main Road. It's a private dwelling now. We know that at one time Hans Appel ran the Five Flags pub and Carl Tolstrup had the general store next door. I like to think the five flags were the flags of Denmark, Sweden, Norway, Finland and Iceland. But I have no idea if that is the case.'

'Oh, that would be very cool,' Kasper exclaimed. 'I hope it was true.'

'But I have kept the best for last,' Michael continued, 'I think you will like this. All those Danish businesses established there and all the patrons who gathered there meant that Campbells Creek had a nickname for about twenty years in the 19th century. It was called Little Copenhagen!'

Yes!' Kasper exclaimed. 'I heard that a few days ago. It's quite amazing!'

'Is that why you came to Castlemaine?'

'No,' Kasper replied. 'I had no idea about any of this.'

Michael had a need to complete the picture. 'Just so you know. By the start of the 20th century some of the Danes, and the other miners, had gone. Gold was no longer something you could find with a pick and shovel. It was still plentiful, but you had to mine for it underground. Many men worked in the mines while other families who had gone into business or farming stayed on. Like us Rasmussens. But the cemeteries still show us some of the Danes who came and never left.'

'What do you mean?' Serene asked.

'Gravestones with Danish names and often Danish epitaphs. Would you like to see some?' Michael replied.

'I sure would,' Kasper replied.

'Well, if you have time, you could go out to the Chewton cemetery and look in the southeast corner. There you will find some Danish graves. I recommend a visit. I won't come with you. I'll let you find them yourselves.' Michael proposed.

Kasper looked at Serene. He hoped she would want to come too. She understood what he was wanting and nodded enthusiastically. He turned to Michael and thanked him profusely then added, 'If you ever want a Danish lesson let me know.'

'I might just do that,' Michael replied. 'But before you go, I have a gift for you.' He retrieved a booklet from his car and handed it over. Kasper read the title out loud: *Gold! Gold! Diary of Claus Grønn. A Dane on the Diggings.* 'Wow!' he exclaimed, 'thank you very much.'

'This is a translated summary by Cora McDougall, Claus' granddaughter. Sadly, I do not have a copy of the original in Danish,' Michael added and went on, 'Grønn was quite a character and wrote a vivid account of his life. He also had a store in Campbells Creek but tragically nine of his children died young. They may well be buried in the Pennyweight Flat Cemetery. Around 200 children were buried there in just five years from 1852. One of the saddest places on Earth.' Michael added, 'visit at your own risk.'

As they left the old courthouse, Michael pointed out the gnarly remnants of a pair of very old gum trees still surviving across from the building.

'Those two trees were used back in the 1850s for a few years to chain up prisoners who were to face the judge in this courthouse. I am sure a few naughty Danes were kept there. Must have been pleasant on a hot day,' Michael remarked ironically.

Serene and Kasper went over for a closer look. They remembered the same story from the weekend workshop. Kasper tried to imagine what it would be like for an illiterate Danish soldier turned miner, with little English, being chained to the tree to await British justice. But immediately another image took over in his head. It was an adult Aboriginal man held in chains here near the creek where he had fished and swum as a child, before the disastrous arrival of the white man just a few decades earlier.

It was a perfect afternoon for exploring a cemetery; cool, overcast and gloomy. They drove out to Chewton. Though just a few kilometres from Castlemaine, it was still a proudly independent town with a rich history of gold mining. Indeed, the Wattle Gully mine had only closed in 2010 after operating from 1853.

They discussed the possibility of rain and agreed that it was likely. Kasper admitted, 'I never wanted it to rain back home. Where I come from rain is mostly a damn nuisance. But at Commonplace everyone seemed to long for rain. Except of course when there is a flood! Rain seems to be of great importance. They talk about it all the time.'

Serene replied, 'well where I come from in Eswatini rain brought hope, greenness and promise for my family on the farm. I really understand what the Aussies are on about.'

Kasper said, 'I am trying to change my attitude to rain, and water. I have heard the stories about droughts in Australia. They must be dreadful. I cannot ever imagine a drought in Denmark.'

Serene chided him for not liking rain. Rainmaking was a very high-status job in her culture, and she had seen it work firsthand. 'Dancing in the rain is one of life's true joys. We should try it some time,' she suggested.

Kasper was no dancer but the prospect of dancing with her was too enticing. 'I will try it as soon as possible if you will teach me a rain dance,' he proposed, 'will it be nude?' he asked cheekily.

She ignored the question. 'So that's a deal,' she concluded, but added 'and you can wear feathers!'

The cemetery was tucked away over Forest Creek just east of the Chewton town. It had the bush around it on three sides. They parked the Commonplace car and tried to work out where the southeast corner lay. Kasper knew where south was. He headed off towards the southeast, calling, 'this way,' back over his shoulder.

'No,' Serene said, 'that's the wrong direction.'

Kasper stopped to argue his case. 'Are you sure? I know where I am heading; to the southeast.' He pointed up to where the sun hid in the sky.

Serene stood there wondering why he had it so wrong. She realised but before she could speak Kasper exclaimed with a shake of his head, 'Oh no, I know what I have just done!'

Serene replied with sarcasm, 'Where is the sun in the southern hemisphere white Scando-northern man?'

Kasper swore in Danish, *'Satans!* In the bloody north not in the south.'

Serene dug him playfully in the ribs. They turned and she slipped her arm through his as they headed towards the southeast corner. Kasper felt acutely every square millimetre of his arm where it contacted hers.

'Okay, okay, a dumb mistake. I admit it,' he confessed. She did not reply just squeezed his arm tighter. He smelt her personal aroma again and remembered it from the workshop weekend.

The southeast corner mostly held newer graves, but it did not take them long to find the old ones from the 19th century. They were weather beaten and eroded and none had been maintained. Some headstones had fallen and broken while others were missing altogether. They agreed that it was sad to see the dead neglected like this. Then Kasper let out a shout, 'Hans Olsen! Here is a Hans Olsen. What a classic Danish name.'

Serene came over and asked, 'what does it say?'

Kasper started to decipher and translate the faded inscription. After a few minutes he said, 'It is hard to read all the writing, but I think it reads; *'Hereunder rests the dust of Hans Olsen, born the 5th of August 1838 in the Holst Parish of Slesvig, Denmark. Died the 28th of April 1864 in Castlemaine.'*

'Aaaw, he was only 25,' Serene said sadly, 'poor, poor man. I wonder how he died.'

'Yeah, I wonder too. And no mention of his family at all. Just him. All alone.' Kasper added and took a photograph with his mobile. 'I will send this to my sister.'

They looked around and right next to Hans lay another Dane. Kasper read out aloud that Peter Wind was born in Denmark on 27th July 1821 and died on 18th March 1865. There were no other details at all on the headstone. Serene noted that at least he had made it to the age of 44 and had died a year after Hans. She hoped they had been friends. Kasper photographed this one also.

A third Danish grave lay further east. It held the mortal remains of Jens Petersen and contained the longest epitaph. 'It will take me a while to work this one out,' Kasper said.

Some of the letters were covered in lichen and others had eroded significantly. He took a photograph and used his phone to zoom in on the writing. After about ten minutes he announced his findings to Serene.

'Okay, this is what I think it says at the top: Jens Petersen born in the Parish of Heldevadt on the 25th of July 1835 and died on the 29th of July 1866.'

'Underneath there's a verse that goes something like this,' he added.

'In the depth of the grave it is so good to rest,
So do not weep now for me
For the angels of the Lord make me smile
And here I am so fortunate and glad.'

'Oh, that sounds so corny!' Serene stated, 'I wonder who came up with that. He was 31 years old.'

'Well, I am sure there could be a better translation, but you get the picture. So, these three men died in different years and were buried here together. So far from home. I hope they were friends. I would love to know about their lives,' Kasper mused, 'but that is probably impossible.'

He stood there in silence for a few minutes, sad and deep in thought. These three men had come all this way and died far too young. He could not tell how long they had been on the goldfields but reasoned it could not have been very long at all. There was no mention of partners or children. He knew his burial place would be very different from this neglected corner of the Chewton cemetery. Roskilde Cathedral is where the dead royals lie in Denmark.

Serene approached him and embraced him. He looked at her with glistening eyes. He felt the quickening of his heart. They stood there for a long time as he breathed her scent before he pulled slowly away. He wondered if she felt more than compassion. He knew he did.

The couple looked around for any more of Kasper's countrymen but found none. So, they slowly wended their way back to the car. With little warning Kasper was overcome by the strangest sensation and for the first time felt his consciousness leave his body and spread far and wide. No physical boundaries, just part of a vast universe. He was out of his body, or rather, his body had expanded to take in the whole world. He felt in awe. After a few minutes, he came back into his body and turned to Serene excitedly, 'Wow I just had the most extraordinary sensation. An out-of-body experience. Did you notice anything?'

'No, you were just silent.' They agreed not to visit the Pennyweight Flat cemetery as she took the wheel for the drive back to Commonplace. She did not tell Kasper she was an unlicensed driver.

As the rain started falling gently, Kasper asked, 'Can I please be excused from dancing in the rain this evening?'

Serene replied, 'Okay, this once, Daneman. But I would like you to dance with me later tonight indoors.' He agreed most readily.

CHAPTER ELEVEN

Kasper had come to stay at Commonplace for three months but extended for three more. He was feeling more at home and could now mostly understand what the locals were saying and even picked up some 'Strine'. He found that the locals would occasionally speak 'Strine' to keep foreigners in the dark. Even those, who like Serene and him, who both learned English from childhood. He still emailed his sister regularly and checked Danish websites occasionally. Life at Commonplace was strange, interesting and busy. After six months, he wrote to his sister about the five things he found most unusual. If a resident was away for a night, a guest would be invited to sleep in their bed. In the laundry was a pigeonhole for common clothes and he could help himself. If you were on cooking duty you had to also do all the dishes and the cleaning up afterwards. The children did not go to school and were expected to speak up on all occasions when they were present. They were also given responsibilities he thought were far too adult, like tractor driving and menu planning. And he was taken by how hard the residents worked, often seven days a week. He also appreciated that there would be reasons for such arrangements, and he was just a Woofer. The members had a saying he had heard them use more than once, 'It's a big life.' He could see what they meant.

With six months of his stay over, Kasper gained permission to attend a Full Members Meeting to put a simple question. The twelve adult members met in the smaller conference room in the Eyrie.

When Kasper took the floor he asked with some anxiety, 'I am sorry to take up your time. Thanks for inviting me. I just want to know whether it would ever be possible for me to become a member and stay permanently?'

Geoffrey was the first to reply. It was not an unusual question for the members to be posed. 'Well, you have really asked two things. And permanence is a long time. So, people can live here semi-permanently without becoming members, though that is rare. But to become a member there are a few hurdles to clear. You would need Australian citizenship or a permanent residency visa. You would then need to be approved by each of the present members individually. Next, you would need to donate or loan interest-free all your assets to the community. We prefer donations,' he added with a little smile before going on. 'You would need to comply with the 'one roof, one purse, one table' rule and you would need to embrace the constitution, ethos and processes of the community and contribute accordingly. Oh, and one final thing; if you have a partner, he or she could not come with you unless they were also approved as permanent residents or members, too.'

Next Irene piped up, 'Well that is the easy part!' Everyone laughed except Kasper.

She continued, 'people have come and gone from

Commonplace over the years for several reasons. You need to know that it is almost a vow of poverty. We do not earn much money from the fees we charge for hosting seminars and running workshops and most of our clients are not wealthy. We have many expenses, so the purse can be empty at times. At times of little income some of us have had to go on the dole, but that's an emergency measure. So, no holidays overseas or fancy yachts. Some people have left because the poverty had ground them down. You can only work for the community so any career plans or thoughts of higher degrees must be dumped. And if you are single and fall in love with someone from the great outside you will not be able to live with him or her unless they can be approved independently as a permanent resident or member. We have lost a few members with that one, too.'

She paused and asked, 'Anything else?'

Simone chimed in, 'Shall we mention the baby issue? It is sure to come up sooner or later. And Kasper may be interested in baby making.'

Most of the others nodded and Kasper noticed a slight collective grimace go around the room before she went on, 'As you know, we collectively raise and home school our delightful children. If you wanted to live here and bring your children with you it is highly unlikely that you would be accepted.'

Kasper was very puzzled and asked, 'Why would that be? I thought you really liked children?'

Simone answered, 'Well we do, but that is not why we are here. Commonplace was not established to raise or educate children but to fight for the planet and a more just world. Other communes may want to focus on children but not us. In the past we used to have lots of single parents come to visit and seeking membership. They could see it would be a great place for their children and for them to get support. But it was no go.'

Geoff spoke again, 'Yes and because we share the childcare and the home schooling, we can well understand how attractive it must look. But we had to turn almost all of them away. This made some people very angry, so we were accused of being anti-child. But we devote a lot of time and resources to our children, and too many children would just get in the way of all the other work we do. And it does not earn any money.' He then added, 'And some of us, me included, believe that humans are a terrible pest species on this earth.'

Kasper thought of his own childhood and the retinue of helpers, the many tables, rooves and the full purses. He imagined there was no problem with overpopulation or big families amongst the royals of Europe.

Irene spoke again, 'And just to complete the picture in case you are wondering, if you are a permanent resident or member and want to have a baby the same principle applies. You would need to get approval from the collective first.'

Simone butted in, 'Yes and this has been one of the most difficult and controversial rules we have had to face. Our detractors and even some of our supporters think that this rule is a gross violation of parents' rights. Which of course it is. We argue that our collective and societal needs just outweigh parents' rights by half a microgram.'

The members glanced at each other across the room and most half smiled and half grimaced.

'You see, decisions that couples make in the outside world remain entirely personal, but here they become a matter for us all,' Simone added.

Kasper had not thought of fatherhood much at all but could see a ready contrast with royal baby making. Producing a line of heirs was a matter for the entire realm and an absolute necessity for the Glücksburg royal house! And his turn would surely come.

Geoff asked if he had any more questions and Kasper replied, 'Well, I am only supposed to be away for a year, so can I stay until my year is up?'

Simone answered with a big smile, 'We think that should be fine, you seemed a little reluctant at first, but you have become a great contributor. You work hard and join in. The kids like you too. One day you might come back and become a member. And even have a baby. Does everyone agree?' She looked around the room and there were nods all round.

Kasper smiled broadly and said thanks as he left the room. There was so much information for him to take in, but he felt certain it could never be for him. He only had one year of freedom, and it was already half gone.

CHAPTER TWELVE

One of the reasons for Kasper's desire to stay on was his appreciation, which developed over the first few months, that Mondays, like a lot at Commonplace, were structured and ritualistic but not always public. At 7.30 am anyone who wanted to get up early met in the sacred ring for the weekly honouring of the divine feminine, called Mother Earth or the Earth Goddess by the residents. Attendances were lowest in the depths of winter and after weekends of celebration but highest on beautiful mornings in autumn and spring. The ring was situated in a secluded and enclosed opening in the bush up behind the Eyrie and comprised 15 upright wooden logs acting as stools arranged in a circle. In the middle was a fire pit.

The ritual consisted of the time-honoured pagan rite of creating a sacred space, first by casting a circle and invoking the four elements, earth, air, fire and water, then by raising the power of the mighty and immanent Earth Goddess and her loyal consort the Horned God. Chanting, drumming, dancing, singing and stomping in the sacred space were employed to bring healing, wonder, empowerment and joy to these earthlings, especially those oppressed, and those in the service of the Earth Goddess.

Each ritual lasted about 40 minutes and ended with the

closing of the circle. The vessels containing the four elements were moved outside. The earth and water were thrown down, the fire and the incense stick were extinguished before the leader said, 'We thank the four guardian spirits of the south, north, east and west for your presence and protection. I release you, your power and your energy, as I close this sacred space.' She swept her left hand around the circle withershins. Everyone stood and recited, 'We end what we start. We close what we open. We continue to serve her.'

Kasper knew nothing of this from the promotional material on Commonplace. His Lutheran upbringing left him unprepared, ignorant and apprehensive about such pagan things, though he knew there were some adherents in Denmark reviving the old paganism of the Vikings. But he recalled that in his religious past, preachers had occasionally railed against exactly these types of gatherings and this kind of 'wicked devil's work'. But despite these warnings, or perhaps because of them, he came to look forward to Monday mornings and, after feeling like an interplanetary alien for the first few weeks, joined in with an increasing sense of connection and wonder. He also noted that the Commonplace members were extremely reticent around talking about these practices and beliefs to visitors or members of the public. His Lutheran roots suggested to him why they were so careful, and he followed suit, even in his missives to his sister. He had planned in the beginning to keep nothing from Isabella but realised that his standing in the Lutheran church, the official state religion, would be ruined if his devotions to the Earth Goddess got out.

After the divine, came the profane. The Revolution Planning Meeting (RPM) took place each Monday morning at 9 o'clock. The term had been coined decades earlier, but no one believed then or now that any revolution was imminent or indeed wise. But the irony was enjoyed by the members.

RPM's attendees used it to plan the work of the week considering what events were scheduled, what groups were coming to use the facilities, what meetings were taking place, what workshops the members were running, as well as any building and maintenance work needed. Alongside those considerations were the routine tasks of the community that needed labour: cooking duty, cleaning, housekeeping, laundry, correspondence, bookkeeping, bill paying, gardening, home schooling, shopping, transporting guests, rubbish tip trips, event planning and website and social media updating.

Over time, Kasper had a go at most of these and enjoyed most that he tried, but not home schooling. He found the interrogation the children subjected him to was too challenging. They had the habit of asking him very personal questions about his intimate life and he often felt a little tongue-tied and embarrassed.

When Sam asked him directly on one occasion, 'How long did it take you to have an organism when you first had sex?' He stammered, 'If you mean an orgasm. I really can't remember,' while thinking, 'Not very long at all!'

He was no prude, but the children's interest seemed too precocious. It was natural for children to be interested in adults' experiences with sex, and other intimate adult activities, and he wondered if his hesitancy egged them on, but it was no fun for him. But the children seemed to enjoy their time with Kasper and often sought him out, especially Sam.

At the RPMs the monthly Peewees: Personal Empowerment weekends were organised. There were three kinds of Peewees: Weewees were Women's Empowerment Weekends, Meewees were Men's Empowerment Weekends, also known as Men's Evolution Weekends by those who thought the last thing men needed was more power, and Saewees which stood for Social Activists Empowerment Weekends and open to all genders.

Commonplace was famous for its Peewees and over the decades thousands of Victorians, as well as many from interstate and overseas, had attended. Some came back again and again. The record stood at 23 attendances by one individual. Kasper was involved each month in the support work needed to make Peewees happen. He helped with cooking, serving, dish washing, cleaning, decorating, flower arranging, housekeeping, bookings, correspondence and fire setting. Each month as he went about these tasks, his curiosity grew about what happened in Peewees. Each month he observed the participants come, then leave with a spring in their step.

Finally, in September, he asked Fran, one of the four members who conducted the Peewees. They spoke in the kitchen when they were both on cooking duty one Tuesday afternoon. There were only going to be about nine for dinner so there was no rush. The menu was chili sin carne (no meat) followed by rice pudding, suggested by Kasper.

As he chopped carrots he asked, 'Fran, do you think I

would be able to go to a Peewee?'

'I was wondering if you were interested. I don't see why not. You have done more than enough work to earn a free place.'

'Thank you. But can I ask you about what happens? I am a little nervous,' he admitted.

'Mmm, well, I don't want to tell you too much, except that we use techniques from group therapy and psychodrama to help people tackle any chronic patterns of thinking or behaving that might stop them doing what they really want to do in life,' she paused, 'Does that make any sense? Oh, and nobody is forced to do anything they do not want to do. It is safe.'

'I understand, a bit. But I have never done any psychodrama or group therapy. Maybe I can read up on them first.'

'Well, I suggest you do the workshop and read up on them second,' Fran shot back.

Kasper laughed, 'Yes I had a lecturer who always said put practice before theory.'

'Wise words indeed but hard for some western minds. You have shown a lot of courage coming here and joining in with a mob like us, so maybe this will be another brave leap into the unknown for you. Shall I book you into a Saewee or a Meewee? Free of charge. Which would you prefer?' said Fran as she went to the pantry to get brown rice.

He considered his options. Which would be less threatening? All men or mixed?

'I think I would rather do a Saewee,' he declared on her return. Having women present seemed a better choice for him.

'Good choice. There is one in October. I will book you in. Feel free to ask me any questions. And, by the way, as a participant you will not have to do any work for the workshop. You will be waited on like a prince.'

Kasper said, 'Well I would be happy to help,' while thinking, 'if only she knew.'

'No, no,' Fran insisted, 'them's the rules.' It was settled.

Kasper smiled. He had just wanted to ask a couple of questions and has ended up with a booking.

The week leading up to the workshop was as busy as ever and Kasper had little time to fret over the weekend ahead, he had thought increasingly about which chronic patterns of thinking or behaving he might want to get assistance with. The cognitive, emotional and behavioural impacts of being born to reign over millions of people were certainly of great interest to him but he could not disclose them directly. Nor did he feel ready to raise all his doubts and uncertainties about his future with Serene. So, Kasper, from being an outside helper, now felt anxious and awkward to being an inside participant.

On 15th October, a few days before the Saewee, Kasper turned 22. A few messages arrived on his phone and laptop from his family, and he replied to each one cheerfully. But he kept his birthday secret from everyone at Commonplace except for Serene. To celebrate, they saw a movie that evening at the Theatre Royal in Castlemaine and sat upstairs holding hands. The Aboriginal classic, *Ten Canoes*, was showing. They both enjoyed it, and the snogging.

CHAPTER THIRTEEN

On the Friday he was on tenterhooks all day, waiting for the workshop to start. That evening he changed into his best clothes and went down to the Polygon where the early birds had started to arrive. He stood around chatting nervously. Meeting new people and small talk were not his forte although he had been schooled in it from birth. Dinner was at 7 pm: pumpkin soup, "lentilherds" pie, green salad and chocolate cake. Fran led the icebreaker exercise. The eleven participants as well as Fran and Luis were invited to give their name, where they were from, one thing that made them joyous and one thing that made them sad.

Kasper had no difficulty with this exercise. 'My name is Kasper, I come from Copenhagen in Denmark, what makes me joyous is the love of my girlfriend and what makes me sad is the imprisonment of people around the world for their political beliefs and actions.' Relieved he was finished; the first hurdle had been cleared.

Before desert, Fran spoke about what was to come. 'Welcome everyone. We meet here on Dja Dja Wurrung Country and I acknowledge the traditional custodians of this land past, present and in the time to come. I also acknowledge that the sovereignty of this land has never been ceded to us white invaders by the first nations. This weekend we encourage you all to be respectful, supportive and cooperative. We are here to work together in a spirit of acceptance and compassion. No one's story is more important than anyone else's and everyone will get a chance to work on their issue. Luis and I will keep you safe and supported, so if you wish, have a go. We also encourage you to play a part in others' role plays if you are asked. But you do not have to. There is no compulsion here. And if you need to step out for any reason, or to go home, feel free. We might follow you out just to see if you are okay. Not to stalk you.' Fran sat down.

Luis rose and spoke for the first time. He was a man around fifty years old who stood 1.67 metres tall and was bald and overweight. He had the nickname "Yoda." Sometimes he really liked his nickname, but on other occasions he absolutely hated it.

Luis began with a big smile and his arms held wide apart. 'First, I must acknowledge but not apologise for my patriarchal birthright: white, male, European entitlement. Please feel free to point out whenever you see it raise its very ugly head this weekend.'

He stopped and walked to the other side of the group. 'The issue you choose to work on is entirely up to you. And if you start and don't want to continue you can bale out at any time. Are there any questions?'

Edna, a young woman in a wheelchair, wearing a striking purple poncho, asked, 'How do I choose an issue? '

'That is the big question,' Luis replied. 'Here are three things you might want to consider. One, do I feel safe raising this part of my life story or will it be too traumatic or triggering for me? Two, is it important enough? You don't want to bring something up that is trivial or unimportant to you. But the decision is yours. And finally, is it too big an issue? If you are recovering from a serious mental health issue or illness, a psych drama workshop like this might not be the best therapy or process for you. Trust your own wisdom and, of course, you can always ask Fran or me.' Luis resumed his seat and out came the cake with tea, coffee and other beverage options.

All through this, Kasper had been thinking hard about what he might bring up if he could muster the courage to have a go. Duncan, an older man sitting on his right turned to him and asked, 'I can't make up my mind. Have you decided?'

'Almost," Kasper replied, 'if I am brave enough.'

'Yes, that's the challenge,' Duncan agreed.

Before the group broke up for the night, Fran rose and called for order again. 'We are sorry. We should have mentioned this important point before. The need for confidentiality. To make this a safe and supportive workshop, confidentiality is key. You will each be agreeing to share your vulnerabilities with this small group. Not the rest of the world. So, no matter how fascinating and newsworthy you will no doubt find other people's stories, please respect their privacy. You can talk about the structure and process here to your heart's content but please respect each other's privacy. Any questions?' Nobody spoke up. 'Breakfast is served at 8 am and we will be kicking off at 9 am sharp. Goodnight, everybody.'

At breakfast the next morning Kasper noticed a certain atmosphere of anticipation and tension amongst the group.

He felt it too. There was not a lot of laughter to be heard. At 9 am, the group of eleven plus the two facilitators formed a circle and Luis opened proceedings. 'Good morning fellow explorers. I think it was Socrates who said a life unexamined is not worth living, Or was it Jung? In any case, wise words I reckon. So please turn your mobiles off or onto silent. So, so, so, here we go. We need a brave and intrepid soul to volunteer first. Who would like this honour and privilege? You will be rewarded richly in your next incarnation.'

Nobody moved a muscle. Kasper was adamant it would not be him. He had taken a long time to fall asleep last night. Two things had weighed heavily on his mind; should he tell the group who he really was? And what personal challenge would he possibly raise? Clearly these two things were linked. Most of all he was very keen to avoid the possibility of being embarrassed or humiliated.

The group sat there in suspense for quite a while. Fran and Luis appeared totally unconcerned and sat in comfortable silence. After a while Luis tried another tack. 'I see a couple of familiar faces. Maybe one of you who has been before could get us started.'

This did the trick. A middle-aged woman called Martha raised her hand and said, 'Okay. I don't want to appear to be pushy but if no one else is ready I will volunteer.' An almost audible collective sigh of relief swept the group and so the workshop began in earnest. Fran replied, 'Thanks Martha. Please be as pushy as you like.'

At the end of the first day, Kasper had not had a turn, but he had found the day fascinating. Of the six participants who had taken a turn, five had raised issues they had with their parents. The mood at dinner was quite jovial but Kasper was pensive. He noticed that the most jovial ones were those who had already taken their turn. Tomorrow, the full glare of the spotlight would be on him whether he had a go or not. After dinner he retreated to his hut and sent an enthusiastic message to his sister Isabella describing the day. He finished with, 'I have never witnessed so much laughing, crying, shouting and raging in one day. And I got to play two roles, a pet dog and a wheelbarrow. It was serious fun.'

Kasper slept a lot better that night. He was now resolved to have a go and was more confident that he would be safe and unembarrassed. He had noticed the subtle skills that Fran and Luis brought to their work. All he had to decide was whether to disclose his true identity.

Sunday dawned a fine, sunny spring day. Over breakfast, Fran announced that one of the group, an older man called Herb, had left the workshop but he had first assured her that he was okay before he departed.

As the day rolled on, Kasper fought an intense inner battle at regular intervals. Each time a facilitator called for a new participant to come forward he procrastinated mightily and someone else beat him. But he knew eventually he would have no competition. At noon they broke for lunch, with three people yet to have a go. Kasper sat quietly eating a cheese and tomato sandwich when Luis approached him.

'How are you going there, Kasper? I notice you are a little withdrawn.'

'I am okay, thanks. Just a little anxious about my turn.

Everyone's issues are so important compared to mine. I haven't had much abuse or trauma in my life. I have been lucky,' Kasper replied.

'Good for you. So, are you thinking of not having a go?' Luis asked.

'No, I want to do it. I just have trouble coming forward.'

'Well, if it would help, there are three places left. You can book one with me if you like and it will be yours.' Luis offered.

He considered briefly and agreed. 'That would really help. Let me go second, or second last,' he asked with a grimace.

'That is a done deal,' Luis replied, 'I will let you finish your lunch in peace.'

Fifty minutes later, Kasper got up at Luis' prompt and stood beside the facilitator. Just get started, he told himself, as he looked around at the other eleven people.

'What would you like to work on today, Kasper? Give us your story,' Luis asked, as he had with all the others.

Kasper had written down a script the night before and was prepared. He just hoped that his story would not blow his cover. 'So, I am Kasper. I am a visitor from Copenhagen in Denmark, and I had my 22nd birthday the other day. I am on a gap year from studying at university. Back home my family is very prominent. For generations we have built up a very large business empire. We own a big portfolio of properties worth hundreds of millions of dollars across the land. Each year the family gets about fourteen million dollars in income. I am the oldest child and since birth I have been raised to take over the dynasty when my father retires or dies. I feel this great pressure on me from my family, especially my father's family. But nothing is ever said. It is all just taken for granted. They just assume I will do my duty, but I am not sure I want to, anymore. I am trying to sort out my life while in Australia, but the year is running out. It will just be so hard, if not impossible, to break away from the family tradition. It would really annoy a lot of powerful people.' Kasper stopped. It was all true but none of it was true at the same time; he had lied by omission but not by commission. So far so good.

Luis stood next to Kasper and said, 'Thank you, young man. You are brave. That was most interesting.' He turned and addressed the group, 'Just appreciate everyone, that every single innovation and invention in human history, from the making of fire, to the development of language, through to the nuclear bomb, came about because some children refused to follow lockstep in the footsteps of their parents. Kasper, can I just ask you one question to help me focus? When you go home is there some imminent challenge or situation that you will have to face?'

Kasper immediately knew the answer and wondered why he had left that bit out. 'Yes, I have to go back into the military, to the Air Force. I only agreed to please my father. To get him onside so that I could take a gap year. I am dreading it.'

'Okay, dread is not good. I can see you will have a lot to deal with back in Denmark. Let us work up a really good psychodrama for you Kasper.' The two were soon in intense conversation.

Five minutes later they were ready to begin. Kasper stood at the head of a line of five people. He had picked the other four and they stood in order of their age, behind him. From the back the order was man, man, woman, and man. They faced Kasper and he faced them. The curtain rose and the drama began.

The man at the back shouted at Kasper. 'Follow me!' as loud as he could. The other three followed suit down the line and after the fourth person had taken his turn all four of them yelled in unison, 'FOLLOW US!'

Luis turned to Kasper, 'How was that?'

'Yes, I have heard them before. In my head, I mean,' Kasper replied. He could feel the heat and pressure inside.

'Okay,' said Luis, 'Let's do it again, you thespians. And this time really put your backs into it! And the rest of us need to get a chant going, 'Follow them! Follow them! Follow them! Here we go.'

They had two more goes and each was louder than the last. The audience got into the chanting and did not stop. It was loud. As the third round of chants was coming to an end Luis went to a large chest of costumes and props that stood against the wall. He returned with an imitation sword and an old-fashioned megaphone.

'Now it's up to you, Kasper,' he said handing Kasper his tools.

Kasper strode to the end of the line as the audience took up the chant again, 'Follow them! Follow them!' Kasper turned to the audience and raised his sword high. With his other hand he lifted the megaphone to his mouth and with a commanding voice ordered the chorus to stop. Luis stepped alongside him and whispered something in his ear. Kasper grimaced and yelled his command, this time in Danish.

'*Hold op for helvede!*' They all fell silent.

Kasper turned on his great-great grandfather and yelled in English then Danish, 'Shut up, you are already dead!' and with his sword he ran his ancestor through. The dying man fell to the floor and had a dramatic end with much writhing and groaning. The audience members cheered.

Next in line was Kasper's great grandfather. By now Kasper was at the height of his might. He bellowed and slayed again with great conviction. The poor victim outdid his own father with his theatrical final act, convulsing and groaning in his death throes. The audience approved.

Kasper turned to his grandmother. Again, he bellowed for her to shut up adding, 'You are nearly dead!' But this time he hesitated with the sword. She saw his hesitation and hissed at him, 'Follow me now, you ungrateful, traitorous, little shit!'

Kasper stepped back and Luis stepped forward. This time Luis yelled, 'Kill the voice!' The audience took up the call, 'Kill the voice! Kill the voice! Kill the voice!' rang out.

Kasper now stepped forward and dispatched the poor woman with a mighty blow of his sword. She fell immediately to the floor emitting a hideous death rattle. The crowd approved both manually and verbally.

Kasper approached the last man standing. His father simply said. 'Be a good boy now and it's all yours.' Again, Kasper raised the megaphone and roared, 'Shut up!' at his father, in both languages.

'Do not speak to me like that son. I am your father. I know what is best for you! Follow me,' the father ordered insistently.

This time Kasper hesitated for a moment before thrusting

his sword forward, immediately as the crowd resumed the chant, 'Kill the voice!' But his father grabbed the sword blade. He was not going to go down without a fight and yelled back at his son, 'You are a disgrace to your family. Do your bloody duty or you will be disowned immediately.'

Kasper was now furious, 'Shut your mouth. I am an adult. I make my own decisions!' He wrestled the sword free and thrust it through his father who staggered back. Clutching his entrails, the final forebear weaved crazily around the room before dying a slow and agonising death, centre stage.

Kasper raised his sword and megaphone in triumph and performed a victory lap around the room. Luis immediately started up a new chant and it was quickly taken up. 'He's an adult. He makes his own decisions! He's an adult. He makes his own decisions!'

Luis quietened the audience after a few more rounds of chanting and spoke to Kasper. 'Well done, Kasper. You will now carry your sword and megaphone with you for the rest of your life. Your sword will bring you protection and courage and your megaphone will give you the voice of truth and justice.' The audience clapped again.

But Luis was nowhere near finished. He went to the chest again and returned with a small bundle in a baby blanket. This part had not been planned between the two of them.

Luis asked, 'Are you a father, Kasper?'

'No, not yet, but I would like to be one day,' he replied.

'Today is that day,' Luis said and handed Kasper the baby doll wrapped in a blanket, 'Congratulations dad. Is it a boy, a girl or another option?' he asked.

'It is a girl,' Kasper answered with a big grin. He was thinking of one person only, Serene.

'Does she have a name yet?' Luis asked.

Kasper thought for a little while before replying, 'Yes, her name is Thula.'

'Oh, that is a beautiful name,' Luis said, 'What would you like to tell her about the work you have done today?'

'Mmm,' Kasper did not have a ready answer and thought for a few seconds before he spoke. 'Well, all I can think of is, 'Thula you can do whatever you want to do when you grow up. I will not stand in your way. But I would be delighted if you became an artist or a musician.' The others applauded.

Luis asked Kasper one final question, 'Tell me Kasper, what is the first thing you will do when you get back home?'

Kasper looked down at the megaphone in his right hand. He thought for a further second then raised it to his mouth, 'I am going to tell my father that I am not joining the stupid Air Force!' he bellowed. The others clapped louder.

'Well said young man!' Luis proclaimed 'Excellent use of megaphone, too. Are you happy to end it there?' Kasper just nodded.

Fran stepped forward as Luis began to put away the props. She thanked each of the four role players and said to each, as they rose from the grave, 'You are not a dead Dane. You are fully alive with all your parts working well.'

Kasper was still on his feet and Fran extended her hand. 'Well done, Kasper. You have now completed your first psychodrama. How are you feeling?'

'I feel great, thanks,' Kasper replied shaking her hand.

'I am happy, sad, tired, and full of energy, all at the same time.' Luis and Fran gave him a big three-way hug as the others clapped yet again. Kasper sat down and took a long drink of water. He was proud of himself and very happy that he had taken his turn, after all.

At 4 am, the workshop ended with three cheers for the two facilitators followed by hugs and handshakes all round. Names and phone numbers were exchanged by most of the participants. Eric appeared to drive some participants to the train station. He exchanged greetings with Kasper, and they promised to catch up later. Kasper helped Fran and Luis take things back to the Eyrie and retreated to his own hut. He lay on his bed feeling drained and replayed the events in his head. But then fell asleep. His last thought was about getting himself a sword and a megaphone as reminders of his workshop and to equip himself for his life to come.

Later Eric knocked on the hut door and called out, 'Kasper it is 7 o'clock, do you want to come down for dinner?'

'I sure do,' he called back, and the two friends went down together.

'How was it?' Eric asked as soon as he could.

'It was extraordinary, thanks, mate. One of the best things I have ever done. Thanks for waking me. I am starving.'

CHAPTER FOURTEEN

By her 16th day of interrogation, Serene realised she urgently needed just to make up a story and some names. Nothing in her upbringing had prepared her for this, although the cruel eccentricities of "the Lion," King Mswati III, and his extensive family were common knowledge across the tiny country of Eswatini. Day after day, the man she just called 'The Interrogator' asked her the same thing in a hundred cunning ways. 'Who were you working for?' He never gave his name, and she did not ask. The hunger, thirst and sleeplessness gnawed away at her but the stench from her cell and increasingly from her own body was really upsetting her.

Again and again, she had simply spoken the truth and had assumed that sooner or later she would be believed and this ordeal would end, 'I did it alone. It was only me. No one told me to do it. I am not in any group. I don't know any communists or terrorists. I did not meet anyone beforehand.' Day after day.

She had grown up in a traditional Swazi household. Her father was the head man and had four wives, all younger than him. She was the second daughter of her father's third wife and had four full siblings and 16 half siblings. By the time she was eighteen she was adamant that she did not want to follow in her mother's footsteps as a polygamous wife, and thus a subservient domestic and agricultural labourer, and baby maker. Luckily her mother wholeheartedly supported her interest in getting educated and they agreed she might become a teacher. None of her siblings had such ambitions and she kept these from her father and uncles.

At eighteen, unmarried young women were obliged to participate in the annual coming of age Umhlanga, or Reed Dance. This traditional and prestigious eight-day female marathon of dance and ritual was performed for the Swazi Queen Mother, known as the She Elephant. It was a big deal. The event drew tens of thousands of young women as well as family members and spectators from across the land. It was a cultural highlight to celebrate the chastity of the females, display their traditional dancing skills and let them pay tribute to the She Elephant and her royal female relatives, especially the princesses, daughters of the king.

Each year a young woman was chosen by the She Elephant to be the captain, or "induna", from among the host of participating female commoners. To her utter horror Serene, who had not wanted to participate in the first place, was selected induna. The induna was expected to have expertise in traditional dancing and just as important, in royal protocol and ritual. Serene did not have, and was determined that she was not going to develop, expertise in either of these things, and moreover did not see why chastity was such a virtue. The thought of having to undergo the mandatory virginity test and to dance bare breasted in public appalled her. Her mother was sympathetic, but her father and siblings were

117

excited at her selection and then dumbfounded when told she was refusing to do it. They argued her participation was sure to increase the standing of her and her family in the community, and equally importantly, her prospects as a bride. Everyone would be a winner. But her resolve did not waver. Where such pig-headed stubbornness came from, she had no idea, but she knew it had been a part of her all her life.

No young woman in living memory had ever refused this prestigious role before and the She Elephant was highly offended. She saw the act as unfathomable treason and a further sign that the forces of rebellion were at large. Recently, she saw a lot of this amongst the poorer class in her country. But Serene knew none of this. A week after her historic act of refusal they came for her late one afternoon as she walked home from the store with some shopping.

On day 17 of her interrogation, the tactics changed. An overweight, bald, middle-aged man in a sharp tailored suit lumbered into the interrogation room. The interrogator bowed slightly. Serene instantly found the man loathsome. He walked around her as she sat handcuffed in her chair. He leered and touched her in a lascivious manner. She flinched. He described her looks and body and announced, 'I am his Majesty's loyal servant, the Royal Procurer, Mr Mtini. Our dear King, the Lion, likes to honour beautiful, young virgins like you, especially naughty young virgins, with an invitation to his bedchamber. You would have the honour and pleasure of giving your maidenhead to your monarch. Should you be blessed with a pregnancy you might even become his 16th royal wife and bear him his thirty fourth child.' He leered again and paused to let the news sink in. 'So, the choice is yours, if you fail to co-operate with the King's Police in this investigation and expose those who would harm him, I might reconsider. Of course, you will be cleansed, clad and perfumed. Now you stink but the Lion will find you smelling like a new infant.' Mr Mtini gave her a final caress and leer. Serene recoiled again. The interrogator nodded and Mr Mtini lumbered from the room.

The interrogator ordered the guard to take her back to her cell, shouting after her, 'Tomorrow you decide!' Serene realised she had to try something new, make something up. The prospect of being raped by the King terrified her, although she fully understood others would never consider it a rape.

As the surly guard escorted her down the long corridor to her cell, she saw another prisoner approaching in the opposite direction. She had seen him twice before in the corridor and had pitied him for his wretched state. This time, unlike before, he made brief eye contact as he drew near, and a smile flickered momentarily across his face. Then he stumbled and reached out to her to steady himself. His guard roared, 'Stay clear of her, you filthy hyena!' She felt a tiny slip of paper in the hand she had reflexively extended towards the wretched man.

Her heart quickened but she made no sign and once back in her cell she lay on the filthy mattress and positioned her back to the camera high above the door and studied the note. It contained three male names, Maxwell Masuku, Noah Thabise and Teri Wandele, followed by a telephone number.

The names meant nothing to her, nor did the phone number. Under the harsh ceiling light, she pondered the message long into the night as she fought the hunger cramps. Towards morning she had memorised the names and the number and had made up her mind. Next, she surreptitiously chewed up and swallowed the note.

On day 18 she was led to the interrogation room early after a "breakfast" of watery milk and a slice of bread. The interrogator was smiling more than usual, 'well young woman, it has come to this. Look we know you are an immature and naïve country girl. We know that offending the She Elephant was not really your doing. If you give us the names you will be treated most leniently. And now you have a new prospect to consider after Mr Mtini conveyed our Royal Highness' generous offer. And let me be abundantly clear. As you might have gathered from seeing the other prisoners, if you refuse to talk or if the King rejects you, your treatment here will become a lot harsher. You will be beaten, burnt and violated until you will surely beg for mercy. Remember, the King is determined to root out traitors. Now, who caused you to insult the King's dear mother, our She Elephant?'

Serene nodded and knew she had to be convincing. She made eye contact with him for the first time. 'Yes, you are right. Three men came to me one evening. I was in the field alone just after I had refused to be the induna. They were very friendly. They said they were democracy activists. They told me they wanted my help to make the country fairer for my family and girls and poor people. They said the She

Elephant was a bad woman who had stolen a lot of money. They said she was very rich, but her people were very poor. They said she needed to be taught a small lesson. They said it would be nothing. They said she would probably just laugh it off.' She paused and held her breathe. A faint cry from down the corridor reached her. Was it the note bearer she wondered, as the interrogator digested her lie.

'Good, good.' He smiled. 'And what did you think about what they were saying?'

Serene saw the trap. 'I did not believe them at first. I was brought up to respect and honour our King and his dear mother. I knew nothing about what they said. I think the King does his best to rule us wisely.'

'Good, good,' he repeated, 'so why did you change your mind?'

'At first, I said no. I did not want to insult our She Elephant. But they offered me money. I said no again, and they offered me more money. I knew it would help my family a lot, so I agreed. We needed seed and food. We are poor. I thought the She Elephant would understand and forgive me. That's what they told me.'

Serene pulled against her handcuffs to cause herself pain. The pain helped her to cry and her tears ran unchecked down her cheeks. Through her tears she pleaded, 'I am so sorry. I did not know how wrong it was. I will never do it again. I was just trying to help my family.'

The interrogator came right up to her and smiled again, 'I understand. It was not your fault. You were clearly led astray. Now I just need the men's names then it will all be over for you. You will be well treated, lots of food, clean clothes, water and soap, no handcuffs.'

Serene felt some hope for the first time since Day One. Maybe she has fooled him. She forced herself to cry some more. Soon she would see. She played her ace. 'Their names were Max Masuku, Noah Thabise and Teri Wandele. But they may have made them up. I don't know anything about them.'

The interrogator exclaimed, 'Great,' and opened his notebook quickly writing down the three names. Then out the door he dashed, without a word. This could be a great day for his career.

She sat there exhausted. What if she had misinterpreted the message? Had she just condemned three men to save her own skin? Was she believable? Was she saved? Would they send her to the King anyway? She tried to force that thought away. She looked around the windowless room. It was nondescript, but she would never forget it. Did she regret her act, she wondered? Not at all, just the appalling consequences. Nobody had warned her. She had been so idealistic and naïve. Her wrists ached and her stomach griped. Now her head hurt, too.

After a long time, the interrogator returned. Immediately Serene could see that he was relaxed and a little cocky. 'Good, good. These men you met. We know them. They are all very bad men, treacherous jackals. You have been most helpful. Well done, indeed!' He immediately ordered the guard standing outside the door to take the handcuff from her wrists. He then produced a document and placed it before her. 'Just sign this and you will be able to eat and wash tonight. Then tomorrow we will release you.'

Serene looked down at the two pages of tightly written script. She did not expect this. It was part confession, part plea for clemency and part statement that she had been treated humanely and compassionately, while freely and voluntarily assisting the police with their investigations in the righteous cause of state security. The final flourish was her vow of loyalty to the King, his mother and all their heirs. She considered her long dirty fingernails and grimy hand as she picked up the clean, shiny pen she was proffered. She scrawled her name. She had no choice.

'Well done, well done,' gushed the interrogator as he pocketed the pen and motioned to the guard to take her away; the handcuffs left off.

That evening she indeed took delivery of a meagre meal of maize porridge, an apple and a lukewarm mug of tea. Later she received a bucket of clean water, a cake of soap and a thin, clean rag. She drank greedily from the bucket first before washing as best she could. She was glad her period had not arrived. But the mattress was still filthy, yet she lay on it and tried to sleep with the tray over her head to shield her eyes from the infernal light. Soon she dreamed she was running hard along a long hallway. Three strange men were pursuing her, but she could not find the exit. Suddenly she was outside with her mother. She dashed across a wide beach and plunged into the ocean. Her mother stood back on the beach and screamed at her to come back. But she ignored her mother. She was desperate to get away and started swimming out to sea. Then she panicked as the waves swamped her.

She feared she was drowning and woke with a start. The tray was under her head with the edge digging into her neck. Reality returned instantly. It was Day 19, and she hoped it would be the last.

A guard bought her a breakfast of maize porridge, milk and a banana as well as a change of clothes. The food was delicious. The clothes were hideous. Sometime later, the guard returned and told her to pack her things. Serene smiled at the notion that she had "things" to pack while tying her dirty clothes into a bundle with the rag. This time the guard did not handcuff her when he led her to the interrogation room.

To her great surprise, she was greeted by a petite, older woman with neat, short, greying hair and dressed in neat, casual European clothes. A teapot, two fine bone china cups and saucers, a sugar bowl, a strainer, and a milk jug sat on the table. The woman held out her hand and spoke in English as Serene shook it cautiously. 'One of the few good legacies of the English, and one I cherish, is a good cup of Earl Grey tea.' Then shifting to Swati, she continued, 'I am Mrs Zena from the Interior Ministry. Let me pour you a cup. Do you take milk and sugar?' Serene just nodded. 'I have heard that you have been most helpful. I congratulate you. It is time for your release but there are conditions.'

Serene felt a wave of anxiety flood through her as Mrs Zena continued without pause, 'we want you to work for us. You are bright, ambitious and strong. Now that we also know how loyal you are, we will assist you in pursuing your dream of becoming a teacher.' Serene wondered how the lady knew this. 'Your path into Teachers' College will be eased and we will pay you a small living allowance while you study. Your family will be relieved of the burden of supporting you. We ask very little of you in return. Nothing more than any loyal subject of the King would happily do as a matter of course.'

Serene thought Mrs Zena was reading from a script. Her speech seemed so practiced and recited. Maybe she employed this speech each time she recruited a spy.

'All you need to do is join in with your fellow students and later your teaching colleagues. Each week or so just report to a colleague of mine, whom you will meet in due course, what certain peers of yours are saying. We know the teaching services harbours subversive types who are out to harm the King and Eswatini, so you should have plenty to report. Your services will be rewarded. But be warned, you have committed one crime against the King's honour already and we will be watching you. If you transgress again, we will make you disappear after a lot of pain. Any questions?'

Serene could not reply. She was trapped and she knew it. There was no escape. She mumbled a 'No,' but then all she could think of asking was, 'how long will I need to do it?'

Mrs Zena was quick to reply, 'Oh, good question dear. Only until you retire. After that we will find you a new role.' A faint smirk of pleasure crossed her face. Serene felt the hair on the back of her neck stand up. Then anger swept through her. She tried to hide it.

'Excellent.' Mrs Zena announced, 'All done. Welcome to the King's service'. She quickly took Serene's hand in hers. Serene now found the touch repulsive and had to stop herself from pulling away. 'You may go now. You are released,' she added airily with the same little smirk and waved towards the door with a flourish.

Serene gathered her bundle from the floor and followed her guard out of the building in a daze. Outside the entrance she stood squinting at the bright sunlight and inhaled the glorious fresh air. She had no idea where she was or how she would get home. The prison frontage bore no signage and there were no street names in sight. As she felt the great desire to get away, she started walking quickly, a taxi drew alongside. The driver beckoned her to get in and called out, 'I am to take you to the bus station. No fare.'

Her arrival at home caused much joy and many questions. Since her disappearance, her family had no news. They were worried that she would never return. They had heard of other families whose daughters her age had disappeared. These young women were known ironically as 'little queens' in the sad expectation that some of them may have joined the ranks of the King's secret concubines. Serene lied about her time away. She admitted she had been detained but stuck to the terms of her statement and said she had been well treated. She said nothing about the conditions of her release. She told them she had learnt her lesson and would not be so foolish again. Her mother knew there was more to the story but did not ask. Her father and uncles lectured her on her shameful behaviour. She cried at this but elicited no sympathy from the adult males.

She did not need the help of Mrs Zena to gain admittance to teachers' college as her high school marks were excellent but there was some stern opposition from her father and uncles. 'Girls are needed on the farm to tend the fields and the animals. In the city you will get into more trouble. And who will help your mother and sisters with the housework?' her father argued. An uncle chipped in, 'We will never see you again. The city is not a place for a girl like you. Your husband will be a city type and there you will stay, lost to all of us.' An older half-brother had his say, 'You will hate the city. You are a country girl.' None of them sought her opinion. Her mother held her tongue. She knew the opposition was more token than real. When alone with her daughter she said, 'I am so proud of you my dear child. Nobody in our family has ever been a professional person before. You have earned it and you will become an excellent teacher.' Serene hugged her in return. She would miss her mother and her home hugely.

CHAPTER FIFTEEN

The female residential unit on the teaching college campus sat in a quiet suburb of Mbabane, one of the two capital cities. Serene settled in quickly. She hoped desperately that she would be left alone by Mrs Zena and her minions, but she duly had a visitor to her room a week later. Her handler, a Mr Ntshangase, smelt of tobacco and sweat and lit a cigarette in her small room. Serene asked him not to smoke but he ignored her. The trauma of her interrogation came flooding back, and for a moment she had returned to that stinking cell. Ntshangase was about forty, short of stature and shabbily dressed in western shorts and a coloured shirt. He did not look like a government agent. He handed her a list of six names and a schedule of meetings. 'These are the suspects we want you to report on,' he explained. 'Get them to trust you and confide in you. Keep a log of what they say to whom, when and where, and who they associate with. We have your bank details and so we will deposit money after I meet you but only if we are happy with your reports. I will meet you in Selection Park according to the schedule. I will find you. Make very sure you are never followed. We have enemies. Any questions?'

Serene was pleased they had enemies and had a thousand questions but decided they could all wait. She wanted this man out of her room as soon as possible. She knew none of the three males and three females on the list. Her career as a government spy would not be easy. She shook her head.

'No questions then?' Ntshangase asked and left his odours and smoke behind as he ambled out.

The next evening Serene felt the time was right. After a long walk from her new home, she found a phone box and rang the number she had fixed in her memory that night in her cell. A male voice answered and did not give his name. Neither did she, 'A fellow prisoner gave me this number,' she said hesitantly,

Before she could say another word, the male broke in, 'Good, we have been expecting you. Hang up now, you will get a mobile. Ring the only number stored in it. Forget the number you used now.' Before she could speak, he was gone.

The next afternoon after class, she was looking for the six names on the lists of students posted on the administrative notice boards when a young woman approached her. She barely noticed as the stranger brushed alongside, slipped something into her bag and moved away.

She hurried to her room and was about to phone the number in the mobile when she realised the danger. Her room may well be bugged. So instead, she found a quiet spot under an impressive acacia across the campus and phoned. She spoke to a Peter for what seemed like ages. He told her he was an activist in the democracy movement and he was assigned to support and protect her. He knew what she had been through. Serene felt some relief for the first time since the day the interrogator had believed her story. And she had one burning question, 'What has happened to the three men I named? Are they safe?'

Peter answered directly, 'One man had been killed before you got the note, one has gone underground and the third is already safely out of the country. So yes, in a way they are all safe, for now. You did the right thing.'

Serene let out a sigh of relief then asked, 'so what is to become of me?'

'After this call, you must remove the sim card, burn it and throw away the mobile. You will get a new mobile when we next have news. We plan to get you out of the country, but it will take time. Do you have a current passport?'

'Yes,' Serene remembered; she still had one from the school excursion she had taken to the seaside in Mozambique.

'Good, keep it safe but do not attempt to leave the country. Not even for a day trip. You are at risk, so it is vital that you play your role until we are ready. Who are the names of those you must report on?'

Serene passed Peter the six names. 'Thank you. We will warn them if need be. Anything they say to you after next week you are free to report to your smelly handler.' Serene smiled at his knowledge.

'But please do not tell him about anyone else at this stage. You may report on just them. I need to go now. Please obey my instructions. Sadly, you cannot contact us until you get a new mobile. Remember, you are greatly admired for your deeds and courage. You have friends around you. Please take care.'

Serene was overcome with intense pride and intense

sadness. Finally, she had an ally, but he had delivered another gut-wrenching twist in the trajectory of her life. If she was fortunate, she would be able to leave her country behind, along with everyone she loved. She sat in the grass and wept tears of relief, grief and despair. She knew it was better for her to cry here than in her room.

For two long years she led the double life of government spy and successful student. She decided she would major in English and History, but she also became absorbed by the social politics of her own land. She read about the poverty and low life expectancy. She became aware of the power and wealth accumulated by the royal family in one of the world's last absolute monarchies. She learned how the government suppressed, sometimes murderously, the democratic and reformist movements. Some teachers had been at the forefront, and she tried to remember their names. She kept these studies to herself.

Mr Ntshangase met her weekly for the first year and seemed happy enough with her copious reports. He said little about her work and she was paid up. He engaged her in no conversation and she initiated none. She thought he probably never read what she reported, just passed it on. At the end of twelve months, he removed three names from the list and gave her four new ones. She knew that two of these three students had left the course and hoped they were safe. She did not ask.

A week later she was passed a new mobile from a different woman. She told Peter of the new arrangements, so he took from her the new names. Again, he told her that she could report whatever they said after a week. He had no news about when she could escape. And as she wondered why it was taking so long; a thought crossed her mind. By now she had read a lot about domestic spying and the craft of espionage and learnt that the security apparatus in Eswatini best resembled the Mossad in Israel. She also realised that she was most likely a double agent and was probably feeding to Mrs Zena what the democracy activists wanted the authorities to know. This possibility pleased her greatly, as did the news that Mr Smelly, as she called him, now only wanted to meet her fortnightly. She still tried to prepare copious and voluminous reports about every little detail. It seemed to have worked so far.

But near the end of the second year Mr Smelly took the initiative at their park meeting. 'You must come to a meeting. Mrs Zena wants to speak to you.' He passed her a note with a date, time and address.

Serene instantly remembered the aroma of bergamot, Mrs Zena's clammy touch and evil little smirk instantly and asked, as politely as possible, 'do you know what she wants Mr Ntshangase? Do I need to prepare anything? Please help me out here.' She wished she had been more friendly to Mr Smelly.

'No idea,' he replied abruptly and stood up from the park bench they occupied. 'May be good, may be bad. I really have no idea. Just do not be late. And maybe bring a toothbrush,' he added. It was not a subtle aside.

His last afterthought appeared to amuse Mr Smelly as he let out a hoarse chuckle which then led to a bout of coughing as he walked away. Serene hoped he had lung cancer. She was immediately alarmed and needed to contact Peter, but how? It had been about six weeks since their last phone call. Later that evening she arrived at a possible solution. It was obvious once she thought of it. She had been in regular contact with two women from the college for nearly two years now. She spied on them. She chose the one she liked the best and sought her out. Her name was Mary Shongwe and she was active in the student association and the debating society. She liked to joke and laugh with Serene and sometimes she told jokes that ridiculed the Lion and the She Elephant. Serene had reported a watered-down version of these in a timely manner.

Serene found Mary where she often was, reading a South African newspaper in the library. She smiled a warm hello. Serene did not sit down but stood there, tongue tied. Finally, she blurted out, 'I need to contact a man you might know. His name is Peter, but I don't know his last name. It's very important.' Mary looked up at her, hesitated and answered in a flat dry tone, 'I know nobody by that name.'

Serene blushed and hurried off. Of course, Mary knew a Peter, she realised, everyone knows a Peter, a very common name.

The next morning as Serene approached the lecture room for her English class with a group of her fellow students, a female she did not know joined her and the others briefly and brushed against her. The mobile was quickly transferred. She silently thanked Mary and knew she would never be able to thank her in person.

Peter listened silently when she rang to tell him of her

forthcoming meeting. It was in six days' time. Peter then replied rapidly. It was clear he was concerned.

'Yes, there is a chance you are in real danger. We may have an informer. We need to get you to safety. Listen carefully. Do not change your schedule or habits in the next five days. The day before your meeting, do not go to class. Instead take a change of clothes and your passport. Hide your passport in your underwear. Put the clothes in your regular day bag as you would your books for class. Take nothing with your name on it except the passport. Leave everything in your room untouched. Exactly as normal. Tell nobody. Head towards your usual class and before you get there you will meet a man you do not know. Go with him to the station. He will give you a different passport and identity papers and will accompany you to Mozambique. Learn your new name and date of birth and the other information in your false passport quickly. You will get all the other information you need from my colleague. Good luck. I hope we can meet in person one day.' Peter hung up. Serene was shocked at the news but knew she had no choice other than to escape her homeland with a man she had never met.

Things went to plan. On the appointed day a man named Moses appeared and took her to the station. They got off at the next station and walked for a long way across the city. Abruptly they doubled back. Next, they caught a bus and after a longer ride alighted in a street of wealthy houses. They walked together for another half an hour or so and finally Moses knocked on the back door of a large house. An elderly, well-dressed woman let them in with a brief nod.

Serene changed into the clothes and put on the wig provided. She studied the photo of her new self in the fake passport and applied make up. Over lunch she tried to memorise the details in her new passport and was quizzed by Moses. After lunch she put her few clothes into a different bag and was given a novel, a return rail ticket, a popular magazine extolling the virtue of the royal family and a mobile phone. She gave her real passport to the kind lady. Moses thanked the lady profusely and they left her house and walked a long way in a different direction.

Moses Jele and his girlfriend Jabulani Dube had an uneventful journey across the border to Mozambique. The border guards stamped their passports with barely a glance and wished them a happy trip. Serene was certain they would notice the tension in her limbs and the sweat on her brow, but it did not happen. She was now a political refugee and her journey to Commonplace was underway.

CHAPTER SIXTEEN

Serene had begun staying from time to time at Commonplace about six months before Kasper turned up. She was now 23 years old, stood 1.82 metres tall and was of slender build. She had a broad nose and a long forehead above her high cheekbones, and she kept her naturally wiry hair short. Her black skin accentuated the whiteness of her prominent teeth whenever she smiled. Despite her travails and status in Australia, she smiled a lot.

Serene was an illegal immigrant and had been hidden and supported by a loose network of people and organisations across the country for the last 18 months. She was just one of the thousands of people with no legal status hiding across the southern continent. At first, she entered Australia on a student visa and when that expired, she sought asylum as a political refugee and applied for a protection visa. For reasons that baffled her, this was refused by Australian authorities, and she had to immediately go into hiding or be arrested. She knew too well that deportation home would mean a long imprisonment, harsh treatment and probably torture, or even death. She was desperate not to go back although she missed her mother, siblings and friends, greatly. She also missed Moses, her first boyfriend, who was now in the Netherlands, on a Dutch asylum residence permit. Occasionally she heard from him.

Thus, she arrived at Commonplace to be sheltered and supported. Commonplace for decades had been hiding certain asylum seekers and refugees on the run from the Australian authorities, to avoid them being sent back to face persecution from the various countries they had escaped. Serene moved between safe houses during her time in Australia and was very hopeful that one day she might be able to get a visa and come out of hiding.

Serene and Kasper had become lovers soon after their visit to the Chewton cemetery and were quite inseparable whenever she was at Commonplace. They spent hours together weeding, watering and planting in the garden and orchard. And in their free time they would regularly run together for miles on the backroads and tracks nearby. But Serene always had an eye on the road into the property and tried to stay out of sight whenever an unfamiliar vehicle arrived. Her deep, heart connection with Kasper had started slowly as both were hiding secrets, and she was also wary of anyone she suspected might report her to the Federal Police.

Kasper had only had one girlfriend before, and that relationship was over. Of course, from a very early age he knew he had to make a suitable match and produce a suitable heir, the kingdom depended on it. His wife needed to be a royal, preferably, if not, an aristocrat or at least someone from a good, upper class, respectable family. And despite his mother being a foreign commoner from Tasmania, Kasper got the firm impression that this was an exception and a wife from among the common people was not the best idea.

For eighteen months he had gone out in secrecy with Mette,

a classmate from his senior high school, or 'gymnasium', and he really thought that she might be the one. Sex had been easy despite his years of anxiety and anticipation about it. The first time was the night of their graduation, indeed losing one's virginity at that time was almost a Danish rite of passage. The festivities to mark the end of twelve years of education were great fun. All stops were pulled out for the occasion. The class had made the traditional great procession on the high floats around the city; wearing naval caps, with the band, the songs, the cheers, the speeches, the hijinks and the booze. Late in the night, Christian and Mette fell into bed together. It seemed so right that he should have sex with Mette that night. He was quite intoxicated but not yet incapacitated, unlike many of his classmates.

During that golden summer, before university started, they were consumed by mutual lust. They travelled down to France where he had spent weeks, all through his childhood. They visited family, friends, and stayed on granddad Henri's family estate, Chateau de Cayx. They helped a little with the grape harvest and slept entwined. Danish royals were less conspicuous in France than at home and they felt less constrained. Back in Denmark, it was time for their next preordained step. Chris enrolled in the University of Copenhagen, but Mette took up her ideal offer – a place at Harvard. Her long-held dream of time in the USA had come true. Chris had not wanted her to go at all. He knew that it would be well-nigh impossible for him to visit her there.

Their relationship was not public in Denmark, but he knew that the media were always speculating about his intimate life or outright inventing partners for him. So far, Mette had not been mentioned except in one trashy article that had listed all his female peers from his class at gymnasium and analysed their attractiveness and suitability as crown princesses. Mette and he had been much amused when the article rated her lowly on both measures. She came to Amalienborg to dine with him for the last time just before she flew across the Atlantic. She wanted to say goodbye and had a heavy heart.

Over pizza he tried one more time to talk her out of going with a hint of desperation, 'I don't want to lose you Mette. I think you are gorgeous in every way and I want you in my life.' He took her hand, 'I am just so worried that with you in the USA we will just drift apart. It will be all too hard.'

Mette did not reply immediately. Then she removed her hand from his and it all flooded out in a rush, 'I have so enjoyed my time with you, and I think you are gorgeous, too. But I just can't let it get any more serious. I don't think it would ever work for me, being with you. I am sorry I lead you along.'

With a sinking feeling Chris asked, 'What do you mean "being with me?" You have been with me for months now and it has been great.'

Mette looked down. 'Well, I mean I just don't want to be a princess or a queen, ever. Sooner or later, we would have to go public, and I know I would hate all that rubbish. Oh Chris, I am so sorry.'

Chris smiled ruefully while feeling his heart rip apart. 'Yeah, I am a very weird package deal.' Inside he raged about the injustice and pain of rejection.

Mette smiled weakly. 'Well, you would be a great catch for millions of girls but just not me. I am so sorry, Prince Christian,' she repeated.

Despite himself, he laughed bitterly. It was the first time she had ever called him that, a term he heard from so many others. 'She must have rehearsed it,' he thought acidly.

She rose and he rose too. She hugged him, 'I want to be your friend forever. Can we stay friends? I promise I will stay in touch.'

Chris felt the twin stabs of disappointment and sadness. 'I don't know. I guess so. But please can you just stay here with me tonight? Just one more night.' But he knew what her answer would be before he asked.

'I had better go, it would be too hard if I stayed. Goodbye.' Mette gave him a final farewell hug.

Chris now knew what a broken heart felt like. He felt a pain across his chest as Mette got her coat and left by the rear entrance, while he stood there rooted to the floor. She hurried away into the chilly Copenhagen night. She hoped she had not been seen, and followed, as she hurried past the great dome of the marble church and headed for the metro.

With Serene it felt both different and the same. What pleased him the most, was his certainty that she was not out to bag a royal boyfriend. In his head he had let go of Mette, but in his heart burned a small, bright flame; a hope that she would come back to him one day. Since his time with Mette, he had worried that no woman he found interesting and attractive would ever want to become his girlfriend or wife. He feared his royal descent attracted the wrong sort of women. Yet he knew he had to marry the wrong sort of woman to secure an heir. This time, Serene had no idea who he really was. Of course, he had thought of the delicious fantasy of returning to Denmark in triumph with a beautiful black African future queen by his side. How scandalous that would be! And with a sinking feeling he knew he had to tell her, sooner rather than later. It could not go on like this. Oh, but he agonised.

Four times already he had tried to tell her and failed. It was not the right time. It was not the right place. He could not find the right words. Something urgent had come up. And he admitted to himself that a big part of him would rather not know her response than have to face her rejection. By the fifth attempt he had worked himself into a real state of tension. He wished he could ask his father for advice. Over and over, he had imagined and rehearsed what to say. What had Dad said to Mum back in the year 2000, in Sydney, 900 kilometres from here? Why had he never asked Frederik? The crazy thought of phoning his dad came and went – just another diversionary tactic. He really did not want to mention Serene to his parents.

So, he found himself alone with Serene one evening, out on the pontoon in the dam. It was warm for early summer, and still. The glowing red sunset faded. Cockatoos, parrots and swallows flew in and out of the dam's circumference finding water. Four kangaroos – two mothers and their joeys, paused hesitantly just above the water line. The joeys were young and clamoured in and out of their mothers' pouches.

Kasper and Serene lay naked on their backs on the warm deck. No mosquitoes bothered them yet. Skinny dipping was the tradition at Commonplace, a culture created by the founders back in the 1980s and since then almost everyone indulged. Nude bathing was quite easy for the Dane, but Serene had found it difficult, at first. She felt the eyes of the whole world on her. Nakedness was discouraged in her culture and nude bathing was unknown for females. But her embarrassment eased after she had seen many other women at Commonplace strip off and plunge in, without any apparent self-consciousness or shame. And with only Kasper she found it much easier.

It had to be right now Kasper told himself, 'I just have to make a start.' He stood up and blurted out, 'There is something very important I must tell you Serene.' His voice sounded high pitched, his guts tighten.

'What would that be, my Viking hero? That you love me even more?' she replied playfully, affectionately placing her arm around his ankles.

Oh, she is making this even harder, he thought. 'I am not who you think I am. I have been using a false identity. I have been lying to you about my life in Denmark,' he started with a shaky voice.

'What are you talking about?' she exclaimed jumping up abruptly to face him, 'You must be joking!' Her hackles rose, but she sensed he was not lying.

'No, it is true,' he looked away.

'Who the hell are you then?'

'Oh God, this is so hard,' Kasper replied. He still could

not look her in the eye. 'I am, I'm...,' just blurt it out he commanded himself, 'actually, Prince Christian, first in line to the Danish throne.'

Relief and fear rushed through him as he held his breath. Now he had to await her response. For several long minutes the silence was broken only by the low drone of the wind turbines on the hill nearby. Suddenly the raucous laugh of a kookaburra mocked him before she spoke.

'No way! Is this a joke? You must be teasing me!' Serene finally snorted in disbelief as she backed away.

'I really wish I was. I am so sorry. I have wanted to tell you for weeks,' Kasper blurted out and rushed on. 'I am having a furlough in Australia for a year, incognito. I am half-Australian. It is a long story, but I will have to go back home one day, and when my father passes on or abdicates, I will be the Danish King. The only true part of what I have told you is that I am at university. The rest is just a cover story. At home they think I am at a college in the USA for a year.'

Serene stood there, speechless, hands on hips. Kasper's heart stood in his mouth. He waited and waited. He looked at her. He looked away. Finally, she laughed, edged forward and took his hand. 'So, Kasper, you are not the nice, cool, middle-class Danish boy I have fallen for. You are a born-to-rule, appointed and anointed by God, royal majesty, a highness full of privilege, pomp and priggishness! Everything I despise! Why would you ever deign to sleep with me? How can I ever believe anything you say again?'

She immediately regretted her angry words when she saw how crestfallen he looked and added, 'I am sorry, that was unfair. I know you are not like that. I just cannot believe this. I have come here to flee the hideous royals in my country only to fall for a royal here in Australia. In a country with no royals! I find myself standing here totally naked on a raft on a dam being told this. It is just too bizarre! How can this happen to me?!'

They stood there on the pontoon, apart. The evening stillness engulfed them. Their eyes did not meet. Minutes passed. Then spontaneously they embraced and kissed. He held her naked body very tight yet feeling weak all over with relief. She had not turned away. He let a deep involuntary sigh escape his lungs. He felt like months of deceit and tension were flooding out of him and he started to sob. He had to sit down on the pontoon again and she sat facing him, their legs entwined. Nothing was said before they swam ashore and dressed.

Later that night, Serene did not go to her bunk in the priest hole down inside the Eyrie. She would take a chance and spent the night with Kasper in his hut. They crammed into his single bed. They talked and talked but Serene did not have the courage yet to tell Kasper her real name. She had told him before of her past, of her escape and flight across the Indian Ocean, away from the security forces of her homeland, and the law of 'lèse-majesté' she had broken. Now after Kasper's confession, all her loathing of King Mswati and the Queen Elephant came pouring out. It was as if the opportunity to tell another royal person why she so detested the absolute monarchy she had fled was impossible to pass up. She told Kasper of the king's 15 wives and 22 children. How he simply abducted other women he desired, how he sought to have people with HIV sterilised and branded. She told of the extra-judicial arrests he had ordered; the torture and murder of democracy advocates and activists of any kind. She named the two dead activists Thulani Maseko and Thabini Nkomonye and expressed her admiration for all those killed. She told of the extraordinary wealth of the king and his family and how their avarice kept her 1.2 million compatriots impoverished. She railed against the rest of the world, especially the rich western countries, for failing to intervene. And especially against the British King, Great Britain, and the rest of the Commonwealth government for letting King Mswati sit amongst the other heads of state while doing nothing to stop his tyranny. Finally, she spat out, 'and so to rub salt into the wounds of my poor Swati people, your dear King Charles has even knighted the despot!' She began to shake with rage and fear. Kasper held her tight. Charles was not his king, but he could think of nothing to say. He just continued to hold her as she cried in great heaving sobs.

It was very late when Serene fell asleep. He then lay there for ages alongside her listening to her breathing while thinking of the centuries when Denmark had also been an absolute monarchy, not that long ago. Was he a living relic of such tyranny?

The next night, they swapped rooms. She led him to her priest hole, the small room hidden in the Eyrie behind a false wall. He had not known of its existence before now. They squeezed into her bunk bed and resumed their conversation.

He was reluctant, initially, to tell her of his royal pedigree but she was keen to know it. He revealed his full name: Christian Valdemar Henri John. He did not really have a surname but was from the Danish royal house of Glücksburg. Or fully; the House of Schleswig-Holstein-Sonderburg-Glücksburg. And his main titles: Prince of Denmark, Count of Monpezat, and Knight of the Order of the Elephant. He tried to keep a straight face, as it all sounded quite ridiculous here with Serene in her underground bunker. They both laughed then kissed again.

She wanted to hear more so he told her he found the old Danish Kings both fascinating and appalling and how he had enjoyed discussing them with his grandfather Henri, a French Count before he married the Danish Crown Princess Margrethe, his grandmother. He revealed that he was most interested in his previous ten namesakes. Mad King Christian VII had become quite famous after his tribulations were featured in the movie *A Royal Affair*. Kasper confessed, 'I have developed a soft spot for the poor, Mad King. He really battled madness the best he could.' Serene had never heard of him.

'But did he know he was crazy?' he asked Serene rhetorically. 'Did he know it was wrong to throw food at his courtiers and masturbate in front of them? Or did he just not care because he was raised to believe that he had the divine right to do whatever he wanted? Plenty of his court pandered to him while some plotting against him behind his back. But this was the time of the absolute monarchy, the strictest in Europe, and any moves to have the king declared insane or unfit and replaced was lèse-majesté and would have meant certain execution. For better or worse he was chosen by God.'

'Yes, I know a bit about absolute monarchy.' Serene commented.

Kasper had imagined himself in that situation with a shudder. He said that Henri was of the opinion that the king knew exactly what he was doing and did not care. Kasper said he was quite sure that he was mentally ill. Serene agreed with Henri. In her opinion, kings did not really care much about their subjects.

'Ironically,' Kasper added, 'the King's father-in-law was mad King George of the UK, and he was stood down as king when unable to function. The British Parliament had rejected absolute monarchy when they cut off the head of Charles I, but we kept it until 1849.'

Serene exclaimed, 'just a shame they continued to turn a blind eye to it in their African colonies! And go Cromwell. A hero of mine; warts and all!'

'So, I am destined to become King Christian XI,' he informed her and told her of the last King Christian, the famous and revered Tenth who had so bravely and cleverly defied the German occupiers during the Second World War. He told of how older Danes he had met recalled those desperate times and spoke to him with such respect and veneration about his great-great grandfather, and how he had been such an inspiration for his loyal subjects.

'Big shoes to fill for the next King Christian, lucky you have been chosen by God,' Serene suggested only half ironically.

'Huge shoes,' he agreed, grimly. Impossibly huge, he thought.

He told her of his horror and amusement at the sheer, bloody violence, betrayal, murder and megalomania of the early Danish Kings. He shared with her his marvel at their fabulously descriptive monikers; Gorm the Old, his son Harald Bluetooth, who apparently coloured his teeth blue as a fashion statement; Sweyn Forkbeard, Oluf Hunger, and also the colourfully named Erics: the Evergood, the Memorable, the Ploughpenny and the Lamb.

'Bluetooth? As in I.T.?' she asked.

'Yes, apparently named in his honour by Ericsson, the Swedish company,' he replied. 'I have no idea why.'

Kasper mentioned that Henri's favourite king was Oluf Hunger. Henri loved to cook and would often tell his grandson with a grin that he was cooking for Oluf Hunger.

'But my favourite king of all, is Eric the Lamb, the only Danish King to ever abdicate. Such a lamb! After nine years on the throne, he had had enough and threw it in. But sadly, he died soon after. He was just 26. So young.' He told Serene he had pondered what had gone through Eric's head, way back in the year 1146. Was he too sick to continue? Or just sick of it?

'Of course, in those days it was more than just reigning. You also had to rule and defend your throne with your sword at the head of your army. How things have changed,' he added.

'What has changed Kasper. I mean Chris?' Serene provoked.

'Oh please, still call me Kasper. I must stay incognito,' he

148

quickly replied. 'Well, these days you just had to be a good boy, keep your nose clean and along comes the throne. No more fighting at the head of your army,' he answered with a shrug.

'Yes, but you would have the army and the police force to enforce your rule. Would you not?' Serene argued. She had firsthand experience.

'So true,' he agreed, seeing her point. 'But I would not have to personally fire the tear gas or rubber bullets, It's the government that runs the army these days. I will just be a figurehead. The last king to sack a government was the same Christian X in 1920. He redeemed himself during the war I guess,' he answered.

'Oh, 1920, that's so long ago!' Serene retorted sarcastically.

Kasper didn't bite. 'The monarchy is hugely popular in Denmark. Unlike here where half the people want a republic.'

'Yes, and I can see why. Stuck with King Big Ears. At least we have our own tyrant. Hey, I've got an idea. You're half Aussie. When Charles dies you could apply for the job. Join the two lands. Austmark or Dentralia? I prefer the former. Sounds less like tooth decay.'

'Great idea,' Kasper replies, entering into the right spirit. 'But it would take years to get the palaces built before I could ascend down under. I would also need an Aussie queen.' He stared at her with a quizzical expression, 'And you are ineligible!'

They kissed and he went on to tell her about his mixed ancestry: his Danish, Scots, and French grandparents and his links to the British royals. He spoke about his childhood and youth, his campaign to be granted a gap year. And the promise he had made to clinch the deal. And he told of Mette too.

They marvelled at the utter contrast in their backgrounds and the sheer chance that had brought them together. They agreed they shared a love of the English language and the wonderful happenstance that they both spoke it fluently. He said he had found her accent totally adorable from the very first time he heard it. She replied that she found him intriguing that same day.

After they made love, he joked that this was the smallest room he had ever had sex or slept in. She answered that neither circumstance applied for her. And they agreed before they fell asleep, hidden deep in the Eyrie, that they did not know what they would do from now on. Their future appeared so full of vast possibilities and crushing limitations. The one certainty they averred is that they wanted to be together and maybe Australia could be their home.

CHAPTER SEVENTEEN

At Commonplace, the residents celebrated the Summer Solstice on the night of December 21st. Most of the members then left over the Christmas period to spend time with family or friends but everyone tried to be there for the longest day of the year. A special ritual in honour of Father Sun was conducted up in the ring at sunset followed by a celebratory dinner. It was the last formal event of the year there, as the days until the new year were the down time. Nothing was done to mark Christmas and no events were planned, while all duties and work commitments were suspended. That Christmas, for the first time in his life, Kasper did not go to church.

Serene was at Commonplace for two weeks over Christmas and Kasper would have her to himself as he had no work commitments and no family to visit and neither did she. She had been invited to stay with trusted Swazi friends in Melbourne but had chosen to spend the time with Kasper. It may well be the last extended period they would be able to enjoy together before he went home, so they had to make the most of it. For a week they borrowed a car and drove first to the Werribee Open Range Zoo to see the elephants. Serene was disappointed that all ten were Asian, not African, but Kasper was very pleased at their facilities; the open space, the mud pools, the waterholes and the barns. He told Serene of his assignment as a teenager with his grandfather at the Copenhagen Zoo, encountering the sad, young bull who warned him of life in a cage. Kasper asked her about elephants in Eswatini.

'Well, they are a source of revenue for our country. The game parks attract many foreign visitors, with the Western African elephants the star. They are protected in the parks except for some rare poaching but when they come near farms and villages they do get killed. Such a shame, but they can do enormous damage. The other shame is that the royals call themselves elephants. What an insult to such majestic beasts! But, oh I forgot. You are an Elephant knight.'

Kasper just laughed. 'And what about you? Do you have a favourite animal?'

'Yes, I sure do,' Serene was quick to reply. 'It's our national animal, the Thomson Gazelle; beautiful, fast, high jumping, long running, horned, vigilant and impossible to find any longer in my country. Just like me!'

Kasper was most impressed. 'I hope we can meet one someday. Another one, I mean, apart from you.'

They continued west to Port Fairy on the coast. They had a house to themselves free of charge. The large Commonplace network meant that there was always some chance of free accommodation around the state over Christmas and New Year. Though it was the holiday season some holiday houses were occasionally available. It was cooler at Port Fairy than at Commonplace. The sea kept the temperatures down and they both enjoyed the coast greatly. The town was packed with visitors, before long he spotted a middle-aged Danish couple. He eavesdropped on their conversation a little but got too close. The plump woman with sunburnt shoulders and legs noticed and asked him in Danish, 'Are you a Dane?'

'Yes,' he said, 'and so are you by the sound of it.'

She was emboldened now and asked, 'yes and you look just like Prince Christian, are you royal perhaps? Do you mind if I get a photo of you with me and my husband?'

Serene could not help herself when she recognised the name Prince Christian. 'Here, let me help,' she mischievously offered, holding her hand out for the woman's phone.

But Kasper was not having any of it and firmly insisted in English. 'No, I am not a prince, and I do not want my picture taken. Please leave me alone. I get enough of this in Denmark.' The woman backed away, disappointed.

Serene was most amused and teased him. 'Famous wherever you go. Even in Port Fairy you are recognised by your fawning subjects.' Kasper was not so amused. He knew that this would be a daily occurrence once he got home. And a beautiful black partner would make it much worse.

After Christmas, as the new year approached, Kasper took stock and discovered he had written over 190 pages in his journal since his arrival. He had recorded all the more formal events as well as the activities he had undertaken just for fun. He made a note of learning to kick the footy and attending an AFL match, swimming in the dam, and at the Expedition Pass Reservoir, playing badminton at the Wesley Hill Stadium, going to the movies at the Theatre Royal, running in the Park Run on Saturday mornings around the Botanical Gardens, riding the neighbours' horse, and picnicking at Dog Rocks high on Mount Leanganook. He also listed his new skills: glass cutting, flower arranging, tractor driving, tree planting, mud rendering, wall painting, joint rolling, driving on the left side of the road, parking in the shade, kangaroo boxing, group hugging, wooshing, casting a circle, dish washing and cooking for many. He even had calloused hands. He wondered if any of these would be of use to him as a Crown Prince or King of Denmark. Probably none. Especially not the callouses. He still had a few weeks of his gap year left and he had some big decisions to make.

CHAPTER EIGHTEEN

There are two positions Victorians adopt about bushfires. Melbournians are concerned about bushfires most summers but are convinced that they will never be in danger (except perhaps if they live on the city fringes). Country folk, however, even those living in towns, know every bushfire season, from October through to the end of March, that there is a small but real chance that their lives could be lost or irreversibly changed and their property destroyed by bushfire. And with global warming, the threat of bushfires across the sunburnt country had increased markedly. Summers were hotter and often drier.

Although Commonplace had a temperate climate, like much of central and southern Victoria, with cold, frosty winters, when a high-pressure system sits for days off the eastern seaboard in the Tasman Sea northerly winds blow thousands of kilometres of accumulated heat from central Australia down upon Victorians and the temperature and wind can both rise. Almost every summer there were scores of fires across the state from a variety of causes: lightning strikes, arson, machinery, cigarette butts, powerlines sparking on overhanging branches and embers escaping from campfires not properly extinguished. For some years, Australians had made attempts to control the risk of fires by adopting a method that the Aboriginals had used for millennia called cold burning, to reduce the fuel load in the bush before summer. But such a method was hard for white people to understand or accept.

At Commonplace, fire risk had been a major concern from the very beginning. It had to be. City people with no knowledge of fire safety, who used the retreat, seminar and accommodation spaces most days of the year, had to be kept safe as the highest priority. And so, too, the residents and their children.

So, the members' pride and joy, the Eyrie, had been designed by architect Celia Sexton to keep fire out, based on what was best practice in the early 1980s. The 110 square "flagship" of the organisation was built into the eastern side of a slope. It featured mud brick and adobe walls, flat roofs with no gables or ceiling cavities and rammed earth floors eliminating sub-floor spaces. Roof guttering was avoided with roof run off being collected from rubble drains. Metal mesh screens were used on all windows, doors and chimney openings. A gravity fed network of metal sprinklers was set up to spray gently the rooves and the large open area of lawn to the south of the Eyrie. Only fleshy and low flammability plants were planted within 50 metres of the building.

During springtime and throughout the summer members held working bees to remove leaves, twigs and other flammable materials from around the building while the grass was kept right down and well-watered. Each evening water from the dam was pumped into the tanks up behind the building to keep them full. Important, too, was maintenance of the building. Any cracks or gaps around windows, doors or other joins had to be filled, so gap filler guns were in the armoury. The other buildings on the property; the huts, sheds, boathouse and caravans were considered dispensable, so little was done to make them safe beyond removing debris from the rooves, slashing any grass around them and keeping the pathways clear.

The fire early that February that changed the lives of many people, including Kasper's, was caused by a young man from Melbourne. He drove up to a camping site on the banks of the Loddon River to visit his father and brother who had been camping there for the five days previously. He arrived at about 5 am, found some shade and knowing no better parked his ute in long dry grass near the other vehicles. The exhaust pipe and motor of his vehicle were extremely hot from the 120-kilometre drive and came into direct contact with the dry grass. He left his tent and other camping gear and went off to find the others who were down by the river in a shady fishing spot. They sat there with their feet in the water, drowning worms, keeping cool and drinking beers from the esky.

When the young man went back up to his ute to retrieve his gear and his beers, what he saw caused him dread, He screamed. 'Fire! Fire!' From under his ute a fire had spread across the grass and headed into the paddocks to the south. He sprinted to the vehicle to save it, but it was already alight. The other two came running and saw immediately that they could not fight the fire. They tried to dial 000 but had no phone signal. They threw themselves into one of the vehicles and raced towards Castlemaine to raise the alarm. But some minutes earlier, the fire spotter in her fire tower perched on the top of Mount Tarrengower, 20 kilometres to the northwest, had seen the smoke and raised the alarm. The fire moved towards Commonplace about 10 kilometres away helped by the light wind.

The smell of smoke arrived at Commonplace just as the warnings came on the mobile phones. There were 16 people on the property that evening, six were in the dam while two were in the kitchen preparing dinner. A group of six elderly visitors were up from Melbourne. Calling themselves the 'Bob Brown Appreciation Society', they were holding a reunion to celebrate their role in saving the Franklin River back in 1983; a historic victory for the environmental movement. Serene was away, having gone to Melbourne to see her lawyer but it was agreed that for her safety she did not have to tell others of her plans.

The decision was clear and took no discussion; activate the fire safety plan. The plan had two simple parts: evacuate safely and ensure that the Eyrie had the best chance of surviving. But each part had complexity and considerable pre-planning. For an evacuation, members each had a personal survival kit they kept handy near the entrance. Each vehicle carried a fire safety kit comprising a fire extinguisher, woollen blankets, masks, goggles, water, local maps and a copy of Joan Webster's *Essential Bushfire Safety Tips*. Spare kits were on hand for visitors' vehicles. For the Eyrie, a checklist was used for preparing it to keep out fire before people left.

This was only the second time that Commonplace had been evacuated for fire; the first, in 1993, was when a haystack spontaneously combusted near Yapeen. But fire did not reach the property on that occasion.

The evacuation this day should have gone smoothly but it didn't. The residents assembled and worked down the Eyrie checklist methodically; hurrying to close all doors and windows, turn off the electricity, check all the screens, turn on the sprinkler system, gather their things and survival kits, fetched the pre-filled water containers, ascertain that the road to town was safe, and agree on the destination in Castlemaine. As Fran briefed the visitors two members of the Bob Brown Appreciation Society, both a little intoxicated, decided they did not want to leave. One was Johnathon, never Jon or Johnno, a gaunt man in his late 70s with a full head of long white hair kept in a ponytail. His hair complemented his black Led Zeppelin tee shirt and black jeans. His appearance complemented his thinking: black and white. He began shouting, 'I survived the Franklin River, I can survive this!' This made no sense but set off an argument. Finally, both him and his mate were manhandled into a Commonplace car while the order of the convoy vehicles was agreed (visitors' cars in the middle.) But one car would not start. The headlights on an old Suzuki Hatch up from Brunswick had been left on. Valuable minutes were spent with the jumper leads getting it fired up before the lead car could start moving. In that car Elspeth suddenly screamed out. 'Oh my God, stop, stop. The Woofers!' She jumped out and ran to find Kasper and Eric, but they were not in their huts. She yelled out to them at the top of her lungs but to no avail. She did not have time to search. She scribbled a note for each hut and rushed back to the car. The notes read; *"Fire coming. We have gone. Shelter in the Eyrie."* The convoy left.

Kasper and Eric had met in Kasper's hut that afternoon. They planned to listen to some Aboriginal music and Eric wanted to play his new didgeridoo. They had both been drawn to this ancient instrument and Eric had been trying to master the circular breathing needed to make that ancient haunting drone. He was beginning to get the hang of it and was keen to show Kasper his progress. But after Eric had made some impressive drones, Kasper had a go and failed miserably. They both laughed, left the hut and went for a walk in the back gully for some fresh air.

In Denmark, 25 degrees is a hot day. Indeed, Kasper mused that the Danes only really have words for warm weather in their language, not separate ones for hot weather. The weather that day was moderately hot, in the high 20s with a light northerly wind. A scorcher by Danish standards. As they walked their conversation turned to their futures, as it had before. Both knew that their sojourns at Commonplace would have to end.

Kasper wondered, 'Will you go back to the US after this? I envy you in a way. You have a great talent for music and no ties. You could go anywhere in the world.'

'Maybe I will, but first I want to go home to Scotland and see my family, especially Mum. After that, who knows? There is always work in the US and Canada for music therapists and the pay is ok. What I really want to do is find a girlfriend and settle down. Maybe my old flame in New York will have me back.' He asked in return, 'and what about you? I envy you too, you know. Loving parents, lots of money, life mapped out. Looks good to me. Even a stint in the Air Force. I'd swap with you any day!'

Kaspar just grimaced and could not reply straight away. How could Eric possibly want his life? And the Air Force? How could that ever be fun? 'Well, that's not going to happen mate, if I can avoid it. I want a way out. Though you could always join the RAF! I'm sure they need good band members,' he added lightly.

Eric just chortled and imagined himself in uniform with short back and sides. He liked Kaspar's dry sense of humour.

It was shady and a little cooler in the gully but the smoke the others smelled passed over them at first. Shortly after, four kangaroos came crashing past them just as the unmistakable smell of smoke reached their nostrils. They looked at each other, not knowing what was happening for a few seconds, said nothing but then started running back to the buildings. The Eyrie appeared to be empty. All the cars had gone. Kasper remembered the safety plan. 'We need to stay in here. We'll be okay inside.' But Eric had other plans. 'No, no, I need to rescue my didgeridoo,' he shouted and ran from the building.

Kasper followed and saw him race up the slope to the hut, but the fire had arrived. The hut was poorly sealed and many embers had already entered under the door and into the ceiling space through the unlined eaves. As Eric dashed inside Kasper realised the curtains and other objects inside the hut were already burning. Kasper did not enter but saw Eric fumbling around in desperation and fear. In horror,

Kasper watched as a firebrand from a gorse seedhead landed by the door, blocking the only exit. Then, too late, Eric knew he had to flee immediately. Kasper screamed for Eric to get out, but he was trapped.

Kasper was just a few metres outside but knew he could not enter, then his instinct for self-preservation took over. He turned and, in a panic, ran helter skelter past the Eyrie and down to the dam. The instructions to shelter inside had abandoned him. Gasping for air with his lungs at breaking point he reached the banks of the dam and threw himself into the water. It was still cool, much to his relief. He swam to the pontoon in the middle and clung to the sides. He dared not climb aboard the platform. He pulled his wet tee-shirt over his head to protect himself as embers rained down. He tried to breathe through the cotton fabric to filter the air. Some embers landed on the wooden deck of the pontoon and he tried desperately to splash water onto them. If the pontoon caught fire, he was in trouble. He drank reluctantly from the dam to slake his huge thirst.

Time paused. He felt the sting of the heat on his exposed hands and arms as he clung to the pontoon and watched the embers. He manoeuvred around the pontoon's edge to face the south, vainly hoping to see Eric appear, but could not. He was alone apart from a wallaby and two kangaroos he could see across in the water. It was maybe 6 o'clock before he noticed that the fire no longer raged around the dam. Indeed, the worst of the fire had passed quickly, he was surprised to realise. He now thought it would be safe to swim ashore. Exhausted, he dog paddled to land and dragged himself up onto the bank. The stench and heat had died down, but smoke still hurt his eyes. He was alive.

He crept carefully back up towards the Eyrie through the blackened garden and onto the unburnt lawn. To his great surprise and relief, he saw that it was still standing. The sprinklers were still working. He realised he would have been safe inside the whole time. But it was Eric he sought. He approached his own hut, avoiding the burning and smouldering grass and bushes with a rising sense of horror. The timber hut had a corrugated metal roof and all he could see was burnt and burning timber and twisted roofing metal.

He approached as close as he dared and thought he could identify a lump that may have been Eric's mortal remains. He could not bear to look closer and did not even think of all his own lost possessions. He hurried away to where Eric's own hut stood and realised that it had mostly escaped the flames. He went inside in the vain hope that miraculously Eric might be there, but no. Yet inside he saw Eric's possessions arranged neatly; his pack, his books, his clothes, his computer, his guitar, his torch, his passport and his mobile.

Kasper sat on Eric's bed and shook in shock and fear. He had lost all his possessions but not his life. He was numb, tired and extremely thirsty but was unable to act at all. He just relived the scene from his hut over and over in his mind. He thought of all the ways it could have been different.

Later he heard the roar of approaching vehicles and looked out to see two fire engines stopping in the driveway. A crew of firefighters methodically pulled out hoses and began to extinguish the few burning and smouldering bushes in the vicinity of the Eyrie. The heat, smoke and wind were still hard to bear so Kasper grabbed Eric's hat and tied his scarf across his mouth and nose as he went outside again. He stumbled down towards the firefighters. One of them noticed him and rushed forward.

'Are you alright', she asked placing one hand on his shoulder carefully.

'Yes' he mumbled and asked for some water. He drank greedily then emptied the rest over his head. All dampness from the dam had long evaporated.

When he returned the canteen, the firefighter asked, 'What's your name?'

'Eric,' he impulsively replied, then added, 'I think my friend is dead.' He led the firefighter up to the smouldering ruins of the hut and said, 'I think his body is in there.'

She looked inside quickly and said, 'the police will need to look at this. You come away now.' She guided him firmly back down the hill.

Kasper went down to the Eyrie and drank a lot more water and tried to eat as he was instructed. The firefighter asked him what had happened. He told her how he thought the others must have evacuated the property but that the two of them had been in the back gully and got left behind. He said that he had survived in the dam after his friend was trapped in the hut. The firefighter asked him if there was anyone he wanted to contact. He said no and he knew what he must do next.

He left the firefighter and went back up to Eric's hut. There were all his possessions laid out neatly as before. He packed

164

them quickly into Eric's pack. He said nothing further to the firefighters who were fully occupied and set out on the walk into town. He took the long way through the bush to the main road. He did not want to meet any of the others on the road into the property. He got a lift to Castlemaine with a neighbour he vaguely recognised and was dropped off at the railway station. He sat there on the platform wondering what to do. No plan came to mind. He was glad he was alive but relived in his mind again and again Eric's final moments: the flames, the heat, the blocked exit, the smoke, the stench, the noise. He just wanted Serene.

Two trains passed through the station. One heading for Melbourne and one for Swan Hill. People got on and off and he barely noticed. He heard an announcement over the speaker saying that the line to Melbourne would be temporarily closed due to the fire, but he took none of it in. In the background were the sounds of emergency sirens and aircraft but nothing registered.

Much later when it was quite dark, he knew he needed a place to spend the night. He left the station feeling dazed and exhausted. He wandered up along Barkers Creek until he reached the Botanical Gardens. He found a secluded spot on some soft earth near the creek bed and lay down on Eric's sleeping bag. Soon he fell asleep under the stars. But he slept poorly, under attack from mosquitoes, and woke at dawn with sore hips and shoulders. He remembered instantly his terrible dream of being immersed in burning oil. The real fear, stench and noise from the day before, gripped him. He wondered how he had slept at all.

CHAPTER NINETEEN

Serene's pro bono lawyer was Zoe Clarke from Mallet and Cross in William Street, Melbourne. But they never met at her legal chambers. As an illegal it would have been stupid for Serene to attend the premises of a law firm that specialised in human rights and was known to represent several illegals in human rights cases. This time she met Zoe in a coffee shop in Footscray. It was a short walk from the Footscray railway station where trains on the Bendigo line stopped. It was also a suburb where many of the African communities in Victoria lived, worked and met.

This was an important meeting for Serene as she had a very difficult decision to make. It was really the same decision she had needed to make from the time she went underground. Her lawyer was convinced Serene had a very strong case to be granted refugee status in Australia and should not have been refused asylum the first time. Zoe had confirmed, as much as possible, all the information Serene had provided her over the months they had been meeting, and she had formed the opinion that Serene had reasonable grounds to believe that if she was returned to her own country, she would be subjected to unreasonable persecution based on her political beliefs and political activities. There were many precedents. If the court accepted this argument, Serene would be granted asylum and a visa to stay in Australia indefinitely with the prospect of becoming a citizen in a few years; a 'new Australian.'

But the problem was, as Zoe had emphatically pointed out, Serene was in the country without a valid passport or visa. She would have to hand herself in to appear before a court and then hopefully get her visa. It was a Catch 22. If she handed herself in, she would be detained and could well be deported to her native land before her case for asylum was completed. She could also be prosecuted for being in the country unlawfully, without a valid visa. At this meeting, Zoe had new information to present to Serene and she would again ask her to hand herself in.

Zoe arrived first. On the way there, she had started to sweat and was glad to feel the air conditioning inside. She chose a table off to the side with a good view of the entrance and ready access to the rear exit. Five minutes later, Serene arrived. She wore jeans, a plain long-sleeved shirt, a sun hat and dark glasses. It was not her preferred attire but was designed to attract little attention. Besides, she had little money to buy the more colourful and flamboyant clothing she much preferred. She was living off charity and donations. They ordered coffee and cake after exchanging warm greetings and a big hug. Zoe always looked forward to seeing Serene. She was such an interesting young woman and had a fascinating case; 'lèse-majesté' in Swaziland was not the run-of-the-mill political "crime" Mallett and Cross usually had to consider.

'Well Serene, I have something new to show you.' Zoe tried to avoid any small talk. 'As you know I am entitled to have copies of any documents held by the Australian Border Force and the Immigration Ministry relevant to your case. I have never seen any documents from Eswatini before now, but I do know the Interior Minister there has been insisting that you would be in no danger if you returned.'

Serene interjected, 'Well of course they would say that! The liars! What I told you is the truth.'

Zoe raised her hand to interrupt and continued, 'But recently the government sent me a copy of this.' She retrieved a document from her briefcase and placed it before Serene, 'have you seen it before?'

Serene looked closely and felt the instant tension and alarm rise in her body. It was if the interrogator and that creepy woman appeared before her and she was back in that room. She nodded quickly.

'And is that your signature, Serene?' Zoe asked quietly. Again, Serene nodded. It was a copy of the release statement she was forced to sign. She had told Zoe of her time in detention and the painful interrogation but never mentioned the document she signed. She wondered why not.

'Well, I fully understand why you had no choice but to sign it, but of course the Eswatini Minister is claiming it proves his case. My concern is that when we apply again this document might be used by the Australian government to deny your claim. It may be a case of reverse racism. You know, a rich white western country reluctant to deny the case made by its poor African cousin. And both in the Commonwealth under our King Charles. But it is not an insurmountable obstacle, though I will need to get all the details from you.'

Serene was crestfallen, 'I am sorry. I was so desperate. I had no choice. But I should have told you about it.' She felt guilty and looked away. Zoe had always been on her side. Now she was thinking that the risk of handing herself in had increased.

'Yes, I can tell you all about it, but I would like to ask you something personal first. Would that still be confidential?' Serene asked.

Zoe quickly reassured her, 'Yes Serene, whatever passes between a lawyer and her client in Australia in strictly protected by the law and must remain confidential.' She did not make mention of the notorious Grollo case when a lawyer was also a police informant. That was an exception. 'Even personal matters,' she added.

'Well things have changed,' Serene started hesitantly, 'it's more complicated because I have met a man I really like. I think I love him. He's from Denmark and is only here for a year. Can we get married? I know my mother would like him.'

Zoe was not expecting this.

She smiled broadly, 'Well congratulations. That is exceptionally good news. I think you can marry but I am not entirely sure what the laws on marriage allow. Do you mind if I make a quick call to my colleague? He knows all about the Marriage Act.'

'Of course,' Serene replied, 'I will just go to the toilet.' Zoe had the answer when Serene returned. 'Yes, you can indeed. But there are two things. First it would be much preferable if you used your real name and additionally, by marrying a foreigner, I mean a non-Australian citizen who is just visiting, it might weaken your case in court for being granted an Australian visa. Marrying an Australian would be much simpler,' she joked, 'but I cannot recommend it.'

Serene chuckled. She had noticed the absence of a wedding ring on Zoe's fingers. Serene was so wanting to tell Zoe the whole story but held back. She had promised Kasper she would not disclose who he really was but part of her was dying to get it off her chest. She ordered another coffee.

Zoe felt she had to try again. 'You still have a particularly good case so if you handed yourself in, we would try to have your appeal all ready to go. I would apply immediately for an urgent hearing. But there are no guarantees. And the courts have refused you once. But by applying for a hearing immediately we would make it harder for the government to deport you.'

Serene heard this but her head was elsewhere. She had an idea and asked, 'can another country grant me asylum and a visa?'

'Like Denmark?' Zoe smiled back.

'Well, yes,' Serene answered, 'why not?'

'Indeed, Denmark might,' Zoe answered, but had to qualify this, 'but I cannot advise you on the Danish laws on immigration or asylum.'

Serene struggled with her dilemma. How much to tell about Kasper? She decided on a limited disclosure. 'What if the Danish man was especially important? Would that help?' she posed.

Zoe smiled. 'Well, again, I must advise you that I know nothing about Danish law but certainly in this country the

Minister has a lot of discretion about who to let in. I would be surprised if it is not the same in Denmark, or anywhere else really. Having a high-profile husband or even a famous and influential advocate might help the authorities or the Minister to just find that extra little milligram of compassion. But there is another possibility. Your VIP partner might get his government to convince the government in your country to drop all charges you might be facing, to annul any arrest warrants and to furnish you with a new passport and immunity from any future prosecution. One country can bring all kinds of pressures to bear on another country to do it a favour, especially a poorer country. Money may well play a central part in greasing the wheels. I'm sorry, you probably already know all that.' Serene just nodded.

'Is there more you want to tell me about your VIP boyfriend?' Zoe asked, then cursed herself, it was too intrusive and none of her business, but she was intrigued.

Serene teetered on the tipping point. There were good secrets and bad secrets. Surely this was a good secret and she trusted Zoe. Since she had gone underground Zoe was one of her very few confidantes. And besides, Kasper did not know all her own secrets, even her real name.

'Well, he is a VIP in Denmark, but he is in Australia for a furlough of one year. He has to go back soon. But he is travelling under an assumed name and identity,' Serene related and immediately felt some relief. It was not the whole truth, but it was true. It felt like a good compromise.

'I see you two have some things in common,' Zoe replied smiling broadly. 'And I can well understand how this would

171

change your thinking. If you marry him here, you may well be able to use his connections and influence. But to get to Denmark legally, the Danes may be able to issue you with travel documents once you are married so you can go back with him. They may even grant you asylum. But the Australian authorities may still want to detain you before you can get on a plane.'

Serene did not reply. This discussion with Zoe had opened a whole new set of options and she had not even raised the possibility of marriage with Kasper, but it had been in the back of her mind. It would not be a simple decision for him to make, she appreciated, and suddenly without warning the title Queen Serene popped into her head. She almost laughed out loud. She would be a she elephant!

Zoe stood up, gathered her things, and made an appointment for another meeting in four weeks. Then they would explore the full details of Serene's interrogation. They embraced and Zoe rushed out the door with her mobile to her ear. On the drive back to her office she wondered if she would be invited to the wedding. Surely Serene would marry for love and not a visa, but then who would blame her if this was her chance at freedom.

Serene sat with her coffee thinking hard. It was clear she had no choice, sooner or later she had to hand herself in. She knew that when she finally did, she had to make sure that she had arranged things so that her chances of avoiding a Swazi prison were kept to a minimum. 'Lèse-majesté' – the crime of offending the dignity of a head of state, or Eswatini itself, was a serious crime. She wondered if the crime even existed in Australia. Hopefully the authorities in Australia and maybe Denmark would appreciate that it was a ridiculous crime from a bygone era. She grabbed her overnight bag and left the coffee shop through the rear exit. She took the train to Flinders Street Station en route to St Kilda. She was going to the beach.

She loved the sea from the first moment she had set eyes on it. Growing up poor in a landlocked country meant that she had to wait. At 15, she rushed home one day with a notice from the school. There would be a school trip to the coast in Mozambique. All her class was invited but each student's family had to pay half the cost of the trip and the passport. She hoped against hope that her parents would pay for her to go. She offered to contribute all her meagre savings and to her surprise and delight they agreed. So, after the bus trip across the border, she found herself rushing down the beach with her school friends and plunging into the waves. She had forgotten about the brine and took a mouthful. Eerk! It tasted ghastly. As she took the tram down to the St Kilda beach, she recalled those happy days of her childhood and wondered if she would ever see the beautiful eastern shores of Africa again.

She alighted from the Number 16 tram on the Upper Esplanade and admired the palm trees as she crossed to the famous St Kilda pier.

Two men drinking on the veranda of the Esplanade Hotel saw her and one shouted, 'Go home you big, coon bitch!'

She ignored them. Nothing new about that commentary from some Aussie white men, she thought. Most Aussie men she did not mind, but there were always a few misogynistic, racist oafs still at large.

It was warm inland but cooler here by the bay with a lovely breeze blowing in from the southwest. The sea was flat with barely a ripple from the waves. Quite a crowd promenaded along the pier. People of many ages, colours and creeds; a cross section of multicultural Australia taking the sea air. Serene was relaxed. The sea had that effect on her, but she still instinctively turned her head away when she saw who she assumed were two black Africans approaching her. Luckily, they did not accost or speak to her. Maybe one day she could give up such an anxious habit.

As she reached the kiosk at the end of the pier and lined up for an ice-cream, she remembered one of Kasper's facts about Denmark; no place is more than 50 kilometres from the sea. That sounded good, she thought, as she walked back licking a pistachio and apricot double cone. She changed into her bathers and from the beach she swam out into the warm flat sea. The water soothed and calmed her. She felt a little more hopeful after the meeting and daydreamed of freedom, of standing up and shouting her name, of speaking out about injustice, of liberating her country from the chaffing yoke of absolute monarchy.

That night she stayed in a safe house in Albert Park. At 10:30 am she was sitting with her hosts, Pam and Robert, in the dining room, drinking coffee and eating Monte Carlo biscuits for supper; feeling safe and most welcome in their home. Such a contrast to all the coming and goings at Commonplace. Suburban normality and solidity. She liked it each time she stayed.

The late news was on the TV in the lounge next to the dining room. Something coming from the box caught her attention. The newsreader intoned gravely, *'a bushfire in Central Victoria near Castlemaine is still burning out of control tonight. It is believed that there have been several lives lost but there are no details at hand. Emergency services including fire bombers and hundreds of CFA firefighters are trying to bring the fire under control. It is hoped that a wind shift and cool change due at approximately 2 am will help contain the fire. We will bring you more details of the lives lost as soon as they are available.'*

Serene heard all this clearly while simultaneously chatting with her hosts who appeared not to have noticed. She made no comment about the news. They did not know that she had any connection in the Castlemaine area and she did not want to alert them to where else she might be staying. She was tired and worried so soon excused herself. In the bedroom she tried to find out more on her mobile phone but there was no additional news. She was returning to Commonplace the next day and Kasper planned to meet her at the station. There was so much she wanted to discuss with him.

Kasper did not reply to the texts she sent him throughout the next morning. At noon, Serene boarded the train to Bendigo, stopping all stations. The line had reopened after the cool change had brought some relief, but there was still no news on the fatalities from the fire. And no messages on her phone. She texted again then ordered herself to stop catastrophising. Things would be alright. He would be safe. Soon enough she will find out what had happened from Kasper himself.

As she stepped from the train at Castlemaine, she could immediately smell acrid smoke. She wondered if the fire had been nearby. And with considerable relief she spotted Kasper. But something was not right. As he approached, she noticed he was wearing strange, loose-fitting clothes and had a backpack on his back. He looked dishevelled, tense and exhausted.

There was no warm greeting from him. 'We need to leave the station straight away,' he blurted out, 'something terrible has happened.'

He took her arm and most uncharacteristically hurried her out of the station and up Kennedy Street.

'We must walk. I don't have a car,' he explained, 'something bad has happened,' he repeated anxiously.

Serene did not reply but she was so glad he was alive. She was compelled to follow him up Kennedy Street and into Mostyn Street. She had never seen him like this before. He led her up the path within the grounds of the Anglican Church. He found a garden seat away from the street and sat down. He looked around in agitation and fear.

'There was a fire Ser. A terrible fire. And he got trapped,' the words tumbled out.

'Who did, Kasper, who,' Serene asked.

'It was Eric, Ser. It was hell,' he answered.

'Is Eric alright?' Serene asked immediately.

'No, he's dead, he died, he burned,' Kasper said looking up at her, 'he was in my hut, there was nothing I could do Ser. It was...' Kasper could not go on. He buried his head in his hands and started to cry. Soon he was crying with great heaving sobs. Serene put her arm around his rolling shoulders. He lifted his head from his hands and buried it into her shoulder. He cried harder, shaking and sobbing with the spasms of involuntary sorrow. Serene tried to stay calm, but his tears were contagious. She recalled poor Eric fondly and thought of him so far from home. Dead in a fire. Her tears came in a rush. Kasper looked up and they embraced cheek to cheek, mingling tears. Nothing was said as they wept together.

Kasper stopped crying quite abruptly and took Serene by the shoulders. 'There's more,' he stated rapidly and intensely, 'I can't go back.'

Serene had no idea what he was talking about. All she could ask was, 'What? Back where?'

'I just made an impulsive decision. I was in his hut with all his things. I had been in the dam. My hut was destroyed. All my things are gone. A firefighter came and I told her I was Eric. I know it is crazy, but I don't want to go home,' his words rushed out as he looked into her eyes. 'I have escaped!' he added.

Serene could find nothing to say. It was just utterly preposterous, so totally crazy, she thought. Is he mad, after such a trauma, she wondered? He will come to his senses later on, she assumed. But then another thought struck her. Maybe it offered her a tremendous opportunity too. She would not lose him. He could stay with her in Australia, after all.

'You are a crazy, stupid fool my prince.' She finally spoke, 'but I love you. Can I call you Prince Eric?' she asked.

A wan smile spread across Kasper's tear-stained face. He

kissed her right there in the Anglican Church Garden on Agitation Hill.

'No, but thank you. It is so good to see you.' Kasper replied.

Serene left him and rushed off to buy him drinks and food. But first she had to ask him for money. Kasper gave her some from Eric's wallet. He ate and drank greedily. Afterwards, they had to decide what to do next. They agreed that he would catch the next train to Melbourne and find a hotel room for the night. Otherwise, he might be recognised around town. Serene felt she needed to go across to the evacuation centre and learn the news of Kasper's tragic death anew. She would join Kasper tomorrow and help him find somewhere to stay.

They set up a rendezvous for 24 hours hence under the rail bridge on the corner of Flinders and Spencer Streets. They parted ways. Serene started walking across to the evacuation centre in the town hall and joined the queue at the entrance. She had almost reached the official at the desk when she came to her senses. They would try to register her, ask for ID and her name, ask other questions. She had not been thinking clearly after her encounter with Kasper. She was still an illegal and her safety came first. And she had to put the wedding plans on hold, too. She backed away and found a spot to wait at the back of the hall. She could see the entrance on the side street. She would just have to wait for a Commonplace person to appear.

CHAPTER TWENTY

The forensic pathologists in Melbourne did not go to the lengths in identifying the remains that they should have. The fire had been very intense but there was still plenty of DNA left to find; however the circumstances were clear and there were no other candidates, once everyone had been accounted for. No need for a DNA check, they decided, against their own policies and procedures. The police report about the circumstances of the death was unambiguous.

The Danish ambassador was happy enough to accept the tragic outcome at first, before he learned that it was the death of the prince. The forensic pathologists had the bodies of all the other fire victims to deal with and some were still unidentified. And later once the Danish authorities found out whose body it really was, they did not want a full public coronial inquest held in Australia and the locals did not object. The Australian Department of Foreign Affairs was justifiably peeved that a foreign royal heir presumptive had been sent to their country with false papers, but the Minister decided in the tragic circumstances not to protest to her Danish counterpart. After all, the deceased's mother had relinquished her Australian citizenship when she became a foreign royal.

But before all that occurred the mortal remains of the

prince were flown home to Denmark and arrived at Kastrup airport in a suitably decorated casket made from Australia hardwood. On the top was attached a cross of Australian gold and inside the funeral director had secreted two objects; a small boomerang and a jar of Vegemite.

The event caused a scandal in Denmark. When the news of the death in Australia of a young Danish man reached the Foreign Office within Borgen there was no alarm. The death of a Dane overseas was no big deal. But when the name Kasper Frederikson was mentioned, and the officials went to find his family they were told this had to go straight to the Minister. The Minister rushed to the Prime Minister who told the King's secretary, who told the King. An emergency session of the State Council was immediately called by the King and it was the Prime Minister who had to communicate the news to all in attendance, including the three young siblings of Prince Christian.

At first there were no recriminations just an unspoken urgency that this had to be conveyed to the media and the Danish subjects in a way that would do the least damage to the reputations of the monarchy and the government. The wording of an official announcement was argued over for three hours. Finally, there was agreement to keep it brief, then the time and place was settled for the King to make the royal announcement. He appeared on the television later that night looking drawn and tired and announced in a firm voice:

'It is my saddest duty to bring you all news of a tragic event. As you may know my dear son Prince Christian had been granted a period of leave from his royal duties over the last few months. He has taken this time to travel in Australia, the place of his mother's birth, to further his education. We have just been advised by the Australian authorities that he has met a tragic and accidental death in a wildfire. Queen Mary and I, our children and all members of my family, are deeply shocked by this tragic event, as I am sure all Danes will be. I declare three days of national mourning to be held from Monday next. On the Wednesday a royal funeral will be held. Arrangements will be announced shortly.'

The TV channels had been given short notice of the King's appearance but had managed to pull together panels of commentators to discuss the bombshell.

A funeral service with all due solemnity and full Lutheran rites was performed in the Church of Our Lady in Copenhagen. The anguish of the prince's grandmother, parents and siblings was clear and heart wrenching. It was his sister Princess Isabella who stepped up to deliver a sad and moving eulogy. For her final words she mentioned that Christian had stayed in touch with her during his time in Australia and told her how much he was enjoying himself. To the mourners and the public's great surprise she then told how he had confided in her a little about the woman he had met and fallen in love with.

And then finally she simply said. 'To dear Serene, I wish you my heartfelt condolences. We offer you our fondest wishes and sincerely want you to know that if ever you choose to come to our small land, we will welcome you with open arms and hearts.'

She stood in silence, finished. The air was riven by weeping. Thousands had already lined the route through the city and along the highway to the Cathedral in Roskilde. A burial site had been quickly prepared in the chapel of the Glücksburg Royal House, right next to Christian the Tenth, and near eight of the other King Christians. He would have good company; somewhere nearby lay King Harald Bluetooth since his sad demise in 985, with his teeth still stained blue.

CHAPTER TWENTY ONE

Ebbe Mosegaard had first heard the news on TV. He was shocked and saddened as he sat on his sofa at home in the small apartment in Vesterbro, Copenhagen. He had been drinking a South African white wine and watching an international handball match featuring the legendary Danish women's team against arch-rivals Germany when the broadcast was abruptly interrupted by a news flash. A very grave looking Gitte Svendsen appeared and announced the tragic news that Prince Christian had died, just 22 years old, in a wildfire in the state of Victoria, Australia.

Ebbe was shocked and sat there stunned. Since he left the Royal Protection service just 18 months ago, he had noticed that the prince had faded from the media's attention and had simply assumed that the lad was keeping his head down at university in the US and that other royal news and fake royal news was seen as sexier. Like the endless speculation about the ex-Queen's health after her abdication.

He loathed the media's fixation with the royals and wondered whether people with this obsession actually had a diagnosable mental disorder. Surely it did them no good at all. And he knew first-hand that at least half of what was written and spouted was pure fiction, invented by immoral gutter journalists and their loathsome and mendacious media bosses.

Ebbe had noticed some reports on TV about a deadly bushfire in Australia, but he never associated it with the dear prince. So that is where Christian had ended up. He speculated that it must have been quite a task to keep that quiet for the last 12 months or so. He felt so sorry for King Frederik and Queen Mary and their three other children and made a note to send them a condolence message. He was sure they would remember him after all the years he had served the family in the cause of Christian's safety. How on earth had this been allowed to happen?

It was an outrage, Ebbe fumed as he turned off his television and grabbed his coat, hat, scarf and gloves. Since he had begun to live on his own six years ago, he hated being alone whenever he felt upset. He had tried to ring his daughter, Stine, in Malmo, but she did not answer. He tried to phone his workmate, Jacob, but the result was the same. So, he headed down the street to his local bar.

Already, on the big screen, the handball match had been replaced by a hastily gathered panel of royal watchers and royal affairs commentators. And off they went, tearing into the government and the bureaucracy for allowing this outrage to occur. Their collective high dudgeon seemed to be based as much on the fact they were kept in the dark about the prince's whereabouts rather than his tragic death. They had every right to know where the prince was at all times and they had been hoodwinked.

'What infamy!' One commentator put it bluntly, 'Surely we should have been told and then we would have kept it secret.'

'As if!' Ebbe thought and almost burst out laughing. The expert went on while the others nodded. 'The Foreign Minister should resign in disgrace as should the head of the Foreign Ministry and the Prime Minister should seriously consider her position.'

This appeared to egg another expert on who jumped in, 'Yes and the King has questions to answer.'

He must have been in a state of severe apoplexy to suggest that His Majesty, the ever dutiful, revered ruler of his loyal people might have erred in any way.

Ebbe had seen enough. He retreated to a side bar away from the demanding and commanding big screen. 'Could it be anyone's fault?' he wondered. It must have been a tragic accident, an out-of-control fire. 'The poor, poor prince,' he lamented to himself. Such a sensitive and considerate young man. Then the sceptical detective in him, who had attended a few suspicious deaths in his career, appeared and the questions arose. Are they sure it was Christian? How was he identified? How badly was the body burnt? Who identified him? Was DNA collected? How good were the Australian police? None of these could he answer, and soon, he realised, he had to accept the facts unless he could get hold of the official reports; the prince had died hideously a long way from his country and kin. What a tragedy!

Mulling it over further, he conceded that Christian had every right to a sabbatical in the land of his maternal forebears. He smiled in appreciation as he thought of the achievement the trip to Australia must have been. Christian would have had to overcome the opposition of his parents, the royal family, the royal household, the royal advisers, the foreign ministry and most of the government. Bravo young man! But it had led him to his hideous death. If only Ebbe had still been by his side, protecting him. He knew that this was just a fantasy, he had no skills or experience in protecting his charge from the risk of fire, but it made him feel a little less helpless.

He decided he wanted to attend the funeral and would apply for leave once the arrangements were revealed. It would be an incredibly sad affair, he appreciated and called for another glass of wine, but changed his mind and went for a long walk instead, past the Tivoli, through the Town Hall Square and onto the Walking Street. He got as far as the King's New Square before turning back.

The funeral had been a sad reunion for Ebbe where he met up with a group of his colleagues from his days at the palace. He had been acknowledged by King Frederik with a handshake and he even got nods from both Queen Margrethe and Queen Mary. Later, Ebbe was the last to leave a boozy informal wake in a bar in Christianshavn. His colleagues had treated him in a very respectful, even deferential manner and all his drinks were free. A week later he still felt disenchanted and hollow. He knew he was drinking too much and had to drag himself through the workday.

CHAPTER TWENTY TWO

That Wednesday shaped up as a real endurance test. Ebbe had to attend a mandatory professional development workshop focusing on cybercrime and cyber security. Ebbe was a cyber dinosaur and his eyelids grew steadily heavier and heavier as the morning wore on. Suddenly his mobile phone went off and he leaped from his seat with a start. He had been daydreaming of walking along a beach in warm sunshine. His boss glared at him and he discovered with embarrassment his phone had not been turned off or set to silent, as had been the explicit instruction by the workshop leader to prevent this exact disruption. He displayed exaggerated gestures of contriteness and stepped into the hallway.

'This is Ebbe,' he answered informally.

'Is that Senior Detective Mosegaard?' a gruff voice asked.

'Yes, yes. You have got me.' Ebbe hastily replied.

'Good, I am Bengt Jørgensen, Under Secretary to the Foreign Minister. We need you at a meeting tomorrow morning at nine.'

Ebbe's interest rose. 'Of course,' he replied, but asked quickly, 'Has my boss agreed?'

'Indeed, indeed she has,' Bengt assured him, 'Come to the Foreign Office at Borgen. Entrance Seven. Excellent.'

Ebbe jumped in, 'Okay but can you tell me what it is about?'

'Not now, in the morning. Goodbye.' Bengt hung up and Ebbe stood there in the hallway wondering. He appreciated being out of the narcosis inducing workshop for now and did not have to rush back in. After all, he had been summoned to Borgen and needed a little time for professional reflection. Professional reflection was all the rage in contemporary policing and now he could use some. He walked the corridors for a good ten minutes before quietly slipping back in. His phone he set on silent.

Pondering what it might mean actually helped Ebbe stay awake for the rest of the workshop, but he had a restless night. Since his divorce and living alone, sleep had been a problem. Alcohol helped for a few years, but the effect had worn off. Stine had been a great source of support and companionship when he first separated. She still had her bedroom in his apartment, but since moving across the sound to attend Malmo University she came to visit less and less, even though it was only 20 minutes across the bridge on the express train from Central Station. Now he visited her more than she visited him.

He cycled across town the next morning to Borgen full of curiosity and parked his bike amongst the many outside Entrance Seven. He showed his badge at the entrance and gave his name. A young man appeared and led him upstairs and down a long corridor to a meeting room. It was ornately furnished and had high windows and a higher ceiling. Quite a contrast to the meeting rooms at Police HQ, Ebbe thought wryly. There were two officials in the room already and a third joined them just after Ebbe entered.

'I am Bengt,' the last man in said, 'we spoke on the phone,' and shook Ebbe's hand while continuing, 'let me introduce you to Annette Rasmussen, our Senior Officer covering Australia and the Pacific, and Anders Larsen, our distinguished Chief of Foreign Affairs. Would you like coffee or tea Ebbe?'

Ebbe did not hesitate, 'Coffee for me thanks.'

The others placed their orders and Bengt spoke briefly on his mobile.

Bengt began again, 'Before we commence, I need to emphasise Ebbe that what we are going to propose for you is strictly secret. You will be familiar with the need for secrecy from your previous role at the palace and this matter is no exception.'

Ebbe simply nodded and his curiosity swelled.

Annette took over, 'We need you to fly down to Australia and investigate the death of Prince Christian. We need to assure ourselves of what happened. We have no reason at all to doubt what the Australian authorities have reported. They have been most co-operative and transparent. But we just need to double check.'

Ebbe was now all ears. But the beverages had arrived, and they were all served coffee by a young man Ebbe thought looked about 14 but must have been older. Ebbe added cream to his strong black coffee.

Annette resumed, 'The Police in the state of Victoria have agreed to cooperate but you will have limited powers. You will not be armed or be able to use a firearm. You will have no powers to detain or arrest, and no status before the courts. You will need to report to us regularly and to keep detailed records of your investigations, of course. So, what do you say?'

Ebbe's mind was racing. He got it. The government and the palace wanted to announce that they had undertaken a thorough and independent investigation in Australia and could confirm the sad facts. Perhaps this might soothe the media a little.

With a smile Ebbe replied, 'well what can I say except yes. I will have some work matters to tidy up and hand over, but I have no personal commitments that might stop me. Oh, I will need a passport renewal,' he remembered.

'Good, good,' Bengt stated, 'we will get right onto the paperwork, and get your passport fixed. Just remember we all need to keep this top secret. We do not want an airplane full of royal paparazzi stalking you all the way. Maybe we will issue a media release later depending on what you report. Now, are there any questions?' he asked, looking first at Ebbe then at the other two. 'Of course, we will provide you with all the reports the Australians have sent us and provide you with a briefing and contacts down there. We understand you have not been to Australia before,' he concluded.

Ebbe momentarily wondered how he knew that but then realised they knew of every Danes' international movements since records began, then he asked, 'How soon do you want me to go?'

'In about a week Ebbe. We think that all arrangements should be in place by then. We will notify you of your flights as soon as they are booked,' Annette replied.

Ebbe next asked, 'Why have you chosen me?' He hoped he knew some of the answer.

Bengt replied, 'Well you knew the prince, you are a skilled and experienced investigator, you understand the need for secrecy and discretion, you have no personal commitments, also the Commissioner said you could be made available at short notice.'

Ebbe was pleased at this reply and murmured, 'Thank you,' as he wondered how much of his personal life, they were aware of. It was clear too, he also gathered, that his bosses saw him as quite dispensable.

'My final question is, how long will I be away for?' he asked.

'Good question. We should have covered that. No set timetable for you. When you have exhausted your lines of inquiry and satisfied yourself that there is no more to discover, or no more that can be discovered, then write a concluding report and come home. We will follow your interim reports with interest, and we trust that you will be focused and disciplined. It is no holiday.'

Then he stood up and was followed by Annette and Anders.

As Annette shook his hand she added with a big smile, 'so, happy packing and don't forget your sunscreen, sandals, hat, and board shorts.'

Ebbe thought that perhaps she was a little too flippant in the unfortunate circumstances and that maybe she was trying to balance Bengt's formality and nose to the grindstone attitude. Perhaps the trip would not be all hard graft and it did remind him that it would be summer across on the other side of the globe. Ebbe formally said farewell and thanks to all three, shook hands with the other two and with a formal nod left the meeting room. The same young man appeared next to him in the corridor as if by magic and led him back to Entrance Seven.

He floated back across town to his workplace. It was a typical winter's day, about minus two degrees, windy with wispy sleet cutting the air, but he did not mind the weather. His day had certainly turned around, he mused as he cycled straight past Police HQ directly to his favourite cafe, The Wet Rooster. Work was not to be endured any more that day. He was on royal business. This was just the fillip he needed for a career going nowhere and morale following close behind.

Although it was only eleven o'clock, he decided on an early lunch, classic Danish open sandwiches, ryebread topped with marinated herring, cucumber and dill with a squirt of mayonnaise and a grind of black pepper. He followed up with a snail pastry and a strong coffee. He was sorely tempted to have a glass of wine or maybe two but knew he was still on duty, kind of.

His phone sounded as he drank his coffee. It was his daughter texting a brief hello. He immediately replied, 'Big news, need to speak, will phone 2000 hours, if you are free,' with two love hearts.

Stine had been to Australia with her mother for a winter holiday about three years ago. All he knew of the land was the usual icons; kangaroos, sharks, beaches, Uluru, boomerangs and bushfires. Very little news from that country ever crossed his path, except for the recent tragedy.

At home that evening he took a crash course in Australian FAQs and downloaded maps and a travellers' guide. Stine phoned just after eight o'clock and was excited at her dad's news. She was sworn to secrecy first then Ebbe grilled her about her trip down under and she was happy to oblige. She noted that her dad had not been so excited about the future for a long time. She explained that Australia would be extremely hot and very big. She had arrived in Cairns in Queensland and travelled down to Sydney. They had visited the Great Barrier Reef, the Daintree Rain Forest, the Atherton Tableland, Brisbane, the Gold Coast, Byron Bay then Sydney and Bondi Beach. It was a fantastic holiday, but it had only been ten days, Stine related, and now it was all a bit of a blur. She advised him to do an online course in Australian English and to have a translation app ready on his phone, as she had trouble at times with the local language.

And she had one more tip for him. 'Just mention Dad, that you know Queen Mary and all doors will be opened.'

Ebbe sighed, thanked her for the advice and they ended the call with the usual fond declarations of love and a promise to meet up for a farewell meal before the departure date. Ebbe knew his English would be a challenge. He had learned the "lingua franca" in school from the age of seven, like most Danes since the Second World War, but his usage was now limited to the infrequent times when he was abroad and during summer when he was occasionally asked for directions by tourists around town, mainly Asians, Germans, Eastern Europeans and Southern Europeans, but he could not recall ever speaking to an Australian. Queen Mary no longer counted.

His tickets, passport, money, vaccination certificates, briefing papers and letters of introduction duly arrived. All was set. He had been for a further briefing at Borgen and had to work for two days in the office to tie up all the loose ends and to receive the usual good-natured teasing about his forthcoming holiday and junket. Ebbe packed the day before he had to fly and even found his board shorts. He had owned them for decades and they led him on a trip down memory lane. He remembered summer days on different beaches and his love of the surf. He had been dead keen to become a surfer back then and engrossed himself in the literature and lore, but it did not happen. Life had got in the way and the surf in Denmark was horrid. But he could recall that Australia had champion surfers and famous surf beaches. Was one Bells Beach or Bay?

On departure day, the taxi trip out to Kastrup was smooth. He loved being driven through snow as it fell and lay on the road. It acted like a cushion and a muffler, and all was smooth and quiet. His plane flew on time, up, up over the sound and the famous bridge to Sweden and his daughter. He waved her a fond farewell from on high.

CHAPTER TWENTY THREE

The 24-hour journey from Kastrup to Tullamarine airport was gruelling. Ebbe could not get comfortable as he swatted up on terms used in Australia for policing and in the law. He lost interest well before the stopover in Bangkok where a whole flock of Danes disembarked for the beach resorts. From there he tried to sleep with the help of wine, but without luck. He thought about his plan of attack. He would travel to the scene and would interview the first-hand witnesses of events that day. He would compare their accounts with what appeared in the reports and he would draw his conclusions. Simple enough, but he knew well that tracking down witnesses and getting their full and frank accounts was as much an art as a science. Especially for a foreigner in a far-off land in a second language. Finally, the long flight across the Australia continent ended and he landed at Tullamarine, Melbourne Airport, at 7 am.

Ebbe was exhausted and knew he could not go anywhere without sleep. He felt unwell and regretted drinking so much on the flight. He could not drive up to Castlemaine just yet. There was a vacancy at the hotel by the airport, so he booked a room and left the terminal. It was already 30 degrees and not even 8 am. He staggered out into the heat towing his bag. Why on earth did he think this would be a simple assignment?

His room was air conditioned and cool. He crashed onto the bed and was barely able to remove his shoes and trousers before sleep hit him.

Five hours later he woke. For a few seconds he had no idea where he was. Then it all came crashing back. Australia, and he had the mother of all headaches! It was 7 am on his body clock. Ebbe showered, dressed and ventured out, though he still craved sleep. Driving was still too dangerous. The heat hit him again as he stumbled to the pool. He swallowed some painkillers with iced water.

An hour later it was 38 degrees. He retreated to his room and checked the weather. It would be 41 tomorrow. The bed beckoned but he knew he had to stay up through jet lag until a more normal bedtime. He cursed himself for knowing so little about jet lag. He sent a brief email to his daughter to say he had arrived safely but was trapped in a hotel room by heat and jet lag. He was only half joking.

By 8 am he was channel surfing on the television. Nothing interested him and his eyes felt like lead weights. At 10 pm he went out like a light, but by 3.30 am he was wide awake. He felt a lot better and went outside. It was a little cooler and he walked across to the airport terminal. As he crossed a roadway, he discovered that the traffic was driving on the wrong side of the road. He cursed himself again. But he had never driven a car that way before. He would wait until daylight and then he would take the wheel.

At 6 am the car hire office opened and he collected his car. He drove north out through Bulla towards Sunbury, driving, to him, on the wrong side of the road. At that hour the traffic was light, but it was still a hair-raising first drive. Once he reached the Calder Freeway, he relaxed a little. He just had to follow his nose to the Elphinstone exit, then just 13 kilometres west he would be in Castlemaine.

Still not 8 am and he had arrived in one piece, somehow. It had been a long way from Vesterbro. Tomorrow he would start work if he could tolerate the heat.

The next morning, he was up early looking for a cafe amongst the fine 19th century buildings from the gold rush era. There were lots of cafes to choose from and most were open at this hour. He chose one in Lyttleton Street, ordered scrambled eggs on toast with bacon and mushrooms. He noticed the espresso machine with pleasure. The Danes had come late to Italian coffee, but he was hooked. He asked the waiter if he knew of Commonplace. The young man told him that after the fire, everyone in town knew about it. Ebbe quizzed him about the place and the waiter said they seemed like nice enough people.

After breakfast he presented himself at the local police station and met Senior Sergeant Alan Spargo. The Sergeant was polite but curt. 'Listen mate, I understand why they sent you, but you will be barking up the wrong tree if you think there is anything dodgy.'

Ebbe did not understand key parts of this, but he understood the attitude well enough. Aussie English, he was beginning to appreciate, was a strange mix of rapid speech and slow drawl with the mouth mostly closed. A good training for ventriloquists.

'Well, I have read your reports for the coroner, and I

just need to confirm a few points,' he continued, feeling a mixture of defensiveness and determination. 'Who were the witnesses at the time of the prince's death?' he asked.

'Prince hah!' the sergeant huffed. 'We had no idea we had royalty in the shire. Nobody told us. We thought he was just Kasper Frederiksen, ordinary Danish backpacker. Until later.'

Ebbe did not reply, he just asked again, 'were there any witnesses?'

'Nah, not really,' came the copper's prompt reply. 'The others had evacuated but they left him behind. What would you expect from greenies and hippies like that? No morals to speak of.'

Ebbe realised that it was a rhetorical question, 'So there was no one with him?' he tried, knowing the answer from the reports he had studied.

'Oh yeah, what was his name? I forget, some Scottish bloke. Poor bugger. He shot through straight away. He would have been pretty buggered,' Spargo suggested.

Ebbe asked, 'What does 'shot through' mean sorry? Was there gunfire?'

The sergeant guffawed. 'No mate. He left town. Nobody got shot, only burned. Ha, ha.'

Ebbe laughed, too, at the black humour; as a policeman he understood it well. 'Did he know anything?'

'Not a lot apparently,' the officer replied. 'He had left before we could interview him, but he spoke to one of the firies,' he added.

'What is a firie?' Ebbe asked.

'A fire fighter. Two fire engines arrived at the property. They came too late, but they found him wandering around. He had been in the dam. Lucky fella.'

He thanked the Senior Sergeant and started to leave.

Spargo ended the conversation with a very rapid, 'See ya, good luck and look me up if you need any more help.'

Ebbe did not offer his hand. He turned and left, thinking that Eric, the only witness to what happened had never been interviewed by the police. Not ideal, he thought.

CHAPTER TWENTY FOUR

The drive out to Commonplace took about 20 minutes. Ebbe could see from his car the burnt countryside and drove slowly. So much of what his senses were experiencing was strange, the heavy smell of summer air, the tinder dry yellow fields, the heat mirages on the roads, the dense formless bush with unfamiliar trees. Some buildings and vegetation had escaped the fire. He could not see why. At the gate to the property, he encountered an armed policewoman sitting under a shade umbrella looking at her phone.

'Listen fella. You will need a bloody good reason for me to let you in,' she drawled.

It dawned on Ebbe that this place would now be the focus of international media attention. A magnet for all kinds of ill- and well-intentioned people. He introduced himself to the policewomen who confirmed his assumption.

'Sorry about my rude opening lines, I am Senior Constable Lorna Gray, we have been inundated: cars, bicycles, helicopters, drones, pedestrians, you name it, even a light plane. Not just the media mate, all kinds of rubberneckers and crazies.'

Ebbe nodded, 'Yes royalty, even Danish royalty, can have that effect.' He had worked out what rubbernecker meant, translated it into Danish and liked it a lot.

'I heard you might come sniffing around, so welcome,' this time she extended her hand.

'Go right in and up to the main building. But they may not be all that cooperative,' she added, opening the gate for him.

Ebbe wound up the window of the car as quickly and as he politely as he could but could not keep the heat out. He drove the 300 metres or so up to the car park near the exceptionally large main building. A boy about ten or eleven years old came out to meet him.

'Hi, I'm Sam, what do you want?'

'Hi Sam. I am a policeman from Denmark. Would I be able to speak to one of the adults?'

'Oh really. From Denmark. Did you know Kasper? He was from there. But he is dead now. Got burnt in his hut.'

Ebbe was a little taken aback at the bluntness of the boy but was happy to confirm this, 'Yes, I did know him. Maybe you could tell the adults that.'

'So do you have an appointment?' Sam was clearly an experienced doorman.

Ebbe said no, and Sam promptly turned on his bare heels and disappeared inside. Ebbe stood in the shade of the entrance veranda and looked around. He noticed the patches of burnt land around him, but the big building had escaped the fire.

Sam returned a few minutes later with the answer, 'Nobody can see you now but please come back at 10 in the morning.'

'That will be fine. Thanks Sam,' Ebbe replied and immediately regretted just cold calling like this. He should have phoned and made an appointment as he would have back home. He wondered where the death had occurred but decided not to investigate. Tomorrow will come soon enough, and who in their right mind would walk around in this heat.

Senior Constable Gray rose from below her umbrella and went to the gate, 'That was quick.'

'Yes,' Ebbe replied, 'I should have phoned first. But they will speak to me at 10 am tomorrow, so I will be back.'

'No worries. I'll be here and could you bring me a large latte with one sugar?' she asked with big smile. 'I have been opening the gate for you!'

Ebbe laughed, 'I will do that for another police officer. That will be fine.'

He gave a little wave as the window went up again. What a boring job, he thought, on the way back to town. Police work was often like that. Ninety-five percent tedium and five percent terror.

He duly arrived back at the gate at 9.45 am the next morning with two coffees. The day was not so hot, around 28 degrees and he even enjoyed the weather that day, although in Denmark it would be a scorcher. He stopped his car and got out with the coffees.

'Do you know much about what happened in the fire?' Ebbe asked while sipping his cappuccino.

'Well, we have been flat out ever since. So much overtime and extra duties. Hopefully, it will die down soon,' she stopped as a large black Mercedes came barrelling up to the gate.

Out she stepped adopting full police status and spoke to the driver briefly. The car did an abrupt 180 degrees and sped off in the direction it had come, gravel spraying from the tyres.

She returned to where Ebbe stood under the umbrella, 'Bloody Hell! Another one just wanting to take a few pictures of where the prince died. Said he had come all the way from Sydney.'

'Did you know the prince?' she inquired.

'Yes, I did. I was his security officer when he was younger,' he replied.

'Okay, then, my condolences mate,' the senior constable offered. 'I can see why you got sent. Such a sad event for you and so many others.'

Ebbe wanted to get the conversation away from him and asked, 'were you part of the investigation?'

'I was indeed. I conducted some interviews,' Lorna replied.

'What about the firefighters? Did you speak to any of them?' Ebbe asked.

'No,' she answered. 'That was a colleague of mine, Sergeant Walter Payton, Wally,' she replied, 'he is still around, you could speak to him.'

Ebbe looked at his watch and knew he had to get to his appointment.

'Thanks so much. I will do that, but now I need to hurry,' he replied with a big smile getting back into his car.

He drove up to the main building and parked. Sam appeared immediately. They entered the very large building and Sam led him down a corridor to a meeting room. It could easily hold 15 people but there were only three waiting for him. They introduced themselves as Fran, Luis and Simone. Ebbe noticed how these Australians did not use their surnames.

They appeared to be in the age range of 35 to 50 and looked a little downcast and solemn.

Ebbe explained who he was and why he was keen to speak to them. He mentioned his connection with Kasper or Prince Christian, hoping it might make them more forthcoming and also apologised for asking them to go over it all again. Simone spoke first and said how well Kasper had fitted in. She described him as a little withdrawn at first but friendly, hardworking and quite shy. Luis spoke about the time that Kasper had asked them about what it would take to become a member and suggested that perhaps Kasper was keen to stay. Ebbe made note of this.

Fran also spoke of their collective amazement when they found out who Kasper really was. She said he had shown no regal or aristocratic characteristics. Ebbe had to smile and thought, yes that would be right. However, their version of events on the day of the fire was no different to the police reports. They had decided to evacuate when they got reports of the rapidly approaching fire. Kasper and his friend Eric had gone off to one of the huts but when they all had to leave there was nobody in either hut. They had called out but decided they had no more time to spare and left without them. Fran added that this decision probably cost Kasper his life and that they felt a deep sense of guilt and responsibility for his death. He was their guest and as a foreigner would not have known what to do to save himself in a fire like that.

They sat in silence for some time heavy with sorrow. Then Ebbe asked about Eric. Luis explained that he had come as a visitor more recently than Kasper, and they had become good friends. The evening after the fire, when they had returned to the property from the evacuation centre in town, they were very surprised to discover that Eric had packed up all his things and left. They were very worried about him and tried to contact him on his mobile but got no reply. Then they tried emailing him, but no luck either. They looked for him on social media and found someone with his name on LinkedIn, but he did not reply to their message either. Suddenly, about five days after the fire he emailed back to say that he was fine, just badly shaken. Eric apologised for leaving so abruptly but just had to get away. He was going home to his family in Scotland and had booked a flight for the next day. Luis told Ebbe they were much relieved that he was okay.

It all made sense to Ebbe and he concluded there was not a lot more to ask them about. But as he was thinking of going Fran asked him about what had happened in Denmark after the news broke. Ebbe summarised the uproar and the outpouring of grief from the Danes in all its forms; denial, disbelief, anger, shock and sadness. Fran added it had been a bit like that for them, too. Ebbe described briefly the royal funeral and burial and how pleased he was to be able to attend. He had an urge to apologise to these people for the deluge of attention and intrusion the death had caused to their lives but thought better of it. It was really nobody's fault.

Ebbe asked if there was anything else about Kasper's stay they thought was worth mentioning. Simone recounted the adventures of Kasper and Sinbad, and Ebbe laughed. Yes, that certainly rang true. He told them of his love of animals from the time of his first pony. Finally, Ebbe asked about Kasper's partner Serene. What did they know about her? Simone answered after a brief pause that they did not know her; Kasper must have met her somewhere else. Ebbe noticed the pause and the slight tremor in her voice. He rose and then remembered a further task. He asked if it was possible for him to see the place where the body had been discovered. They readily agreed and Luis said he would show him on the way out. Ebbe expressed his thanks for their time and wished them well. He shook hands with two of them and left with Luis. Sam appeared as soon as they left the room and tagged along.

They walked the 70 metres up to where the huts were situated above the main building. Luis showed Ebbe the remains of the hut with the fading police tape still draped around to form a cordon. Ebbe lifted the tape and took a brief look closely. He was no forensic expert but could see how hungry the fire had been. Twisted roofing metal and some charred remnants of wooden posts and beams were all that remained amongst the ashes. He walked away with a heavy heart and noticed in stark contrast a hut nearby that appeared to have been untouched by the fire.

'That was Eric's hut,' Luis noted when he saw Ebbe's look. 'The fire spared that one. It seemed so bloody capricious,' then added, 'Kasper's hut was pretty much the same.'

Ebbe nodded and took a quick look inside. So, this is how Christian had spent the last year; no palace, very spartan by royal standards, but he could understand the attraction.

Sam asked, 'would you like to see our dam? It's great and

even has a pontoon. You could have a swim. That's where Eric went. He saved himself, you know.'

Ebbe thought for a moment and replied, 'no thanks young man. I have seen all I want to see.'

Ebbe, Sam and Luis walked in silence back to the car. Ebbe said goodbye to Sam and shook hands warmly with Luis. He drove very slowly out of the property. On the way out, all he could think of was how it must have been on that fatal day. What a terrible way to die. And the heat. He thanked the Senior Constable at the gate and wished her well. He did not stop to chat; he could barely manage a smile.

He was pleased that he had made the visit, seen the ruins and spoken to the residents. In a way it had reassured him that Christian's gap year, and final year, had been a happy one. He had even been interested in staying.

Ebbe again visited the police station, and Wally Peyton could see him now. The Sergeant was everything a Police Sergeant ought to be; tall, round, gruff and to the point. He said that he had led the investigation but that the detective branch was also involved initially as it was an unexpected death. After he had assured himself that no crime had been committed, he then had the role of organising a detailed report for the coroner who would make the ultimate determination of the cause of death and the circumstances. The four firefighters who had been the first responders were interviewed separately. He produced the records of their interviews and handed them to Ebbe.

One interview interested Ebbe particularly. It was with firefighter Valerie Metcalfe. She had met and spoke to Eric shortly after the fire engine arrived. Ebbe skimmed the report of what Eric had told Valerie Metcalfe and knew it was consistent with what he had already read. Nothing seemed out of order. Peyton explained how the state coronial service then took over the site and removed the body, or what was left of it, to the state mortuary in Melbourne. He said from then on, his job was done and, apart from keeping the curious and depraved at bay, as far as he was concerned there was nothing out of the ordinary with the death.

'People die like this in fires almost every summer,' he added almost with a shrug. Ebbe asked him what had happened to Eric who had been at the scene. He already knew the answer but wanted to hear the police line on this.

'Well, he cleared off and is out of the country,' came the succinct reply.

Ebbe knew that this did not put the witness out of reach of the police by any means, but he decided it was time to leave Wally alone.

He stood and thanked the police officer for his time and as he was leaving, the Sergeant added, 'If I had known he was a Danish Prince I would have done exactly the same things.'

Ebbe nodded and kept walking while thinking, well that is utter rubbish, you would have had your hands full with a horde of foreign office officials from two different countries, a separate horde of media and every senior police officer in the land as well as a few from Denmark. Ebbe left in a good mood. He was getting close to the eyewitness now.

But Valerie Metcalfe was hard to track down. He discovered that the Castlemaine Fire Station was empty that afternoon.

He phoned the number on the notice board and spoke to the captain. Ebbe was told that the fire engine in question was not from the Castlemaine Fire Station but had come from the nearby Harcourt Station, a village 12 kilometres to the north, at the base of Mt Alexander (Leanganook). He phoned the Captain of the Harcourt fire station and the captain confirmed that Valerie Metcalfe was one of the volunteer firefighters, but he was not prepared to give Ebbe her number. The captain explained that she had taken leave from her job as an orchardist, and from her firefighting duties, and gone away with the kids. The fire had been traumatic for her. She was not to be disturbed. The police were already told everything she knew, anyway. Ebbe decided not to push him. He knew from extensive experience there was more than one way to skin a cat, especially in a country town.

He ate lunch in a Castlemaine eatery. It was not an easy choice. For a town of eight thousand there were about 30 lunch options including fare from India, China, Italy, Greece, Thailand, the Middle East, Japan and France. He vowed to himself he would listen to his doctor and eat healthy in Australia. No more pizza, burgers and fries followed by pastries and cakes, washed down with beer and wine. So, he found himself eating at the Melon Cauliflower in Lyttleton Street, with an eclectic menu heavily influenced by Asian and vegetarian traditions; his newest favourite.

On his laptop he searched for Metcalfe Orchard, Harcourt. After lunch he phoned the landline number of the business and a gravelly male voice answered. Dean Metcalfe confirmed his daughter was Valerie. Ebbe explained who he was and asked if he could speak to her. Dean said she had gone down to Apollo Bay with her two kids for a few days. But he was happy to give Ebbe her mobile number. He asked if it could wait until she got back home on Sunday. Ebbe was non-committal and thanked Dean for being so cooperative.

Ebbe had never heard of Apollo Bay and knew that Castlemaine was a long way from the coast. He rang the number he was given and had to leave a message with Valerie. He planned to ring again in a couple of hours but did not have to wait more than one hour. Valerie rang back and apologised for missing his call as she had been at the beach body surfing with her children. Again, Ebbe explained who he was and asked if he could ask her a few questions. She said she had told the police everything she knew but would be happy to talk to him on the phone. Ebbe said he would much prefer to speak to her in person if that was possible and added that it would not take very long. Reluctantly, she agreed, stating that she would be home on Sunday and they could make a time after that, but she would be very busy.

Ebbe then had a brainwave. An Aussie beach with surf sounded more than interesting; surely he had to visit one on this trip. So, he suggested that if she had the time, he would be happy to drive down and speak to her in Apollo Bay. Valerie thought this a fine idea and they agreed to meet at 2 pm the next day. Ebbe was very pleased. Two birds with the one stone. He was careful to include his board shorts. Perhaps Valerie would be his last port of call and he could wind up his visit in a day or two, or even squeeze in a couple of days' leave after he finished his final report and before the long flight home. So far, his reporting back home had been very plain and routine and surely his bosses would allow him some time off after coming all this way.

CHAPTER TWENTY FIVE

Ebbe set off at 9 am on a four-hour journey, thinking that this may well be his last chance to see some more of the countryside and the coast. He drove southwest though the wide, ancient landscapes, past extinct volcanoes, hills, bushland, plantations of European trees and the vast open plains. He conceded that the dry, yellow land had its own beauty, a harsh beauty, with its vast horizons and huge sky, so different to his small green homeland the Danes often called affectionately "Little Mother Denmark."

The coast was another story. It was exquisite. Golden beaches, the ancient headlands, the open sea and the tangled coastal vegetation. So familiar to him yet so strange. He loved the sea back home. It was always quite close by. His country was very much a land of islands, coastline, sand dunes, bridges, boats, sailors and ships.

Apollo Bay appeared and he parked the car amongst the cypress trees huddled on the foreshore up from the beach. Barefoot, he strolled along the warm sand. A cool sea breeze ruffled his thinning hair. He felt so good, no jet lag, no deadline, no boss watching over him, and, as his favourite Aussie term insisted, no worries. Just before 2 pm he knocked on the beachhouse front door.

A girl of about thirteen opened it and let him in, saying,

'I'm June. Mum is expecting you. She is just getting lunch ready. She thought you might be hungry.'

'I'm Ebbe and I am very hungry,' he replied with a grin.

June led him through to a large open plan kitchen, dining area and lounge. Valerie came forward and extended her hand. She was a woman in her mid-forties, quite short with dark hair and complexion, tanned from lots of sun. With a big smile she introduced herself and said that lunch was ready. Ebbe said that he was not expecting lunch at all but would definitely have some.

Valerie called down the hallway towards the front of the house, 'Tom, lunch is served. Get off your computer and come right now. Our guest is here.'

A lanky, lean lad of about 15 years appeared. He stood about six inches taller than his mother, about the same height as Ebbe, 1.80 metres. He looked healthy.

'Hi, I'm Ebbe,' the detective said extending his hand.

'Are you really a Danish Detective?' Tom countered before quickly adding, 'I'm Tom by the way.'

'Yes I am.' Ebbe replied.

Then June chipped in, 'So do you know Queen Mary?'

Ebbe admitted that he had met her and explained that he used to work in Royal security. Before the interview could continue, Valerie interjected and they sat down to eat. The lunch consisted of grilled calamari, Greek salad, pita bread and tzatziki dip. Ebbe tucked in. It was delicious.

'Are you Greek?' he asked Valerie.

'Oh no,' she replied with a laugh. 'I just like what the Greeks eat and it is easy to purchase.'

Tom was the first to finish lunch and turned to Ebbe, 'Do you want to go body surfing down at the beach? It is way cool.'

Ebbe looked at Valerie. He wanted to for sure, but it was not up to him.

'We'll see, maybe later Tom,' she said. "But I need to talk to Ebbe first. He's come a long way to see me. Can you two leave us alone for a while?'

The children seemed happy enough to disappear up the hall and Valerie closed the door. They sat across from each other on sofas in the lounge area, each with a cup of tea.

'Well, I just want to speak to you about what happened with the fire. I am sorry to ask you to talk about it again. I hope it is not too hard for you,' Ebbe stated with all the compassion he could find.

Valerie smiled very briefly and replied, 'I understand that it is important for you. You have come all this way. I am very sorry about what happened to the prince.'

Valerie related the events of that fateful day again. How she had met Eric, dirty, shocked and very thirsty. Her account offered nothing new.

Ebbe asked a few questions. How did Eric appear? Was he injured? Did you see the body in the hut? Was he being clear? What did he say?

Valerie answered each question calmly, 'I did see the body from outside the hut, but it was just a lump. I could see that it was a body but that was about all. I did not get too close and I wanted Eric to come away. He was obviously shaken and shocked, but he was not burnt or injured. He said he had sheltered in the dam and his clothes were very dirty. I could not see his face clearly. He had a hat on and a scarf around his mouth and nose. The air was still hot and smokey so that made sense. But he did speak with a foreign accent.'

It sounded right to Ebbe. He knew Eric was a Scot. 'Right, he was a Scot. Did he sound like one?' He asked.

'Really, is that right?' Valerie replied, 'I have not been told that before now, but actually he sounded like you. But I didn't know where he came from.'

Ebbe felt a sudden surge of adrenalin rush through his body. He hid it from Valerie as best he could.

'So did you see the media reports of the death?' he asked.

'Yes, some,' she replied. But I tried to avoid them.'

'So, you would have seen pictures of the prince,' he stated, half asking.

'Yes, I saw a couple, poor fellow,' she answered.

'And had you ever seen him in real life? Before or after the fire?'

'No, I don't think so. Is it important?'

Ebbe did not answer. Instead, he asked, 'do you mind if I just show you some pictures? I will need to get my laptop from the car,' he said as serenely and politely as he could.

'Not at all,' Valerie assured him. 'I'll just put the kettle on again.'

Ebbe stood up slowly, he did not want to appear in a rush. Outside he could smell the ocean, he fumbled with his key in the car boot lock before grabbing his laptop. He could not help rushing back inside. Valerie was standing at the kitchen bench putting tea leaves in the pot. He stood beside her and from his computer opened a folder with the name

'Photographs' in Danish. He clicked on a file. It took a second for the file to open and for Chris and Eric's faces to appear.

Ebbe turned to Valerie and pointed to the photo of Eric, 'Is that him?' as matter-of-factly as he could manage.

She looked closely, 'No, I could not see his face much but I'm pretty sure that's not him. The eyes look different.'

'Okay,' Eric replied, 'what about this one" he asked and pointed to Kasper's picture.

'Maybe. The eyes are very similar. But I'm not really sure. As I said it was very smokey and his face was covered. Is it important?' She asked again.

'No, not really,' Ebbe lied. He thanked her and closed the laptop casually. He noticed that his heart was beating fast, but he knew how to stay calm. He remembered someone once called it the "deep acting" of a police officer. He had no more questions. He put his laptop aside and they drank tea again and soon the children reappeared.

Ebbe asked June about the orchard, and she told him about the apples, pears, and cherries they grew to sell and the other fruit and vegetables they grew for themselves. Tom explained that the cherry season was over but soon the pears would be ripe and after that the apples.

But Tom had other things in mind. 'Can we all go to the beach now Mum? I am sure Ebbe would like to,' he asserted.

Ebbe and Valerie laughed simultaneously. 'Well, that's okay by me. But Ebbe may have to go back,' she replied.

'I would love to go to the beach Tom,' Ebbe agreed, 'And I even brought my board shorts just in case.'

But all Ebbe could think of was what he had uncovered.

Was it an act of audaciousness, madness or maybe desperation?

They all got changed into their swimwear and loaded themselves up with towels, sunscreen cream, hats, boogie boards, a beach tent, a bat and ball, drinks and snacks. The beach was just a leisurely walk of 400 metres through the town. The children rushed ahead and Valerie felt the need to explain that she had been divorced from their father for eight years now. Their father lived in Adelaide and saw them far too infrequently in her opinion. Ebbe followed suit and told of his failed marriage and of his divorce 19 years ago. He had never re-partnered although he got close a couple of times. He spoke with pride of his 24-year-old daughter Stine now at university in Sweden, but luckily just a short train ride away from his home.

They arrived at the beach and had to find the children. They had pitched the tent and laid out the towels. Ebbe's summer tan was now faded, and he was relieved to find he was not the palest person on the modestly populated beach as he applied the sunscreen cream liberally. He took in the whole scene with delight. So, this was an Australian beachscape in summer. He noticed the waves breaking. There was a nice swell and a group of surfers in their black wet suits bobbed out there waiting for the next decent wave.

Tom and Ebbe grabbed boards and went off to catch waves. The water was colder than he expected and at first, Ebbe was hopeless. He had not caught a wave for more than 30 years and it showed. But he improved each time and after a while was able to keep up with the two children. He was hoping that Valerie would join them, but she stayed on the beach.

'Someone had to mind their things,' she said, but she really wanted to check out the Dane. Ebbe then tried body surfing without the boogie board and eventually caught a wave that way, too.

The four of them stayed for hours, surfing, seashell hunting, playing beach cricket, sandcastle constructing, boat spotting and observing the board riders. Tom insisted that he be buried up to his neck in sand and Ebbe obliged. The afternoon seemed endless and the sun sat still in the western sky. Ebbe had not had this much exercise for years and started to feel it. At 6 o'clock Valerie gently suggested that if Ebbe wanted to get back to Castlemaine at a reasonable hour then he would need to consider leaving shortly. Ebbe checked the time on his phone. He jumped up and started to gather his things.

But Valerie had a suggestion, 'why not stay the night with us Ebbe? We have a spare bedroom and there are some fine restaurants in town. I think the kids would enjoy that, especially Tom. And I would too.'

Ebbe sat down again. It was an easy decision. 'I would like that a lot,' he said, 'I am sorry I did not check the time earlier. It has been such a wonderful day.'

At 7 pm Valerie called the children and they packed up their beach things.

Valerie announced, 'listen kids, we will be having an overnight guest. Do you have any suggestions for dinner?'

In unison Tom and June shouted, 'Fish and Chips Mum, please!'

Ebbe answered too, 'What if we all go to a restaurant

instead and I pay?' he proposed, 'you have all been so kind and I have enjoyed myself so much.'

The others readily agreed and then a restaurant had to be agreed. There was a choice of Indian, Chinese, Thai or Italian. Indian won the majority vote three to one and a table at the Agra Taj was reserved. They did not bother going back to the house as the restaurant was almost on the way.

Over dinner the children plied Ebbe with questions he did his best to answer or deflect. No, he had not shot anyone. Yes, he did have a gun, but it was back home. Yes, he had arrested bad guys. Yes, he had seen dead bodies. Yes, Queen Mary now speaks good Danish. Yes, most Danes speak English and it is compulsory in school. Yes, there is snow and ice in winter, and you could skate on the lakes some winters. Yes, he knew how to skate and ski. No, the Danes do not play Aussie rules, rugby, cricket or netball, instead they play soccer, handball, tennis and badminton. He had to explain handball.

Now it was Ebbe's turn: where did they go to school, what subjects did they study, what careers did they want to follow? What sports did they play? What was it like living in an orchard? What fruit did they like best? What music did they like? He had great fun. These were the first Australians he had spent proper time with. And he had no meaningful contact with children back home now that his daughter was grown.

Ebbe understood when he agreed to go to the beach that it was probably unethical for him to spend all this time with a key witness. Especially after what Valerie had innocently disclosed. But he was not a real policeman in Australia, and he even thought he might try to claim the dinners on expenses.

They arrived back at the house a little before 10 pm and Valerie warned the children that it was soon their bedtime. It took her about 20 minutes to convince them of this fact and Tom was most reluctant. But finally, they had said polite good nights to Ebbe and left the two adults alone.

Ebbe and Valerie settled down with coffees. They shared their life stories. Well, all they chose to tell; the presentable bits. Valerie told of her childhood in Harcourt then her university studies in Biochemistry at Monash University. She had worked in medical science labs until her mid-30s. Three events then changed her direction completely: her mother died, her marriage failed, and she lost her job. Bad luck in threes, they say. Her dad invited her to bring the children home to Harcourt and help him run the orchard. They could both earn a living if they were careful. She agonised over the decision for a long time and eventually agreed. Her career as a biochemist had to go on hold, but it had been the right decision for all concerned. Now her dad was semi-retired and she increasingly ran the business. It was going well. Her children were happy. But was she single? Ebbe wondered but did not ask.

Ebbe did ask her about her firefighting. She proudly told him that, again it was her dad who got her involved. The Country Fire Association was a venerable institution in Victoria of mostly volunteer firefighters. Volunteers did almost all the firefighting outside of Melbourne. She joined up in the beginning to meet some locals and make new friends, after all her time in the city, but she found the intense training and the camaraderie very rewarding. She was a key member of the Harcourt CFA with about 50 other volunteers.

Ebbe was full of interest. 'How could you possibly fight a fire in summer? You would roast.'

'Oh yes, it can get terribly hot,' Valerie agreed, 'but we are used to the heat. We grow up with the heat. And we need to wear protective clothing, of course, to protects us from radiant heat. And we drink lots of water. But if the fire is too hot, we must retreat. There is nothing anyone can do to stop a raging fire on a hot, windy day, and too many firefighters have been killed over the years,' she added.

Ebbe thought this might have been the case on the day of Christian's death.

Valerie must have read his mind. 'The recent fire just took off like an express train even though the conditions were not truly severe. With a fire like that, we can only try to stop it by making fire breaks a long way ahead of the front. But the embers jump miles ahead anyway. Otherwise, we just try to limit its spread to the sides. But the water bombers can make quite a difference. Otherwise, on the ground we just come along and mop up once the fire front has passed. And find the bodies,' she added ruefully.

'Kasper was most unfortunate. He was left behind, but he would have survived anyway if he had sheltered in that big building. It was well protected. But he went to the hut instead. He was from overseas,' she added. 'It was far too late when we arrived.'

They sat there in silence and sadness, deep in thought. There was no need to say more. Ebbe could not bring himself to tell her who she had really met that fatal day.

Finally, Valerie asked, 'How long are you planning to stay in Australia?'

He answered honestly, 'I am not so sure. I have a few things to finalise, then I need to write a report. Maybe another two weeks.' After the revelation today, he was not sure what to do next. He had to let it all sink in.

'Well, I need to go to bed soon,' Valerie stated, 'it has been a long day.'

She got up from the sofa across from Ebbe. 'But I want to invite you up to the orchard in Harcourt before you go back home. I will cook you a nice dinner and it will not be Greek. I'm sure the kids would like to see you again.'

'Sure, that would be great,' Ebbe responded as he stood up, too, and took the coffee cups to the kitchen. 'And thanks for a lovely day, Valerie. It was what we call "hygge" at home, meaning friendly, even cosy.'

He stood there not knowing what to do.

Suddenly Valerie chuckled, 'Oh dear, I forgot, you just came for a brief interview. I will show you to your room and find you a toothbrush.' Ebbe followed Valerie to a bedroom at the front of the house. It contained two single beds on adjacent walls. Valerie's family had furnished it in that vintage style he recognised from holiday houses back home. 1970s pine with macramé wall hangings.

'Sorry it's not five stars,' Valerie said, 'but at least you have a choice of beds. The bathroom is the second door back down the hall on the right. I will be just across the hall from you if you need anything in the night.'

Ebbe said a fond goodnight, 'Thanks for a lovely day. I am

so glad I came to visit the three of you.' He wanted to hug her but settled for extending his hand.

'How very formal,' Valerie said lightly and shook it happily. She liked his touch, not too hard, not too weak, just right.

Ebbe fell asleep quite soon to the sound of breaking waves and the occasional croak from a koala. The best day in Australia by a mile, he thought, and Christian was almost certainly alive.

He woke around 7 am and lay there going over the events of yesterday. He saw himself on the beach catching waves with the boy, in his old board shorts.

Suddenly he leapt out of bed and grabbed his laptop. Was it Bells Beach or Bells Bay? He recalled the days long ago when he was a surfing fan and dreamed of big hair and big waves. How far was he from that famous beach? Did they have a surf school? 85 kilometres to the north-east, according to the computer. About 75 minutes' drive along the Great Ocean Road. He dressed and packed his things and went to wash in the bathroom. Valerie was up already and was emptying the dish washer. He offered to help but she turned him away.

'How did you sleep Mr Danish Policeman?' she asked playfully.

'Very well, thank you. I think "like a log" is the right expression.'

Valerie laughed. 'Or like a baby. The choice is yours.'

Over breakfast he told her of his surfing fantasies as a young man and how he had remembered a place called Bells Beach. Valerie replied that Bells Beach was along the Surf Coast, a Mecca for board riders all year round.

'Have you ever been to Bells Beach?' he asked.

'Yep, back when I lived in Melbourne, I went there a few times. It was a wonderful place to surf,' she replied casually.

'You can surf. Oh wow!' Ebbe exclaimed almost leaping up on the spot. 'Maybe it is not too late for me after all,' he said.

Valerie just smiled and poured them each a cup of coffee.

He did not go north again via Bells Beach. He had things to do, and it was a long detour. He drove back to Castlemaine daydreaming of surfing at Bells alongside Valerie. In his mind she had taught him well and he was standing up there on his board as proud as punch. And she rode alongside with her perfect smile.

CHAPTER TWENTY SIX

It was easy for Ebbe to find Chris once he had done the detective work. He was grateful the local police had been willing to help. The explanation that Eric was the vital witness and needed to be located was readily accepted. Some key databases the police searched revealed that Eric Anderson had not left the country and that his bank card was being used in Melbourne along with his mobile phone. Eric was somewhere in the inner northern suburbs of Melbourne. His exact location was a little harder to pin down. But the police helped Ebbe find a real estate agent who had leased a flat to an Eric Anderson. The agent identifies him from a picture Ebbe produced.

Ebbe waited outside from 7 o'clock in the morning and at 3 o'clock in the afternoon Chris came out of the white Northcote block of flats in Elm Street and headed for the station on foot.

He did not look a lot different to the dozens of images Ebbe had seen of him through the years. His hair was long and tied back in a ponytail, and he sported a full moustache and beard. His time in Australia had aged him a little and darkened his Nordic and Celtic skin to what everyone once called a 'healthy tan', before they discovered skin cancer. The Danes, however, judging by their addiction to lying in the sun all summer, were still not convinced.

Ebbe followed him to the platform and onto the train to the CBD. He wanted to speak to him alone and waited for a chance. Chris bought a coffee and sat down at a cafe near the main entrance to Flinders Street Station and its old clocks. This was the right time and place.

Ebbe approached and asked calmly in Danish, 'Do you mind if I sit down?'

As his ears pricked up, Chris took a split second to realise someone had addressed him in his father's tongue. Occasionally he heard Danish around town, and he found he could recognise Danish at a hundred metres across a crowded room. He did not mind sharing the table, especially with a Dane, and said simply without thinking, 'That's fine.'

Then after a few more seconds Chris knew. He recognised Ebbe and froze. The horrid realisation struck him.

Ebbe spoke first, 'I came to Australia to see what happened Christian, they thought I would be the best person for the job.'

After a silence Chris finally stated very quietly, 'So you have found me.'

'Indeed, I have.' Ebbe replied calmly and with no sense of triumph. 'But I'd like to hear what you have been up to since we last met.'

Chris' face slumped and he closed his eyes; downcast and defeated. In his soft, posh Danish accent, modelled on his paternal grandmother's clear, approved diction, he countered defensively, 'You do know who I am, but I do not have the slightest wish to tell you anything about my time here. I have a new life now. Or at least I had one.' He felt bitter defeat.

But to Chris' astonishment Ebbe said with a grin, 'I understand completely. I am preparing my report for Borgen and Amalienborg now. In it I will find that there is no evidence at all for doubting that you died in the fire and that your mortal remains indeed lie in Roskilde Cathedral with most of the other King Christians.'

Chris looked up wide eyed and incredulous. He had trouble speaking, all he could manage was a mumbled, 'Thank you, a thousand thanks. But why?'

'It seems that you like it a lot here in Australia, too, even though there are no wild elephants,' Ebbe added. 'Your reasons for becoming Eric must be sound.'

Chris smiled and remembered the scene at the zoo many years ago, then he looked around at the scores of travellers and commuters rushing to and fro. He had rapidly changed his mind. It seemed that Ebbe may be on his side and he needed allies. The temptation was too great.

'Well, it has been a wild ride,' he said, then added quickly, 'Look I'm running late for work, and I do have to earn a living now I am no longer royalty. Can we meet again soon, I think I might need your help?'

Ebbe readily agreed. He admitted to himself that he had planned to leave Australia in a few days, but this would be an excellent reason for staying on a little longer.

'Can you come for dinner in two days?' Christian asked, 'there is someone I would like you to meet. You know where I live.'

'I would be most honoured,' Ebbe replied and offered the smallest of bows, a habit he had still subconsciously followed.

'Please Ebbe, not so formal. I have quit, remember. I'm Eric now,' Christian said with a smile extending his hand. Ebbe shook it warmly and the two men parted.

Chris thought about the forthcoming dinner for the next two days. He had not had a conversation in Danish for ages and he had a feeling that Ebbe might well be sympathetic and useful. He hoped Serene would understand him wanting to introduce her to a Danish police detective.

The couple had to be careful. Serene could not just move in with Kasper, as her constant presence might attract attention. Now Kasper, as Eric, also had a whole raft of problems to solve. It was not easy taking on a dead man's identity in the 21st century even when you have all his possessions. Passwords for one thing. Photo ID for another. And of course, he could not touch any of Christian's old accounts or communication channels. Luckily Serene had been a major help. She was in touch with several of her country folk living in exile in Australia and she had her own skills for getting things done with no legal status, and without genuine identity documents.

That night Chris phoned Serene to report that he had been tracked down by his former bodyguard. He recounted his meeting and his relief at Ebbe's collusion.

He added, 'I invited him to dinner in two days so you will be able to meet him.'

Serene was not at all pleased with these arrangements. Cops to her were amongst the enemy. She had feared them from her youth and the fear had grown ever since.

'How dare you just assume I would be okay with having a copper for dinner!' she complained angrily, 'you can't just make royal decrees and have me fall into line. Damn you, your bloody royal highness,' she spat.

'I'm so sorry,' Chris replied, 'you are right. I should have checked with you, but I just grabbed the chance. If you don't want to come, I would fully understand.'

'Can he be trusted, Eric?' she asked, 'that's the main thing for me. He may be on your side, but I do not want him to turn me in. Cops do that you know,' she argued.

She had agreed to use his assumed name whenever she could so it might become a habit in public. But mostly she forgot.

'I am sure we can trust him. Please come. I have known him since I was a little boy. He's okay. It will be fun,' he implored.

He now understood, of course she would have a totally distinct perspective on the police from his.

'Well fun for you, perhaps,' she rebutted, 'this time I am prepared to take your word for it. But we do not have to tell him that I am an illegal. Would you agree to that?'

'Sure,' he conceded, 'thank you, you are a gorgeous human being,' he added gratefully. Perhaps his buttoned up Danish royal reserve was fading a little when it came to Serene.

Chris was relieved. He had one more request in mind but now decided he would leave it alone. He decided not to ask her to cook an African dinner, he would cook a Danish one instead. If he could cook an edible dinner for fifteen at Commonplace, then surely three should be a breeze.

CHAPTER TWENTY SEVEN

Chris prepared a typical everyday Danish dinner: boiled potatoes, beef rissoles, peas and carrots under a butter and parsley sauce. Starters were rye bread squares topped with pickled herring, cucumber, hardboiled egg and mayonnaise. He tried unsuccessfully to find some real Danish rye bread and had to settle for pumpernickel. Danish beer and cider were the drinks.

Ebbe arrived right on time and Chris introduced him to Serene with the simple words, 'This is Serene, my girlfriend,' and then turned to Serene and said, 'this is Ebbe my old bodyguard and a very generous man.'

Ebbe and Serene shook hands. Ebbe the detective was most puzzled. Why had nobody mentioned her before? The Commonplace residents had not, nor had the local Police. Where did she come into the picture? Something was nagging at him and then, of course, he remembered, he had heard her mentioned before. Not here but back in Copenhagen. At the funeral of Christian. In Princess Isabella's eulogy. The cryptic message of condolence to Serene. She must be his partner. He cursed his forgetfulness as he remembered the woman at Commonplace hesitating at his mention of Serene's name. This piece of information, this line of inquiry, should have been explored, not forgotten. And here he stood shaking hands with her and with the prince standing right beside her. He had so much to ask them both, but it had to wait. This evening, he was a guest, not an investigator.

The three of them dined and talked politely. Serene ventured nothing about herself, so they talked about Christian's childhood, family, and time in Australia, and a little about Ebbe. It was in English out of courtesy to her, but she said little. Chris spoke about how he had met Serene at Commonplace and Ebbe filled in the gaps for Christian about his own life and work since they saw each other last and described how the authorities summoned him to Borgen out of the blue.

'How did you know it was not me who died in the fire?' Chris had been itching to find out.

'It was the firefighter. Her name is Valerie. The one you spoke to and said you were Eric."

'Sure, I remember her. She was very kind,' Christian replied, 'she wore very funny clothes, big yellow pants with red braces and a shiny helmet. I remember those braces.'

Ebbe imagined Valerie in her firefighting garb but went on, 'Well, she said you spoke like me. Eric was a Scotsman. So, I showed her Eric's picture. And she said, 'That's not him.' So, I showed her your picture. And she recognised your eyes. If I hadn't spoken to her, nobody would have known.' Ebbe shook his head and realised what he had said. "Well, you two would have known.'

'Well, I barely said more than a dozen words to her, with a scarf over my mouth. I was a little distraught at the time and did not plan it very well, or at all really.' Christian felt the need to defend his slip up.

'It must have been hellish. I am so glad you survived,' Ebbe added.

He turned to Serene and asked, 'where were you that day?'

Serene was surprised by the sudden attention and simply said, 'I wasn't there.'

This did not satisfy Ebbe so he asked, 'So, did you evacuate with the others?'

Serene had no intention of elaborating and repeated more forcefully, 'No, I was not there that day.'

Ebbe let it be and Christian stood up.

'Is it time for cake and coffee?' They readily agreed.

Christian produced a classic Danish Kransekage. The rich smell reminded both men of home. Chris proudly placed it on the table with a container of crème fraîche, but he had to admit, 'I am no baker, so I confess that Serene helped me with this.'

'No, he helped me,' she corrected, and they all laughed. Ebbe noticed the ease they shared.

She was pleased that the detective had not shown much interest in her, though he must have been curious. And she was also glad that she had not given too much away. But now she was thinking, maybe Ebbe is alright. She could see that Chris seemed to think so.

After coffee she rose and excused herself, saying deadpan, 'you may speak Danish now.'

The two men grinned and immediately obeyed her instruction. Ebbe related all the royal gossip and news, how the Danes had responded to Christian's death, the media furore, the funeral at the cathedral, the procession to Roskilde and the entombment in the family chapel. Christian remained silent, his eyes downcast, absorbed by deep feelings of sympathy for his family, and guilt. Not many people get detailed accounts of the mourners' behaviour at their own funerals.

Ebbe thought now was the right time to broach the subject and said, 'I had heard of Serene before, you know. Your sister made a brief mention of her at your funeral, but I had forgotten until tonight. She called her Serene.'

Ebbe realised what he had said, paused and shook his head. 'I am sorry. It was not your funeral. I must think of something else to call it.'

'Well, it was certainly not Eric's funeral,' Christian added, 'much more mine than his. I did see a bit of it on the Danish news but not what Isabella said. Most impressive event I thought,' he added. Both men smiled – more at the bizarreness of the situation than anything amusing.

'What did my sister say?' Christian asked.

'Not much, she just sent her condolences to Serene,' Ebbe responded.

'Really? I had been keeping my sister updated and Serene was getting quite a mention in my emails. So, I am not really surprised. Nice touch really,' Christian explained.

Christian hesitated and Ebbe sensed he wanted to say a lot more, but he held back.

Ebbe ventured, 'Well she is obviously a lovely woman. I can see that you two are very close. I truly hope that you can make it work out. But I can see that it will not be easy.' Christian thanked Ebbe and agreed.

Serene had retired to the only bedroom. She removed her sandals and lay on the bed. She looked around at Kasper's sparse space. On the dresser she noticed his imitation sword and toy megaphone and remembered his account of the psychodrama at Commonplace. She knew he was a brave man. She heard the murmur of the male voices through the wall. There, hung a blue and white flag of St Andrew. She smiled at the subterfuge as a car purred past on the street outside.

She lay there wondering how on earth she had ended up in this situation; dining with a Danish prince impersonating a Scottish musician so he can be with her, and a Danish detective sent to find him. Yet she was pleased the evening had gone well. She had taken a chance with a police officer and it seemed to be okay. She deeply distrusted the police, but she would always be an illegal unless she took a chance with a police officer. She recalled Zoe's advice about asylum in Denmark and now soon after, unexpectedly, a Danish policeman appears in her life. Half guiltily she wondered if she could take advantage of this confluence or would Ebbe simply hand her over to the local Police. He might be loyal to Kasper but obviously he had been working hand in hand with the police in Australia, and he was still a white, western policeman, and probably as racist and sexist as the average white, male copper.

People walked past the apartment on the footpath and she could hear their voices; two women in an argument. She thought through her options as she had so many times before, but this time there was a new element. Even though Kasper had taken this extraordinary gamble to stay in Australia with her she knew she only had three options, and all had risks: stay an illegal indefinitely, hand herself in and apply for asylum again, or try the Danish gambit, even if it meant separating from Kasper for a while.

She decided to try a silly game she had used since her childhood to help make decisions. She used it to decide if she would refuse to perform for the She Elephant. If the first noise to reach her ears from outside was a pedestrian she would stay as an illegal. If the first sound she heard was a car, she would hand herself in, but if it was a tram along St Georges Road, she would ask Ebbe to help her find asylum in Denmark. The universe would decide for her or at least point the way.

She got up and turned off the light at the switch by the door. Some light still filtered in through the blind on the window as she lay back down. In the murk she listened hard. She heard the Danish voices continue to rise and fall, she heard the wind rustle the trees along the nature strip and she heard a solitary bird give a plaintive cry, perhaps a gull, but she was not certain. Australian bird calls were tricky. She noticed her heart. It was beating faster, despite her repose. The minutes passed as she waited with her ears pricked.

Finally, a rumble reached her from afar, but she was not sure what vehicle it was. It grew louder and then she heard that unmistakable Melbourne squeal of metal on metal. A Number 11 tram glided by. She sat up and turned on the light. Would she go with it or use her loophole of seeing what came next? She stood there looking in the mirror and asked herself; 'how does it feel in my guts?' The reply was clear; it felt right, but she knew Kasper may well disagree.

She checked herself in the mirror and tidied her hair as she heard a car rumble by. She slipped her feet back into her sandals, and before leaving the room she rubbed the lucky elephant statue Kasper kept on his desk. She noted with approval that it was an African, not an Asian, she elephant.

The two men stopped speaking when Serene suddenly re-entered the room. She went to the kitchen bench, put the kettle on, and sat down with the two men.

She addressed Ebbe, 'Ebbe I want to tell you about me, as I think Kasper has not told you much.' She glanced at Kasper who shook his head to indicate that he had not.

'Maybe you can help me,' she added. Kasper did not know where she was headed but hoped that she did.

Serene went on to tell her story briefly; her childhood, her insult of the royal family, her interrogation, her spying, her flight, her asylum rejection in Australia and her time in hiding. She even admitted to them that it was a big gamble telling a foreign policeman, but she was keen to push on. The two men sat listening attentively.

'On the day of the fire, I had a meeting with my lawyer. I told her my boyfriend was a Danish VIP. That's all. Not a prince. I asked her if we were able to marry in Australia. She said yes and that it might help my case especially if he was an Australian. I came up to Commonplace the next day to ask you to marry me, Kasper.' She paused. 'But you had become Eric.'

She noticed that Kasper's eyes shone deep and liquid, but he did not speak before she went on. 'My lawyer also thought that I might get travel documents from the Danes and go there and get asylum, especially if my boyfriend was a very, very important person. Or perhaps even the Danish government might get my King to pardon me and give me a passport. And bloody hell, now I cannot marry you Kasper, or should I say Chris, 'cos you're bloody dead. But perhaps the Danes might still help me. I need help.' She turned abruptly towards Ebbe. 'Can you help me Ebbe?' She stopped, breathed out forcefully, then looked him right in the eye. 'Is there any chance? What a pity the Danes have never heard of me,' she added anxiously.

'Yes, they have!' Chris interjected, 'My dear sister offered you her condolences at my funeral. I had felt a bit guilty about mentioning you in my emails to her. No details. But now I am glad I did.'

Chris rose and squeezed her tight from behind her chair. Serene was not at all upset. She thought this might be a lucky break.

'Ebbe, will you take on my case? Please. You must have some good contacts back home. I will do all I can to help, and I am sure my lawyer will, too,' Serene pleaded.

But it was Chris who spoke first. 'Oh, Serene I had no idea, I would have said yes, yes, yes to marriage! It all makes sense, your plan, I mean.'

He stood with his arms around her. But Serene's eyes did not leave Ebbe's. Ebbe had been thinking hard. He had not expected this googly to come his way. He imagined what the tumult at Kastrup airport would have been like as the proud prince and his bride stepped from the plane. But that was not possible now.

Serene took up her cause again, 'So as the de facto widow of your dear Prince, so tragically stolen from his loyal people when merely a callow youth, I might have a chance?'

Ebbe did not answer right away but he had formed a firm opinion. Surely, he could help leverage all the grief and sorrow, all the human sentiment, the sympathy, and the urge to put things right when they never can be again. Harness all that emotion to support a grieving (de facto) black African widow, a democracy activist being hounded by her own vengeful King and government, so unfairly. Surely such a cause he could make succeed. What's more, she would never be the queen of Denmark now. Just the widow. Surely Christian's good parents, the government, the church, the human rights advocates and lawyers, the African aid organisations and the unions would join the cause. It might just work.

'Okay, I will do it,' Ebbe finally agreed. 'I think it is possible.' He smiled and quickly looked up at Christian asking, 'But where would all this leave you?'

Christian took his arms from around Serene and raised them in the air in mock surrender, 'I have no idea,' he replied, 'all I know is I have made my bed and now I must lie in it. If Serene can get asylum and a visa in Denmark that would be a wonderful thing.'

Serene beamed at them both and had one more thing to announce. 'Eric, or Chris, I should have told you this months ago. I am sorry for hiding it from you. My real name is Senty, and my surname is Jele. Senty Jele. But I want you never to call me Senty Jele in Australia. Okay? I am just Serene.'

Both men nodded and Serene went to make a pot of tea. It had been a dinner to remember, and she was proud of herself. The universe had been kind to her on this occasion.

Ebbe declined a cup of tea. He had to get back to his Castlemaine motel and had a lot to do. He was hatching a plan he was sure would detain him in Australia a bit longer. It had been an extraordinary evening and he felt energised, even enthused. Serene had made quite an impression on him. In his head he began to draft his next report to his superiors. This one would not be humdrum. He started putting it on paper as soon as the train headed north to Castlemaine. There were few passengers on the last train late that night, and most had their ear buds in and their eyes closed.

After Ebbe departed, Chris and Serene toasted the plan with cups of tea in Swazi and Danish, then did the dishes. In bed they talked well into the night. And when they eventually turned off the light, they bid each other a good night with, 'Goodnight, Eric,' and 'Goodnight Senty.'

She jabbed him in the ribs, 'Serene, please.'

He corrected himself, but as Chris fell asleep a shadow crossed his thoughts. Would he end up separated from Serene, forever by 20 thousand kilometres?

CHAPTER TWENTY EIGHT

The next day Ebbe got stuck into his new assignment as he breakfasted at the Melon Cauliflower. Four days later he sent a lengthy, carefully crafted report to Borgen marked Highly Confidential. In part it read:

"I have finally been able to locate and interview Ms Senty Jele who was in a relationship with Prince Christian at the time of his sad passing. It is clear this relationship was close, mutual and sexual. Ms Jele is a citizen of Swaziland (Eswatini) and has known the prince for approximately 9 months. She was not present at the time of the fire in which the prince sadly perished. I am particularly keen to report on her dire circumstances in the hope that some assistance may be provided to her by the Danish state. Her status in Australia is most precarious as she entered the country two years ago to seek asylum as a refugee on the grounds that she is facing persecution in her own country for her political views and previous political actions. A country she has fled. Unfortunately, and unjustly, her request for asylum was rejected by the Australian government and she is facing detention and repatriation back to Swaziland to almost certain imprisonment and punishment, with possible death. She has no residency or work status in Australia, and is supported by charities and ex-compatriots, as she seeks to avoid detention. She plans to appeal the initial rejection of her asylum claim. I have spoken to her lawyer Zoe Clarke, who was able to confirm the facts above. As the de

facto widow of Prince Christian, I believe strongly that Ms Jele would be a most worthy candidate for support in whatever forms possible by the State of Denmark. I am sure that this would be a fitting expression of the late Prince's wishes and would bring great credit on the Danish government and kingdom both at home and internationally."

Ebbe briefed the Danish ambassador and was also able to speak to Christian's parents briefly after quite a few attempts. They seemed sympathetic. He also briefed Zoe Clarke who recommended that Serene seek legal representation from the best human rights lawyers in Copenhagen, and after some research, Ebbe sought the services of Bang and Laudrup on Serene's behalf. Zoe also raised the possibility that the Australian authorities might be glad to see the back of Serene. Ebbe suggested to Zoe that he would be the right person to escort her on the flight back to Denmark if the plan succeeded and Zoe agreed. Zoe also raised the need for Serene to prepare a media pack with the most favourable multimedia material including a personal plea from Serene to the Danes for help.

She suggested that Ebbe coach Serene in a few suitable phrases in Danish like, 'I really loved Prince Christian. He was a wonderful man.' And 'I am very frightened of being sent back to Swaziland.'

Ebbe readily agreed to raise it with Serene.

A cautious reply from the Ministry in Copenhagen arrived a week later. Ebbe arranged to meet with Serene under the rotunda in the Castlemaine Botanical Gardens. She greeted him warmly with a hug. Despite himself, Ebbe wondered whether this was the first time he had been in the embrace of a black woman. They sat down in the shade as a flock of resident ducks approached looking for handouts, and after some small talk he trepidatiously translated and read her the most telling part of the reply from Copenhagen:

"We are considering what support we might wish to offer the young woman. We are keen to ascertain before we might make any decision three things:

a) whether she has borne a child during the time she has known the prince,

b) whether she is currently pregnant,

c) whether she intends to claim that any child or children she has, or might have due to a current pregnancy, are fathered by the prince.

DNA testing would need to be carried out to our satisfaction to support or disprove any claims she may make about paternity. Other relevant material such as gynaecological reports would also be important to establish the validity of any such claims.

Further to any decision we might make, the woman would be required to formally relinquish any claims she or any of her offspring or family members might make now, or in the future to royal or aristocratic status, or on the state purse."

Serene threw back her head and laughed sarcastically. 'I am tempted to tell them I am expecting twins just to make them shit their royal pants. But that might be self-sabotage. The answers are no, no and no!'

Ebbe had not been looking forward to raising these matters with Serene, nor with Christian, and was most relieved she was not insulted, and her answers were three straightforward "no's". But part of him could not avoid imagining the delicious scenario – a black half-African claimant to the Danish throne.

Son or daughter of Prince Christian or perhaps twins! If a son, he would have to be christened Frederik and surely Margrethe if a daughter.

CHAPTER TWENTY NINE

It was a long time before Chris would see Serene again. In the beginning he was mighty relieved and proud that she had been granted asylum in Denmark. He recalled vividly the day she had flown out with Ebbe. Chris had spent the day before with her in Melbourne. He had taken time off from work and went with her down to St Kilda for lunch at the pier cafe and a swim in the sea. In the afternoon a summer squall came up the bay. A band of thick black clouds arrived with rain carried on the wind. The temperature fell ten degrees. Sand blew up the beach and all the bathers grabbed their things and ran for cover. The Esplanade Hotel offered them refuge and they dashed inside laughing and rubbing their eyes. An episode of Melbourne's fickle weather was a fitting last day for Serene.

In the evening, they attended a farewell dinner for Serene at Pam and Robert's safe house where he was introduced simply as Eric, a friend of Serene's. The other two guests were Tandzi and Sabelo. Serene introduced them as her Swazi friends and supporters.

Chris recalled that Serene was on edge that night, as tomorrow she had to face the authorities at the airport. Zoe Clarke had assured her that a diplomatic agreement between Denmark and Australia meant that she had free passage out of the country, but Chris knew it had not really assuaged Serene's fears. She was preoccupied with the thought of being detained. Seeing her compatriots over dinner had triggered her recall of the details of the several deaths in detention of activists in her homeland. Serene made a brief speech after dinner where she thanked everyone for the love and support she had received in Australia.

She hoped she would come back one day and added, 'If tomorrow I end up in detention, please do not forget me.'

Chris recalled that a shiver went down his spine at the possibility as he reassured her that it would not happen.

They went to bed late and before turning off the light Serene had something to ask. 'Look I know this is really none of my business, but I will probably have to meet your family once I get to Denmark.'

Before she could continue Chris interjected, 'yes I have been thinking of that for ages.'

'So, what will I say? Have you told any of them?' she added.

'No. Oh I have so wanted to. But Ser, I know it will be very hard for you, but can you please not tell them that I am alive. It would ruin everything.' he pleaded.

'Not even a secret chat with your sister?' she gently suggested.

'That is so tempting but I am so scared it would leak out. If the police here found out I would get arrested. Please do not,' he implored.

'Okay. I can keep a secret,' she assured him. 'In fact, we are both very good at that.'

They could not sleep, being both full of the same anxious

energy and after a while they got up. In the end they started watching the Danish classic "Babette's Feast" but fell asleep halfway through, around 3 am. It seemed like ten minutes later that the doorbell awoke them. It was 8 am and there stood Ebbe and Zoe, all smiles, behind them a silver top taxi stood idling in the street. It was a cool, overcast morning and the streets were still damp from yesterday's rain. Chris longed to go with them to the airport, too, but knew he must not. He stayed inside, out of sight of Zoe. Serene clung to him, and they both tearfully vowed their eternal love before she left the flat.

'I will come back as soon as I can,' were Serene's parting words; an element of truth given in that pledge.

At Tullamarine they had no difficulties. Zoe passed Serene the travel documents and the three went to the check-in desk. When Serene presented her papers the airline clerk showed no interest. At the security barrier she presented her papers again. The officer asked her to wait and made a phone call. He spoke briefly on the phone. Serene felt sweat appear on her brow.

But a big smile spread across his face as he waved her through with the parting words, 'I am sorry we did not treat you better.' It seemed that he was expecting her.

Serene knew she had been holding her breath and let out a massive sigh. Ebbe followed her through, and they turned and waved to Zoe. She gave them a big thumbs up. Serene and Ebbe headed for the departure gate. In 45 minutes, they would be in the air. 24 hours later they passed smoothly through Kastrup airport and were met by an officer from the Foreign Office. Her life had entered a whole new chapter.

CHAPTER THIRTY

The next two years dragged on for Chris. He had a foreign name and identity, little money, few friends and he could not contact his family. He remained anxious, worrying that someone would recognise him. He missed Serene terribly. But the worst was his nagging guilt at how he had misled Isabella, in particular, as well as his parents and the twins, to believe he was dead. Time after time he wanted to send her a message, something cryptic that she would understand. He brooded often over the many ways he could do this and ask for her understanding and conspiratorial silence. But every time he hatched a plan and was at the point of acting, he paused and put it off until another day. But he knew one day he must do it.

He had finally found a job and that was hard. He had no contacts, nor did he have qualifications or training and no work permit; everything bosses required. Eric, he discovered, had been in Australia as a tourist. Eric's money was almost gone, and Chris thought he might have to abandon the apartment and live on the streets. His job was kitchen hand in a big hotel, The Pilgrim, in Collins Street.

Along with most of the other hospitality staff at the hotel, he was employed illegally and paid cash in hand. He learned that this was a long-standing practice in Australia, as it kept the labour costs modest and the profits high for the employer and gave an income to people without a legal right to work. His pay was meagre, but he could scrape by.

Chris did not mind the work. It got him out of the flat and out of his head. He slowly connected with people. But it was another world from his time at Commonplace. His colleagues were a mini United Nations of people. He did eventually make two firm friends. One by the name of Harry Lim, from Hong Kong. He overstayed his student visa after dropping out of his Masters degree at Monash University. He was about 30, short, overweight and jovial. He had no intention of returning to Hong Kong as he had been heavily involved in the pro-democracy movement there as a younger man.

The other called himself Said Zaheer, from Pakistan. He had come as a tourist five years ago under the misapprehension that it would be easy enough to get a work permit and a good job. He was supporting his wife and two children in Lahore, so he worked long and hard. He was thin and serious, a devout Muslim and a cricket tragic. Harry and Said had both trained in engineering but had no prospects in that field in Australia. The three friends occasionally played badminton together, a sport they had in common. Chris found four racquets in an opportunity shop for eight dollars. They were not the most modern weapons but would do for a hit and giggle.

After three months as a kitchen hand, Chris' boss offered to promote him to waiter. The boss explained Chris appeared to be intelligent and polite and spoke good English. Chris thought he might possess another characteristic that had influenced the boss' choice; white skin, but he did not raise it.

It would mean a higher wage and Chris readily agreed to the new role. He had done a little waiting at Commonplace when they had paying guests. He also thought the chances of him being identified were slim and he could always laugh it off.

Waiting on tables was better than washing dishes; more pay and the occasional tip and much kinder on his hands. Occasionally he was asked where he came from and after saying Scandinavia for a few months he deigned to say Denmark. He learned that most locals knew almost nothing about Denmark and was always secretly amused when diners asked if he spoke Dutch.

At home he spent hours on face time with Serene. When he got in from work around midnight it was 2 pm in Denmark and a good time to connect. Serene entertained him with her vivid descriptions of her first encounters with the Danish winter. How her eyebrows and nose mucous froze as she walked down the street. She reported her fondness for hot mulled wine she bought on the street corners and for the little Danish sausage vans plying the streets. But the cold and severe lack of sunlight got her down.

Serene reported that she had been received with great kindness by the Danish authorities and people. The media had pestered her for a while, but she had refused all requests for interviews. From incognito to minor celebrity was quite a leap, she told Chris, but the attention had died down after the first few months. She had been to Amalienborg and met Chris' family, but she had felt very awkward keeping her huge secret to herself. Serene also reported that Isabella had plied her with questions about the fire and Chris, and that she felt comfortable replying that she had not been there and so had no personal account of what happened.

But the hardest challenge for Serene, she reported, was when Chris' family took her to Roskilde Cathedral to pay her respects at Chris' tomb. Like any royal outing it attracted a crowd of onlookers who were kept beyond the cordons. Yet despite the cold, mournful atmosphere, long faces and solemnity she had great trouble keeping a straight face. Luckily, she could manoeuvre her long winter scarf over her mouth to hide it at strategic moments. She told Chris she was so glad to get out of there without giving herself away.

Serene happily described how she had found a room in the apartment of a middle-aged Swazi couple from Lobamba who had lived in Copenhagen for 15 years and taken out citizenship. They had no children and had treated her like a daughter from day one. She had learned the uniquely Danish word *hygge* and began to experience with her hosts what it represented; cosiness, snugness and connection. The apartment was in the suburb of Amager, and she was able to walk along the beach each day, enjoying the icy water and the sight of ships passing under the great bridge to Sweden.

The Danish state had granted her asylum and given her a small allowance. She was spending her time as a volunteer at a refugee support service and taking Danish lessons. She tried out her fledgling Danish on Chris each time they chatted with much amusement from him. At his teasing, she had to point out that she already spoke Swazi, English, Afrikaans and Zulu but those guttural Danish vowels were trickier than those in Afrikaans.

Serene told Chris she was given a three month's visa, but she was not to leave Denmark in that time. Further extensions for three months then six months followed but her lawyer advised her each time that, as she had no Danish passport yet, it would be difficult, if not impossible, for her to travel freely to countries that required her to produce one. Of course, she asked when she would be able to travel back to Australia. Reluctantly she told Chris that the advice was clear. She had to get a visa from the Australian government to get into Australia. But she also had to demonstrate that she was committed to Denmark, so that she would be allowed to re-enter. Her lawyer advised her that after a year in Denmark, it would probably be seen as okay by the Danish authorities for her to apply for a visa and leave for Australia, if she got it.

As the first year of their separation dragged on Chris understood that a reunion would not happen any time soon. He missed her greatly and felt sad, especially when not at work.

His other nagging concern was Eric's family. After the fire they tried to make contact with their family member regularly. He could see from Eric's previous emails that Eric had been in regular contact with them. At first Chris had no idea what to do when the cheery request for news arrived. Should he tell them that Eric was alive, or indeed dead? One was a lie and the other could expose him and his own deceit. In the end he decided to ignore all correspondence from Eric's family or friends. Slowly the messages came less frequently, but every single time he opened Eric's email he felt a pang of anxiety and guilt at the prospect of another plea for news from Eric's family.

In August of that first year, it came to a head. One Friday afternoon he was asleep before his usual evening shift. At 4 pm two police officers knocked loudly on his door, rousing Chris from a deep slumber. He threw on some track pants and went to the door. The sight of the police made his heart leap into his throat.

Constable Meyers and Senior Constable Everett introduced themselves. The constable asked, 'Are you Eric Anderson?'

Chris answered yes and invited them in. They came into the small lounge and kitchen area and remained standing.

The constable said, 'Your family in Scotland has reported you as a missing person. Did you know that?'

Chris was thinking fast, 'Well no, but I am not surprised.'

'Why is that?' the senior constable asked.

'I am sort of estranged from them,' Chris replied, 'I don't want to contact them, not since my father died,' he added hoping desperately this would be an okay thing to say. He felt his face redden.

'Okay, well look, that is your decision,' the senior constable replied writing in her notebook. 'We will have to notify them that you are alive and well. We will also report that you want no contact. We cannot force you to. You are an adult.' She closed her notebook and motioned to her colleague that the visit was over.

Her colleague spoke up. 'Look mate, why don't you do your family a big favour? Just send them a bloody message! No skin off your nose and it will put their minds at ease. What do you reckon?'

Chris knew he had to agree, 'You are right. I should have

done that months ago. I don't really want them to worry.'

'Good man,' the senior constable replied as she led her colleague out the door. 'Our job is done. Sorry to wake you,' she added.

'That's okay,' Chris said as he closed the door behind them.

As the police officers reached their car, Constable Meyers stopped abruptly and said to her colleague. 'We really should have checked his ID you know. Shall I run back and get it?'

'Nah, don't bother,' her more senior colleague replied. 'He looks like the real deal. Besides, I want to finish this shift on time. My motorbike's at the mechanic's. I must retrieve it.'

Chris had two hours before his work shift started and he sat brooding as the kettle boiled. Why was it Eric and not him who ran into the hut? He knew that if the police had asked him for ID or had checked out his visa status he might have been in extremely hot water. It was a near thing.

Chris spent his second anniversary in Australia quietly. There was little to celebrate, and he was waiting to get the news from Serene. He had pleaded with her to apply for an Australian visa as soon as her year was up. It had not been easy for her, she told him, as everyone who knew she wished to return had just one question; 'after the way they treated you why on earth would you want to go back down to Australia?' She was never able to offer the main reason or any reasonable explanation. In her tourist visa application, she stated that she wanted to have a holiday and visit acquaintances.

Chris checked with her every night and for two weeks she replied each time, 'No news yet.' He kept his fingers and toes crossed. If he had any faith left, he would have prayed.

Then Serene contacted him unexpectedly as he was preparing for work at 5 pm. The moment he saw her face appear on the screen he knew what the answer was.

'They said no Chris,' she said bursting into tears, 'They will not let me come back.'

'Oh no. That is terrible!' Chris screamed. 'How could they do this?' he added, sad and furious.

'They gave no reasons. I don't know why,' Serene replied bitterly. 'I am so sorry Chris. They told me it might fail but I didn't really believe them.' The words spilled out of her, 'they said I can appeal but it would take a long time and they said I would probably fail again. It is just hopeless. I might never see you again.'

Chris did not know what to say. The implications were dawning on him. He had always assumed she could come back. Without another option he blurted out, 'Well, I will have to come to you.'

But he had no idea what he would do. He just wanted to be reassuring and to carry some hope. All he was certain of is that he would have to spend a lot more time apart from her. He promised to chat with her again as soon as he got home from work that night. Sadly, they signed off.

Chris stormed around the apartment yelling at the walls, 'Trapped, trapped, trapped!' But soon he had to get ready to catch the train alongside St Georges Road to The Pilgrim. He stared blankly out the window feeling sadder than he had in a long time. It was going to be a hard shift.

CHAPTER THIRTY ONE

It took a fortnight for Chris and Serene to decide upon a plan. Chris was to organise a British passport with his photo in it and save enough money for an airfare, one way. Serene would travel to Stockholm as she could cross the bridge to Sweden without a passport or visa. He would meet her there. Their plans after that was anyone's guess and they dared not discuss a future together.

On his meagre income Chris could only save about 50 dollars a week. He lamented to Serene that it would take years for him to raise the money. He looked for a second job without luck, though his boss gave him extra shifts from time to time. He spent hours alone in his apartment ruminating about his childhood. He appreciated that the genesis of his decision that fateful day to utter the word "Eric" probably lay way back in his past.

He came to understand, the idea that something was wrong with his destiny, had taken hold of him after he met the elephant at the zoo, and had developed over the next few years whenever he remembered the elephant's words and sorrow. A feeling of unease and displacement had arisen, also, whenever he was in church. And royal princes must do a lot of churching in Denmark. Lutheranism, the state religion with the monarch at the head meant he was often dragged along to services, or funerals. Around this time, he had also discovered that the Danish monarch is legally required to be a member of the Lutheran church in good standing. So much for religious freedom in the 21st century. In his loneliness, he pondered why he was so sceptical or even cynical at such an early age. Often, he felt so angry with who he had become. He was born to privilege and entitlement. Why could he not have just toed the line and enjoyed his birthright like his father and the queen? They had rationalised it in terms of duty and service to the nation. Surely not such a hard ask for him?

It had come up, too, when he was at school. Perhaps it was because he was the first of Danish royal descent ever to attend a state school. School for Christian had been no festival of hygge. His unique status had attracted a lot of attention from his fellow students, the staff and the parents. And of course, the omnipresent media. He had been unprepared for the bouts of bullying he got both at state school then at Herlufsholm, the private toffs' boarding school he attended for a while. It started when was nine; in his third year. In English class, two boys had discovered that the word for king in Danish "kong" had a different reference in English, "King Kong." So, some boys had taken to calling him "Ape". They had found it highly amusing. He had not. And probably because of his discomfort, the taunting escalated: 'Ape, ape, ape!' had followed him around, day after day, and even followed him when he was sent to Herlufsholm. School had become an ordeal. Then he had a further ordeal, his conscription into the Hussars. His anxiety soured. He had tried to hide it as best he could.

Why did he hide it, he now wondered. Surely his parents would have intervened if he had told them. And they would have had it stopped forthwith. All he could conclude was that he would have been very embarrassed.

It is just so damn unfair, he had felt back then, that every other young person he met has some say about what they want to do with their lives, and what they want to believe and follow, except crown princes. No matter how determined a father could be to have his son join him in the family business, others had some choice. But his life, Christian had known from his teens, had been set in granite from the day of his birth. No matter what interests, education, qualifications or skills he might pursue, they would all be of no importance in determining what he would do in his life.

'This is such anathema,' he had thought back then, 'to the great, proud Danish culture of: choice, freedom, social mobility, education, skills development and self-actualisation.' By the time he was eighteen, his classmates had their career plans: pilot, architect, psychologist, chef, doctor, teacher, and so on. Well, he could have trained to be a ship's captain, he loved being out on the ocean, but he had doubted that he would be allowed to travel much. And not at all, once he became King, whenever that was to happen. Not that he had ever wanted to stay in the military, unlike his male ancestors but he had done his compulsory duty anyway. His father had been in the Army, Navy and Air Force - all three. He did not want such a career, he had thought, even back in his early teens.

Chris' stood up suddenly. He had been lying on his bed

fully absorbed in his past. He remembered with a sudden jolt that now he would never have to join the Air Force as he had promised. Perhaps the bushfire had been his sword. It had cut away his past and freed him of his pledge. He made a cup of coffee and felt a little better. He ate a bowl of muesli and prepared for work. There was the whole Australian experience outside.

But the next weekend his ennui and black mood were back. He woke on Sunday with an annoying tickle in his throat. He lay there thinking of Eric's death, as he did every morning, and then of his own. Nobody would miss him if he put an end to his misery. His family already knew he was dead, and he could not find the courage to tell them this was not true. Only one other person mattered to him, and Serene had taken full advantage of his royal status once he had told her and freed herself from the clutches of the Australian and Swazi police. She was busy creating a life for herself as a minor celebrity in Copenhagen and would not need him anymore. The annoying irritation in his throat returned and he forced himself out of bed. He took aspirin and returned to bed sucking a lozenge. Death preoccupied his thoughts, as he recalled in great detail his first encounter with death.

2020 had been a huge year for Chris, and the rest of the world. He had turned 15 years old, and humanity was reminded of how fragile we all are in the face of a virulent, invisible, viral enemy: Covid19. The Danes had no tradition of wearing face masks or social distancing. Indeed, for some, the full body hug had become popular in social culture, but the handshake was still very much the norm. For the first few months of the new year as the news was spreading about this nasty virus coming out of China, the Danes noticed some Asian tourists were wearing masks. Scandinavia was just coming out of winter, so there were only a few visitors at the Little Mermaid and along Ny Haven.

Chris had gone about things as usual but soon everything changed for the worse. His school closed and he found himself mostly confined to the palace as the number of Danes with the virus was soaring. Masks suddenly became an annoying necessity, even for members of the Royal Family. The physicians that looked after him had reported that a lad of his age was most unlikely to get the virus, but they still had to be careful. If they contracted it, they could infect older, more vulnerable members of the family. So, when Chris felt the first signs of a cold coming on, he had not been concerned at all. He had suffered spring colds before, and this seemed no different. But by the third day he knew something was wrong. The doctor was summoned with a Covid test kit. The swab had gone up Christian's nose and tickled his brain, and to his alarm he tested positive. The doctor said it should not be too serious and he would probably throw it off in a day or two, but Christian soon developed the strong belief that he was going to die.

The doctor moved him to a suite in the guest wing of the palace away from his family and his spirits plunged. He was very worried and extremely sick. His breathing became harder and harder, and his throat became sorer. The doctor fitted him with an oxygen mask and that helped a bit, but swallowing was still agony. He had never been this sick before, and he was very afraid. Thousands of people had been dying in Denmark and around the world, and he believed he might, too. Dying terrified him. In the last few years, he had all but given up his belief in God. His rational, sceptical mind was unable to concede that a Lutheran God was up there in heaven with Jesus and the Holy Ghost alongside, directing traffic, gatekeeping, throwing down the occasional miracle, inspiring good deeds, receiving prayers, punishing some sinners, forgiving others, curing some, letting others die, and overseeing the appointment of priests and church officials. His faith had been severely weakened despite what the Danish Constitution had in store for him. His attendance at church services had become only tolerable for the music and singing and the occasional interesting sermon.

He kept his lack of faith to himself. Yet in these desperate hours he was unable to fully concede that he would just totally cease to exist after his death. No soul, no spirit, no afterlife, no ascension to a heavenly kingdom or paradise, or descent to hell, no divine right to protect him. During those long days while his immune system fought hard for his survival, all these ideas and fears, doubts and deliberations had crowded in and had taken up his febrile waking hours. And his sleeping hours, too. He had dreamt repeatedly of being locked in a long hall, a bit like the knighthood hall at Rosenborg Castle, one half of it was ice cold while the other half was boiling hot. He was naked except for a crown affixed to his head. Nowhere in the room was he able to find a bearable temperature or any comfort. He had alternately frozen and roasted as he ran back and forth. Outside the room he had been aware of crowds of people cheering and applauding, in ebbing and flowing waves of sound. He had shouted for help, but none came.

The royal media unit had predictably sent out carefully crafted statements assuring the public that the young prince was okay. Yes, he did have the virus, but it was not serious. All those in the royal household and in the government who knew how sick he really was, had hoped and prayed that he would pull through. Prayers for his recovery had sounded out from churches across the land even though the congregations were absent. Slowly his crisis had passed. He had fought the virus off with the tenacity of Luther and he needed the oxygen mask less often. The horrid dreams had faded and on a most memorable day his doctors had declared him fit and well.

When his physician had brought him the news and given him another lung capacity test Chris' mood had been almost chirpy, 'I feel as if I have dodged a bullet doctor,' he said proudly.

'No,' the doctor had replied, 'you were hit by a bullet. But we have no idea who fired the gun.'

Chris had been thrown into a deep reflection as his strength and appetite had slowly returned. Why had he been singled out? What could he have learnt from this? His thoughts had returned to three ideas. He was given a second chance. He was strong and healthy, and he had to make something of his life. No-one else in his family had been infected, he was relieved to learn, and when the vaccine arrived eight months later, the government rushed the royal family to the head of the queue. But about a year later his mother got Covid, too, and he supported her as best he could. She recovered quickly.

Chris returned to the here and now when his stomach rumbled. Suicide was a choice he could never make, no matter how, at times like this, it appeared to be a solution to his problems. He was guilty about what he had done but felt no shame. He would find a better solution. He reminded himself of those he loved and the many joys of his year in Australia, and he had his sword and megaphone to help him. He sat up and looked at the Scottish flag on the wall, the cross of St Andrew, and wondered why Anderson was a Scottish name, not Andrewson.

CHAPTER THIRTY TWO

Financial salvation came from a most unexpected quarter six months later when an email appeared in Eric's inbox amongst the junk mail and spam. It was from a Melbourne solicitor making contact to finalise the estate of the late Magnus Anderson. Chris had completely forgotten that Eric had come to Australia to see his father who had promptly died. This explained why there were never emails from his father. He chastised himself for forgetting why Eric had no contact from his father. But now he knew, because Eric was being contacted to take receipt of 300,000 Aussie dollars from his father's estate. Chris could not believe his good fortune.

The money would get him a top-quality and undetectable alteration to Eric's passport, an airfare, and some warm winter clothes that fitted him. He rushed to tell Serene the good news that night after work.

She was much less ebullient. 'But Chris, this is not your money. You should not touch it. If you do, it is akin to theft.'

Chris was unmoved. 'Well, you may be right, but I just cannot let this chance go by. Do you know it means I will be able to come to you much sooner? Without it I will take years,' he appealed.

'Well, alright. But only take as much as you need. Maybe

one day you will be able to pay it back,' she agreed. It had not been too hard to convince her of the merit of his position.

Chris had not thought of it as theft. This inheritance windfall was something that at one level he felt was his entitlement rather than something he was stealing. Up until the fire and his new identity he had hardly thought of money at all. It was just something that appeared in his bank account every month. A massive sum of money he appreciated. Especially now he was a cash-in-hand waiter and knew a whole community of poor working people at The Pilgrim. Money had become a preoccupation for Chris, as it was for so many others.

He enjoyed his time as a waiter but not the poverty. Now, all that was coming to an end. He told his boss that he had come into some money and was leaving as soon as he could get his travel plans in place. The boss was indifferent and simply asked for as much notice as possible.

CHAPTER THIRTY THREE

I t took Chris another four months to get the arrangements in place. The hardest job was getting his photo into Eric's passport. His facial features were not a lot like Eric's, and he knew he could not just go to the UK High Commission and request a new passport with his own photo. Serene suggested he contact Tandzi and Sabelo from her farewell dinner. They were able to put him in touch with a reliable supplier of fake and forged passports. For $10,000 they would take Eric's existing passport and return it with Chris' mugshot. They guaranteed the fake photo would be undetectable. Chris paid up in advance and provided new passport photos. Four weeks later the passport came back, and he thought it looked the goods. He knew there would only be one way to find out and thought it would probably be easier to have it pass muster in Stockholm than in London.

There was a lot he had started to miss over the last year or so. He missed Commonplace and all the characters there, just 112 kilometres away, but totally off limits. He missed his sisters and brother more and more. He started following them and his nephews and nieces in the media. He also missed his friends from the past and looked for some of them on social media. To his surprise he also missed the uniquely Danish culture and customs; the hygge, the smørrebrød, the candles, the frozen lakes, the songs, the handball, the rye bread, and the bridge to Sweden. But his strongest regret was over what he had avoided. He had to hide from Eric's family, and they did not know their son was dead. He had just vanished from their lives, and he had ignored the efforts they had made to contact him. He had not followed up the police officer's advice to make contact. It would be just wrong to let them still think that Eric was alive. Now his lies began to gnaw at him.

Then, as Chris knew it surely would, the inevitable occurred in his family that year, the death of Queen Margrethe. She had achieved the impressive age of 88 and had reigned for exactly 52 years before her abdication in January 2024. Not too bad for a smoker, he thought. He was fond of his grandmother but had never felt very close. It was her late husband Henri he had felt connected to.

He watched his family mourn closely from afar and noticed Crown Princess Isabella wearing her royal Order of the Elephant. He watched intently all the ceremonial events that followed the Queen's death; the lying in-state, the funeral, the procession on the special funeral train out to Roskilde and her interment at the cathedral in the family chapel right alongside him. She had designed her own sepulchre ten years before and it was certainly more eye-catching than his. The traditionalists in the aristocracy and patriarchs elsewhere argued after Isabella's elevation that, as a female, she should be bypassed, and Prince Vincent should be the next monarch, but the government held firm. A big part of him longed to be with them.

On the Saturday, after his last shift at The Pilgrim the

previous night, he played badminton with Said and Harry for the last time and they went for dinner at the Delhi Belly in Little Lonsdale Street. He picked up the bill for his friends and wished them the fondest of goodbyes. Then he gave them each one thousand dollars in crisp hundred-dollar notes. He knew Serene would not approve and the men protested briefly but he knew they were really delighted. Together they hugged him out on the street. He remembered nostalgically the group hugs at Commonplace.

CHAPTER THIRTY FOUR

Chris landed at Arlanda Airport outside Stockholm wearing a face mask and a heavy cold. His nose dripped like a leaky tap and his throat was sore and rough. His cold distracted him from his passport photograph and he passed smoothly through the immigration checkpoint. He did, however, get escorted to the virus control station. He was asked if he had ever had Covid19 and if he had been vaccinated. He said yes to both without thinking and was asked for documentation. He cursed himself. He had no idea about Eric's viral history and no documentation.

He replied, 'I am so sorry. I forgot to bring the papers.'

The officer asked him to wait and made a phone call.

Chris understood Swedish well. He liked the sing song delivery, so different from its Danish cousin. The officer asked, 'He's not well and has no vaccination papers. He's English and was in Australia. Will he need seven or 14 days?'

Chris could not hear the reply. He longed to ask the officer what the answer was but knew he could not. He was a Scotsman and did not understand Swedish. But he was sure he did not have Covid19 of any variant. His cold was nothing like the illness he had survived as a teen. But he was facing a fortnight's quarantine anyway.

The officer turned to him again and asked in crisp English,

'Are you prepared to take a rapid Covid test?'

Chris replied. 'Of course.'

The officer directed him to a small clinic off the main hall and a clinician dressed in white with a blue cross on her shoulder administered the nasal swab. The clinician withdrew the probe and asked him to wait five minutes for the result.

Chris sat there and watched the hands on the wall clock crawl agonisingly slowly clockwise. Would he see Serene in 15 minutes? Or would it be two weeks, even if his test was negative?

After what was more like 20 minutes than five, he was convinced, the clinician returned and said blandly, 'The test was negative. You are free to go.'

Chris stood up and felt like hugging her. Instead, he spluttered, 'thank you, thank you very much.'

He retrieved his bag from the luggage carousel and pulled out his new winter coat and his woollen green and gold beanie. It was minus 7 degrees Celsius outside. In the exit hall milled a throng of people meeting the recent arrivals. Chris stood still while intensely scanning the crowd. Where is she? He searched the faces and the hand-held signs. He could not see her and felt the panic rise in his body. He stood there rooted to the floor trying to contradict the voice screaming within, 'She did not come!'

She approached him on his blind side. She was carrying a handmade A3-sized sign reading ERIC in big red letters. She was just inches from him when he sensed her presence and swung around.

'G'day mate, howya goin?' she asked in a fake Aussie drawl

as she leant forward and pecked his cheek.

Chris cried out in surprise and relief, 'Ahh you did come!'

Serene dropped her sign and Chris dropped his bag before they fully embraced. A Danish freelance journalist, who was at the airport meeting his Swedish friend, thought she looked familiar and snapped the couple's long embrace, just in case. No one else noticed.

The reunited couple had made a reservation at the Budget Inn for seven nights. It was cheap and close to the central station, but was no palace. After two days Chris' cold had subsided, and their two-year sexual hiatus ended. Like all good language students Serene had developed a new Danish sexual lexicon and used it freely. Chris approved and was able to teach her some of the finer nuances. He was also able to brush up on his basic Swazi vocabulary on the same topic. They only went outside every second day.

On the fourth day, Serene checked her phone and rushed to show Chris a message she had just received from a friend in Copenhagen. It was an article from the tabloid magazine *Nu Bladet*. Under the headline, "Has her prince come?" was the picture of their airport embrace. A breathy piece followed underneath in which the author wondered who the mystery man with widowed Senty Jele might be. It appears she had moved on. Chris was not mentioned but he sat there crestfallen and annoyed, nevertheless. He told Serene that he thought it now would only be a matter of time until his identity was revealed. He realised that he would have to bring his plans forward and get it done as soon as possible. Otherwise, it would be taken out of his hands.

That night he told Serene of his decision. He had assumed she would be dead against it. He also feared she might end their relationship, as he had many times before. But he was wrong on both counts. She accepted his plan with equanimity. She said it made a lot of sense. He was doing the right thing. She would stand by him. Her idea for their future together was to settle in the UK if she could not return to Australia, but she was happy to let it slide. His plan trumped hers, well and truly. They made detailed arrangements well into the night.

The next morning, he started to steel himself to make the call. He expected that this call would be the hardest conversation he had ever had in his life. Even harder than the one on the pontoon in the dam on the other side of the Earth. Luckily, he still had Isabella's private mobile number in his head. At 11 am he called her, and it took him three attempts to get the number right. He hoped she had not changed it. He had written down what he would say if she answered.

'Hello there, is this Isabella?' He croaked.

'Yes, who is it?' came her hesitant reply. Just occasionally she would answer callers whose names did not appear on her screen but usually she hung up immediately if she did not recognise the voice. Her private number was a state secret, but nuisance calls still got through. This time there was something about the voice that made her pause.

'You might recognise my voice Isa wizza. It's your brother Christian, I know this will be a big shock to you, but I am not dead,' he blurted out in a rush. His throat felt sandpaper dry. She hung up immediately.

Chris threw the phone onto the bed and went to get a glass of water. Maybe he would not be able to speak to her before he returned to Copenhagen. What a damn pity, but he could not blame her for hanging up.

His phone rang two minutes later. He grabbed it in total haste and saw her name appear. He fumbled for the button. It took him a further moment to get his name right and he answered, 'this is Christian.'

'Is it really you? You are dead. Are you a hoaxer? What is going on?' he heard his sister exclaim. 'But you called me Wizza. It must be you!'

'It is me. I am not dead. I am in Stockholm. I am so sorry. It was someone else who died in the fire, and I stole his identity. I have been such an idiot. But I had my reasons,' he said.

Isabella was lost for words for a minute. So many implications competed in her brain. She realised immediately that she would not have to be queen after all. She immediately dismissed the thought. Suddenly a rush of words, 'Hell Christian, how can you possibly be alive? Who is buried in Roskilde Cathedral? Oh, I am so happy, you are alive. What happened? Why are you in Sweden? Are you coming home?' Isabella poured out her surprise and disbelief.

'Yes, I am coming home as soon as possible. I am longing to see you again. I have missed you so much. Are you okay? Are you busy now? Can I tell you what happened?' The words tumbled out of him as the relief rushed in. He had done it. He would see her again, soon.

In reply Isabella asked the obvious question, 'Do Mum and Dad know yet? Oh my God, they will be amazed!'

'No, they do not know yet, Isa. I am too embarrassed to tell them. I thought if I told you first then maybe you could warn them,' he admitted.

She laughed aloud with shrill, sharp exhalation, 'You are such a coward! First you force me to become the Crown Princess and now you want me to do your dirty work. But I am so pleased that my big brother and heir apparent is alive, and so I will. And I will give them your number.'

'A thousand thanks and if you feel like it, please tell the twins, too. I have been following all of you on the internet like crazy.'

Two hours later they finished the call and Isabella rushed off to find the King and Queen and Vincent and Josephine.

Next, he made calls to Ebbe Mosegaard and to Morten Sand, Serene's lawyer at Bang and Laudrup. These calls were much, much easier. They decided on a plan and schedule very rapidly, and also set the date, time and place for the event. They had to hurry; time was certainly against them. The couple packed, checked out of the hotel and with their beanies pulled low and their scarves tugged high headed for the train en route to Senty's Copenhagen home.

The King and Queen did not attend, but Crown Princess Isabella joined her older brother at the media conference in Borgen. She sat on his right side; alongside her was Annette Buch, the head of communications at Amalienborg Palace. On Christian's left sat Serene and alongside her was Morten Sand. Christian had both a new haircut and new grey suit. He wore a red tie, and in his lapel shone a tiny silver elephant. He was clean shaven for the first time in more than three years.

273

Despite the short notice, the media centre was packed. At the appointed time, Morten Sand stood and held up both hands, palms facing the throng as the buzz subsided. He only spoke briefly, 'Thank you all for coming at such short notice. Christian will be making a statement. Annette Buch will then make a brief statement. Please turn your phones to off or silent during these statements. No questions will be taken afterwards.'

He sat down. Without further ado, Christian rose slowly and looked down at the assembled media and blinked three times. He could even remember a few of the faces from earlier times. Tightness gripped his abdomen. He took out his statement, found the first page and paused. 'Just get started,' he told himself. 'It will be better once you start.' Total silence awaited him as he drew breathe and began reading.

'First, I thank my dear sister Isabella, and my precious partner Senty Jele, for supporting me here today. I appreciate their care and love greatly. Next, I wish to sincerely apologise for all the pain I have caused many people since I faked my own death, withheld the truth and stole the identity of Eric Anderson, two years ago in Australia, after his tragic death. I particularly must apologise profusely to the family of Eric: his mother Helen, his brother Andrew, and his sister Joyce. I plan to travel to Scotland as soon as possible to offer them personally my profound condolences and to apologise for my cruel deception and fraud."

He paused and took a few sips of water for his dry throat.

'I also apologise to my dear parents, all my family and my friends here in Denmark and abroad for causing much unnecessary loss, grief and expense in such an uncaring and utterly selfish way. I have been deeply moved by the warmth and acceptance my family has shown me in the short time since my re-appearance, and I deeply regret the emotional distress and cost I have put them through in the last two years. In the time I have been away I have come to the difficult decision to give up my royal status. This means that I will be stepping down as Crown Prince and relinquishing and returning all positions, titles, honours, privileges and resources that I would be entitled to as a member of the Danish royal family. I wish to be known henceforth as Christian Frederiksen and to become an ordinary citizen and commoner. I will also be applying for joint Danish and Australian citizenship and hope that one day that might be possible. I also fully acknowledge and admit my culpability for the several crimes I committed as a result of the identity theft during my time in Australia. I plan to return to Australia to face justice and to make recompense for my wrongdoing.'

Christian paused again. He took another drink and looked to his left. He caught Senty's eye. He quickly looked back at his statement to stop the sadness and tears from welling. He clenched his buttocks hard and the urge to cry subsided. He returned to the statement:

'Finally, I must also apologise to my dear partner Senty Jele for implicating her in my deception and for convincing her to use my falsehoods as part of seeking asylum in Denmark. I am, however, so very grateful that she has found sanctuary here amongst kind, compassionate Danes and I thank my parents and the government wholeheartedly for giving her a safe place, free from the prospect of unjust persecution. I hope that my deception does not place her status in any jeopardy. We plan to marry immediately after this event. Thank you.'

Christian stopped. He could not immediately look Senty in the eye and instead looked around the media centre. He heard a very brief smattering of applause then a roar of voices struck him. He quickly sat down and glanced at Senty. She nodded and beamed at him. To her, Christian appeared pale and drawn as he smiled wanly back. She saw the tiredness and tears in his eyes, and she knew he had hardly slept last night.

Annette Bach now stood and waited for the uproar to abate, but it did not for some time. She stood there unmoved until it reached a level to her satisfaction before she spoke. 'The Palace asks all members of the media and the public to respect the privacy of the Royal family, and Christian and his partner, during this challenging and unprecedented time. Further statements will be issued by myself, and no doubt by the government also, to clarify any new arrangements that will need to be made. This will include organising the repatriation of the mortal remains of Mr Anderson to his next of kin in Scotland.'

The five of them stood as a wave of voices hit them from the floor. They turned and moved towards the exit door at the rear. Christian walked arm in arm with Serene on his right and Isabella on his left.

The legal, royal, diplomatic and administrative entanglement that ensued for the next 18 months in Denmark and Australia (and Eswatini) was unprecedented. Never before had a Crown Prince returned from the dead, abdicated at the same time, sought to marry a refugee from another monarchy who had gained her refugee status through falsehoods and then applied for dual citizenship, and sought citizenship of another country.

King Frederik was in a pickle. He had to consider carefully articles 21 and 25 of his special powers under the archaic Kings' Law. The first article meant that royal princes and princesses could only be taken to court with the approval of the monarch. There were calls for Christian's prosecution and he could make his son above the law. The second meant that princes and princesses had to seek his permission to marry and the leave the country. In the end agreement was reached.

The wedding was a small and private affair within Fredensborg Palace. Chris and Senty arranged for her parents to be invited and for their airfares to be paid, but they were denied passports. No media were invited, just 12 guests. Afterwards, a collection of 30 photographs from the wedding was released to the public. The Danish Air Force protected the airspace above the palace during the event, calling it a training exercise.

The Eswatini government sought Senty's immediate return and heavily lobbied the Australian Prime Minister Barty, seeking her help in pressing the Danish King and government to return Senty. The Prime Minister made a token attempt to cooperate but through back channels sent the opposite message to the Danes.

The citizenship matter was a thorny one for Australia. Both

the hard left and the hard right opposed granting Chris, and his wife, citizenship. Hostility towards Chris, Senty and the Danish authorities was fanned at the extremes of the political spectrum.

The parliamentary leader of the Australian New Front party, which held just two seats, Tibor Vallence thundered in parliament; 'The Danish Queen who was once our Mary has turned her back on her fatherland and renounced her citizenship a very long time ago. Why should we honour her son's criminal and deceitful behaviour with the great privilege of citizenship in our fair land? We no longer afford royals of any kind the rights and privileges they once enjoyed based entirely on birthright. The Danish authorities then had the effrontery to deceive us into hosting her reprobate son so he could carry out his criminal acts. Meanwhile his black, radical, leftie wife, another master of deception and deceit, hid here illegally with no right to be in our land, while she sponged off us and refused to face the law in her own land. Enough is enough. Their marriage is clearly a sham of convenience, so keep both these unwelcome foreigners out we say.' Later he 'corrected' the Hansard draft to remove the word 'black.' But Tibor was disappointed at the near total lack of interest the mainstream media showed in what he believed was his principled stance and Churchillian oratory and the speech passed with little fanfare into history.

Another pro-monarchy faction near the political centre had formed and took an entirely different approach. They argued that the British King should be ditched, and Christian installed as the King of Australia. After all, if the monarchy had to remain, at least he was half Australian, and the country would get a local head of state. Further, if Christian did not agree then Isabella must be queen of both lands; a new partnership for the third millennium.

More sensible views eventually prevailed as many voices expressed great sympathy for Chris and Senty. After all, Australia, according to them, was an inclusive and welcoming country full of misfits, refugees and others escaping their past for a fresh start. Indeed, it was the antipodean equivalent of the same groups of people in Denmark that had convinced the Danish government to grant Senty asylum.

A deal was finally struck that the Australian government could argue was in the national interest. Chris' admission of guilt and willingness to face the music and make reparation was a telling factor. Indeed, putting a royal in court in Australia had a clear appeal to moderate republicans and it meant the Danish King could avoid any court case in Denmark.

CHAPTER THIRTY FIVE

The dinner at the big farmhouse in Harcourt was a happy affair for all seven of the residents. Two married couples, two youths and the infant were all in high spirits. The table was decorated with cherry blossoms and wattle. They celebrated the spring Equinox and the first birthday of the gorgeous girl Thula.

Each of the four adults had prepared a dish. Valerie baked an apple birthday cake topped with a big beeswax candle. Her husband Ebbe tried his hand at scalloped potatoes with butter, peas, carrots, and parsley sauce. Senty had wanted to serve roast ostrich, a Swazi favourite. She even considered emu but settled instead for mealies with a spicy beef stew and greens. Her husband Chris served up grilled salmon with mörk, a chocolate syrup. Chris tucked in. It might be the last chance for him to dine with his family and friends for a while. Tomorrow Mr Frederiksen was being sentenced in the Castlemaine Court.

THE END

ACKNOWLEDGEMENTS

Many thanks to my daughter Holly Thomson, to the members of the Elphinstone writers' group: Amy Coburn, Anthea Matley, Iain White and Jenny Nestor, and to my other generous readers and friends, especially John Sawtell, Lynne Bird, Lynne Waddington, Neriman Kemal, Niels Zahle and Tristana Freeman, for all their support, suggestions and encouragement. I offer special thanks to my editor Katherine Seppings, Seven Pens, and my publisher Marcus Fielding, Echo Books. Their expertise, knowledge and support have been essential. This book was written on Jaara Jaara Country. I acknowledge the Jaara Jaara traditional custodians of the land and pay my respects to their leaders, past and present. I particularly acknowledge and thank Maya Coff from the Nalderun Education Aboriginal Corporation, Castlemaine for reviewing, correcting and approving chapters 8 and 9. I acknowledge that the dreaming stories of Barramul, the emu, and the fight between Tarrengower and Lalgambook in chapter 8 come from the traditional teachings of the Jaara Jaara people. I also thank Chicago University Press for permission to use the Hannah Arendt quote above.

ABOUT THE AUTHOR

Originally from Barham NSW, Gavan Thomson decided to write books at the age of ten when he won a *Biggles* book for the best essay in Grade 5. Sixty years later he has finally succeeded. *Royal Descent* is his first novel. In the meantime, he has had a diverse career as a biochemist, health researcher, counsellor and mental health social worker before retiring four years ago. From 1978 to 1981, he first lived and worked in Denmark, began studying Danish and has had a love affair with the Kingdom ever since. He has been back many times and works as a freelance Danish-English translator, and plays badminton. Gavan has been an activist in the anti-nuclear, environment and community health movements since the 1970s. Once he lived on a commune but now lives in Elphinstone, Victoria on a small orchard in the middle of town.